THE EXILE

OMEGA TASKFORCE: BOOK THREE

G J OGDEN

Cover design by Laercio Messias
Editing by S L Ogden
www.ogdenmedia.net

If you like Omega Taskforce then why not check out some of G J Ogden's other books? Click the series titles below to learn more about each of them.

Darkspace Renegade Series (6-books)

If you like your action fueled by power armor, big guns and the occasional sword, you'll love this fast-moving military sci-fi adventure.

Star Scavenger Series (5-book series)

Firefly blended with the mystery and adventure of Indiana Jones. Book 1 is 99c / 99p.

The Contingency War Series (4-book series)

A space-fleet, military sci-fi adventure with a unique twist that you won't see coming...

The Planetsider Trilogy (3-book series)

An edge-of-your-seat blend of military sci-fi action & classic apocalyptic fiction. Perfect for fans of Maze Runner and I am Legend.

Audiobook Series

Star Scavenger Series (29-hrs)

The Contingency War Series (24-hrs)

The Planetsider Trilogy (32-hrs)

CHAPTER 1
HERE WE GO AGAIN

CAPTAIN LUCAS STERLING stepped onto the bridge of the Invictus and paused for a moment to drink in the view. The ship was still docked inside the Fleet Dreadnaught Hammer while it underwent repairs, but the bridge had already been fixed up. Returning to it felt like opening the front door of his house, hanging up his coat and dropping into his favorite chair after a long, hard day.

The notion of "home" was as alien to Sterling as the Sa'Nerra's waspish language. Since joining the United Governments Fleet, over half his lifetime ago, Sterling had lived wherever his duties had taken him, with no one place feeling any more unique or special than another. The Invictus was different, however. This was his ship and his crew. The act of stepping onto the bridge of the Marauder-class warship was as close to a feeling of belonging as Sterling had ever experienced in his life. An icy cold shiver ran down his spine as he realized how close he had come to having it all taken away.

It had been two days since the destruction of G-COP at the hands of Emissary Clinton Crow, but barely a minute had passed without Sterling reflecting on what happened. They had managed to repel the Sa'Nerra this time, but the attack had just been a prelude to a full invasion. The alien war fleet was en route to G-sector, but rather than face them the War Council had ordered a retreat. G-sector was being surrendered to the Sa'Nerra in what was one of the biggest defeats of the fifty-year war.

However, while Fleet forces were withdrawing to F-sector, Sterling was preparing to go against orders and head in the other direction. Officially, the Invictus was also to withdraw to F-COP, but an Omega Directive from Fleet Admiral Griffin had ordered them back into the Void. Their mission was to find and retrieve disgraced and exiled Fleet scientist, Dr. James Colicos, at all costs. It had been Colicos' experimentations that had led to the creation of the neural weapon and he was the reason the Sa'Nerra had it in their possession. Only Colicos could undo the damage he'd caused and find a way to reverse the effects of Sa'Nerran neural control.

Unfortunately, the War Council had not agreed, which was why the burden of retrieving the scientist fell to Sterling and his crew alone. However, this time Sterling would not have the cover story of the "Void Recon Squadron" to shield him from scrutiny. Obeying Admiral Griffin would require disobeying a direct order from the Secretary of War. Yet Sterling still believed in the Omega Taskforce. Sometimes doing what is necessary means breaking the rules, he told himself.

Sterling had been so deep in thought that he hadn't noticed Commander Banks also enter the bridge. She was now standing alongside him with Jinx – their surprise stowaway beagle hound – trotting along in tow.

"It always amazes me how quickly they can bang these things back together," said Banks, who was also inspecting the spruced-up bridge. "The Invictus looks like it's fresh out of the shipyard."

"That's what fifty years of war does for you," commented Sterling, smiling over at his first officer. "The engineers on the Hammer are some of the best and most experienced in the Fleet. This sort of work is no more taxing to them than tying their bootlaces."

Sterling advanced and stepped onto his command platform, then caught Lieutenant Shade glancing at him out of the corner of her eye. Shade was at her weapons control station, as always. Sterling wondered idly if she'd ever left it. He nodded to Shade to acknowledge his weapons officer and she nodded back respectfully before returning to her work. Jinx the dog then jumped up next to Commander Banks at her station and let out a contented "yip". The sound almost caused Shade to jump out of her skin. The weapons officer reached for her sidearm and spun on her heels, aiming the pistol at the dog, before stopping herself and doing a double-take.

"Don't ask," said Sterling, as Shade's confused eyes met his own.

"Aye, Captain..." replied Shade after the shock of seeing a dog on the bridge had subsided. She holstered her weapon and scrutinized the miniature intruder for a few more seconds before returning to her work.

Sterling smiled as he glanced over to Ensign Keller who was also at his station. Sterling could see from his captain's console that the helmsman was busy finishing off a diagnostic to recalibrate the helm controls. This had been necessary because of a much-needed engine tune-up that the Hammer's repair crews had performed while they had been docked to the mighty Dreadnaught. Sterling allowed the ensign to finish, considering that it may well be the last opportunity they would have for some time to perform routine maintenance. There were no advanced repair facilities in the Void, and the few adequate facilities that did exist would likely not welcome a Fleet warship into their dock.

"How is it coming along, Ensign?" asked Sterling, drawing the gaze of his pilot.

"Almost done, sir," replied Keller, the tone of his voice sounding almost as breezy as their ship's quirky gen-fourteen AI. Sterling wondered what had caused the ensign to be in such a chipper mood when he noticed the glint of metal just beneath the collar of Keller's tunic.

"How are you feeling, Ensign?" Sterling asked, remembering that his pilot had been officially dead only a few days ago. Commander Graves had managed to resuscitate the ensign then replace several organs, as well as his sternum and half of his ribs with technological substitutes. The fact that these cybernetic enhancements were highly-experimental and entirely illegal hadn't bothered Sterling in the slightest. All he cared about was that his ensign was alive and ready to resume his duties.

"I feel amazing, Captain," beamed Keller. "Though Commander Graves said that might be the result of all the drugs I'm taking."

Sterling suddenly felt a familiar neural link form in his mind. He accepted it and prepared for the inevitable snarky or sarcastic comment that he was sure would follow.

"That's just great... Our pilot is as high as a kite," said Commander Banks through the link. She was looking at him out of the corner of her eye from her station beside Sterling's. "Are you sure you still want him at the helm?"

"I'd trust a spaced-out Keller more than almost any other pilot," Sterling replied, smiling over at his first officer.

"It's your funeral," Banks replied. Then she frowned. "No, wait, it'll be mine too..."

Sterling huffed a laugh, glad that his first officer was also in high spirits, though he guessed that this was largely due to her new furry companion. He closed the link then returned his attention to his helmsman.

"I take it that you're up for some more daredevil piloting then, Ensign?" Sterling said to Keller.

"Of course, sir," the ensign replied, still with a carefree nonchalance to his speech and mannerisms. "I'll be finished long before we're scheduled to depart the Hammer."

"Change of plans, Ensign," replied Sterling, more sternly. "We're leaving now."

This statement caused the helmsman to stop work and spin his chair around to face Sterling.

"As in *right* now?" asked Keller, raising an eyebrow.

"Is there another now that I should be aware of, Ensign?" Sterling replied, his answer causing a corner of Banks' mouth to curl up.

"No, sir," replied Keller, smartly. The ensign then spun his chair back to his helm controls, looking a little red-faced, but no less jaunty.

"All the crew is on board, sir," said Commander Banks, this time speaking out loud. "We're light on numbers, though. Fifty-four in all, including twenty commandoes. We weren't scheduled to get replacements until we docked at F-COP."

Sterling sighed. "It will have to do, Commander," he replied, wearily. "What about the status of the ship? Were the Hammer's engineers able to finish the repairs that were initiated at G-COP?"

Banks worked her console for a few seconds then half-nodded, half-shrugged. "Yes and no," she began. Sterling saw the status report flash up on his console then Banks skipped across to join him at his station. "The important systems are all back online. Weapons, engines, armor..." Banks went on, tapping her finger on the various systems while she talked. "But several crew sections are still out of action and parts of engineering look like a building site. The former isn't really a problem, considering we have fewer crew than usual."

Sterling nodded. "So long as we're fighting fit, it doesn't matter if we still look a little beat up in places," he replied. He scanned the ship's stores and his brow furrowed. "This might be a problem, though," he said, enlarging the readout so that Banks could also see it.

"Ah, crap," replied Banks before also letting out a weary sigh. The first officer glanced up from the screen and met Sterling's eyes. "We're light on food packs, water and parts. We can't requisition them from the Hammer, since they know we're getting resupplied at F-COP. That means we'll have to stop in the Void to re-supply."

"More importantly, we're not carrying enough fuel to make it to the Void and back," Sterling added. "We can go on rations and try to fabricate any parts we might need in the workshop, but fuel we can't magic out of nothing." Sterling noticed that Banks was looking at him like he'd just spat on her shoe.

"Go on rations?" Banks repeated, sounding utterly appalled at the suggestion.

"I'm sure you can manage for a few days," replied Sterling, shaking his head. Jinx yipped and made a strange growling sound.

"See, our new acting ensign agrees with me," said Banks, pointing to the beagle hound.

"The dog doesn't get a vote," Sterling hit back. "Neither do you for that matter," he added, unsympathetically.

"Fine, but I should warn you that I can get pretty grouchy when I'm hungry," said Banks.

"Noted, Commander," replied Sterling, remaining blithely indifferent to his first officer's plight. "We'll find somewhere to take on supplies as soon as we're into the Void," he continued, clearing his console. "First, we actually have to get through the aperture with half of the Fleet and the Hammer standing guard.

"Diagnostics complete!" Keller announced. The ship's helmsman still sounded annoyingly chipper. "Lieutenant Razor reports that engines are ready. We're standing by to detach from the Hammer. I've locked in a course to the F-sector aperture and can engage as soon as we're clear."

"Belay that, Ensign," Sterling called out, causing the ensign and Lieutenant Shade to stop what they were doing and become alert. "We're not going to F-COP, anymore," Sterling added. The expression on his helmsman's face suggested that his statement had come across sounding more foreboding than he'd intended it to. Shade, however, simply stared back at her Captain with blank, unreadable eyes.

"Where are we going, sir?" Keller finally plucked up the courage to ask.

"We have new Omega Directive orders, which means we're going back into the Void, Ensign," Sterling answered, confidently. "Unfortunately, the other Fleet ships in the sector don't know this, so I'm going to be in need of your talent for creative flying once again."

Ensign Keller's eyes grew wide, but then to Sterling's surprise the pilot smiled. "I never liked F-COP anyway, sir," Keller said, with a hint of rebellion. "Setting a new course now."

"Here we go again," said Banks, smiling at Sterling then hopping back across to her own station.

"Here we go again," repeated Sterling, though he muttered the words under his breath.

Sterling turned back to Ensign Keller, who was still eagerly awaiting his command. A sudden silence fell over the bridge with only the familiar thrum of the ship's engines as a backdrop. It was like the distant rumble of thunder that suggested a storm was on the horizon. Sterling leaned forward and gripped the sides of his console. His fingers slid into the familiar grooves that he'd worn down over the last year of commanding the vessel. He sucked in a long breath and let it out slowly.

"Take us out, Ensign," Sterling said to his pilot. "And prepare to run like hell on my order."

STERLING'S HANDS didn't leave the sides of his console for the next ten minutes, nor did his eyes leave the viewscreen. Dozens of Fleet ships continued to buzz around the sector on regular patrol routes, many flying so close he could read the serial numbers on their hulls. Every chime from Sterling's console sent his pulse racing, expecting it to be from a warship demanding to know why the Invictus was heading for the aperture. So far, though, no-one had challenged their progress toward the inter-stellar gateway.

Ahead of him on the viewscreen, Sterling watched the flashing beacons that surrounded the aperture grow larger and brighter. However, the beacons were not the only objects close to the perimeter of the gateway. Dozens of Fleet warships were also watchfully guarding the aperture in case the vanguard of the Sa'Nerran invasion armada decided to surge through and survey the battleground. Suddenly, Banks' console chimed an alert, causing Sterling's pulse to spike even higher. He cast his eyes across to his first officer's station, waiting for her report.

"It's a message from the Fleet Heavy Destroyer Falchion," said Banks, peering down at her console screen. "They're the lead ship in the current taskforce guarding the aperture."

"Let me guess, they're warning us to steer clear?" said Sterling.

Banks smiled. "Right first time," she replied. "They're being pretty insistent too, and not very polite."

Lieutenant Shade's console then chimed an alert and Sterling turned his attention to his weapons officer.

"The Falchion has turned toward us and locked weapons, Captain," said Shade. Her tone and expression remained level. However, Sterling knew Shade's tells well enough to see that the destroyer's brazenness had riled her.

"You're right, that's not very polite at all," said Sterling, glancing back to Banks.

"Should I turn away?" asked Ensign Keller, his voice betraying his unease at the fact one of their own ships had targeted them.

"No, hold your course and keep it nice and steady, Ensign," replied Sterling, assertively. "But be ready to put on a burst of speed when I give the order."

"Aye, Captain," replied Keller, briskly.

"Shall I charge weapons?" asked Shade, sounding eager to match the destroyer's aggressive stance.

"We do nothing to provoke them, Lieutenant," replied Sterling, again maintaining an assertive, level tone. "They're just posturing. The Falchion won't shoot at us."

Banks' console chimed another alert. "Another message from the Falchion, sir," said the first officer, still focused on her screen. She then looked over to Sterling, eyebrow raised. "It's Captain Anders and he's demanding to speak to you."

"He's *demanding* to speak to me?" replied Sterling, with a rising intonation. Banks merely smiled and nodded. Keller and Shade also shot astonished glances in the direction of the captain's console, clearly eager to see how their captain would respond. "Well, you'd better put him on the viewscreen then," Sterling finally answered, standing tall and pressing his hands behind his back. The viewscreen changed to show an inset image of the Falchion's captain in the center. Captain Anders was a tall, thin man, with straw-like yellow hair, cut-razor close along the temples so that it looked like a bird's nest had been placed on his head. The yellow stripe across Anders' tunic denoted that the officer served in the Second Fleet, under Admiral Grayson. Their usual domain was D-sector, which had largely kept them out of front-line action in the more recent years of the war. Anders, however, was a veteran who had seen plenty of combat.

"Captain Sterling, are your systems malfunctioning?" asked Anders, peering down his nose at Sterling.

Sterling saw Banks wince out of the corner of his eye. The condescending and snooty manner in which the question had been asked was exactly the sort of attitude that got Sterling's goat.

"No, Captain Anders, our systems are working just fine, thank you for asking," replied Sterling. He'd managed to force his lips into a thin smile, though the act of doing so was already causing his face to ache.

"Then why are you still on course toward the aperture, Captain?" Anders hit back. "I issued clear instructions for you to steer away."

The captain of the Falchion had switched from condescending to downright disdainful. It was as if the officer were speaking to an insubordinate malcontent, rather than someone of equal rank.

"If that was your question, Captain, then you should have just asked it the first time, rather than play games," Sterling replied.

Sterling's veneer of politeness had already cracked. He now wished he'd allowed Shade to charge the weapons so that he could blast a warning shot across the destroyer's bow. However, he had to remind himself of his own advice, which was to avoid provoking his fellow Fleet officer. Even so, it was clear that Sterling's snarling response had already caused Captain Anders to bristle and puff out his chest like a strutting pigeon.

"Very well, Captain, since you prefer that we speak plainly," the officer began, clearly working up to deliver an ultimatum. "Turn away now or I am authorized to fire on your vessel. Our orders are clear. No-one is to enter the Void, not even the fabled 'Void Recon Unit'."

The sneering manner in which Anders had said "Void Recon Unit" only served to rile Sterling up even further.

"I realize that the Second Fleet doesn't see much action in D-sector, Captain," Sterling replied, giving as good as he got. "But firing on your own side isn't generally the done thing." Moments later he kicked himself for rising to the bait.

"From what I hear of your taskforce, Captain, you would know far more about that than I," Anders hit back.

There was an audible intake of breath from the station beside him. Sterling glanced left and saw that Banks was almost ready to leap at the viewscreen and punch her fist though the image of Captain Anders.

"In any case, there is no need for threats, Captain," Sterling replied, managing to rein in his own combative tendencies and speak more calmly. "We're simply running some quick shakedown tests to calibrate our engines after the recent repairs."

"Calibrate your engines in the other direction, Captain Sterling," Anders replied. Unlike Sterling, he had made no effort to take a more civil tone. "I will not warn you again."

The image of Captain Anders on the viewscreen vanished. Sterling allowed his stiff posture to relax, though his heart was thumping hard in his chest. Then he noticed that Ensign Keller had twisted his chair around to face him, awaiting further orders. The young officer still appeared to be full of doubt, but Sterling commended his relatively green pilot for holding his tongue.

"Full power acceleration, Ensign," Sterling said, feeling his hands again tighten around the sides of his console. "Keep going straight for the Aperture, no matter what that destroyer does."

"Aye, Captain," Keller replied, with slightly less assuredness than before.

"You think he's bluffing?" asked Banks, casting Sterling a quizzical eye.

"I think he'll try to confirm the order to fire on us before he takes any action," replied Sterling. "And I'm betting that Admiral Griffin will take her sweet time to answer his call."

Sterling then felt the kick of the engines push him toward the rear bulkhead before the inertial negation systems adjusted to compensate. The pulse of the engines through of the deck-plating quickly rose as the Invictus powered its way toward the aperture.

"Power surge from the Falchion," said Banks, raising her own voice above the beat of the engines. "Anders is definitely getting ready to fire."

"Hold your course, Ensign, and prepare to surge," Sterling called out, heading off any doubt his helmsman may have had in that moment. He then turned to Lieutenant Shade. "Regenerative armor to maximum, and charge the weapons, just in case," he said. Shade sprang into action almost before the breath carrying his words had exited Sterling's lips. His weapons officer had clearly been eagerly awaiting the order to active their own defensive and offensive systems.

"Thirty seconds to the perimeter of the aperture," Banks called out. "If Anders is going to shoot at us then he's leaving it to the last minute."

Sterling didn't answer and continued to peer out through the viewscreen. *Come on, Captain Anders, let's see if you have to balls to do it...* Sterling thought, almost willing his fellow officer to take the shot.

"Ten seconds... I think we're clear," announced Banks. "Five seconds..."

Sterling smiled then felt the universe collapse into nothing, so that only his disembodied thoughts remained. His mind dwelled on what had just happened. Sterling had called Falchion's bluff, as he knew he would. However, his primary sensation wasn't relief that his gamble had worked, but anger that it had done. Anders should have blown the Invictus to atoms. Sterling had disobeyed orders and made a run for the Void. For all Anders knew, Sterling and his crew could have been turned. By taking no action, the officer may have allowed an advanced warship and battle-hardened crew to join the ranks of the enemy invasion armada. It was an act of cowardice, Sterling thought, as he waited for the surge to complete, and it was all because Captain Anders was not like him – not an Omega officer. If it had been the Invictus guarding the aperture and the Falchion trying to run, Sterling wouldn't have hesitated. He'd have launched everything he had and reduced the Falchion to dust. That was the difference between himself and the other Fleet captains. And ultimately that was difference between winning and losing the war. *Fleet will learn this to its cost in the days ahead,* Sterling considered as his disembodied thoughts continued to fill the absence. *Hopefully, the cost will not to be too high...*

Sterling and the Invictus exploded back into normal space on the other side of the aperture and a cacophony of strident alarms immediately blared out onto the bridge. Sterling was suddenly bathed in the crimson hue of the battle stations alert lights, and he quickly realized why.

Ahead of him on the viewscreen were three Sa'Nerran Skirmishers and the Invictus was heading straight for them.

Sterling stood tall and tapped his neural interface, opening the link to the entire crew.

"All hands... battle stations..."

THE FLASH FROM THE INVICTUS' plasma rail cannons lit up the Void and moments later the lead Sa'Nerran Skirmisher had been obliterated. Impacts from the debris of the enemy warship hammered into the hull of the ship as its momentum carried it through the wreckage. Sterling glanced down at his damage report screen and saw a dozen sections of their regenerative armor turn from green to dark amber. However, just as quickly as the damage had been sustained, their self-regenerating protective shell began to knit itself back together again.

"Full-power turn, Ensign," Sterling called out. "Get us behind that second ship before it has a chance to react."

"Aye sir," Keller called out.

The starfield on the viewscreen became a blur as the gifted pilot maneuvered the Marauder-class warship in pursuit of the second enemy vessel. Sterling was forced to put his weight forward and grip the sides of his console again to compensate for the delay in the inertial negation systems. It was like standing on a bus while it was taking a sharp corner and being forced to grip onto the handrails more tightly.

"Torpedoes away!" Lieutenant Shade called over the weapons control console.

Sterling saw the weapons race out from the aft launchers of the Invictus and pursue the third Sa'Nerran Skirmisher. Like Shade, he doubted that the torpedoes would reach their target before the alien ship's point defense guns took them out. However, all they needed to do was distract the enemy warship and buy them enough time to deal with its companion. The second Skirmisher came into view ahead, though Keller's alien counterpart was doing an admirable job of evading the Invictus' guns.

"I'm switching weapons to manual," Shade announced, as three hard thuds reverberated through the deck from incoming plasma fire. "The Sa'Nerran jamming fields are blocking our targeting sensors."

"Direct hit broad on the port quarter," Banks called out, as another thud shook the deck, forcing the first officer to steady herself against her console. "Regenerative armor failing. Minor hull breach."

Sterling silently cursed the alien gunner who'd managed to poke a hole in his vessel, then turned to Shade. "Lieutenant, we can't hold this course for long," he said, noting more sections of their armor turn dark amber or red. "Take them out, now."

"Standby..." Shade replied, her gaze laser-focused onto the manual targeting display. Sterling saw the glowing reticule dance across the viewscreen then land on the enemy warship's engineering section. "Locked on... Firing!"

The viewscreen briefly went white as the rail guns fired again, but the display compensated in time to show the plasma blasts tearing through the starboard beam of the Skirmisher. Crippled, the enemy vessel listed out of control, spewing fire and arcs of electricity into the Void.

"Target neutralized, weapons resetting," Shade called through gritted teeth. Combat was the only thing that made Opal Shade come alive and she was relishing every second of the encounter.

"Coming about!" Keller shouted, turning the Invictus away from the stricken vessel.

Sterling gripped hard to his console again, but the final Skirmisher had predicted the move and remained on their tail. Seconds later, more powerful impacts thudded through the deck. Sterling didn't need his console to tell him that the damage was serious – he could feel it, as if the ship was an extension of his own body.

"Hull breach, cargo bay," said Banks.

Sterling glanced at his console and saw that in its eagerness to score a hit, the Skirmisher had left itself in a bad position.

"Zero safeties on the aft torpedoes," Sterling called out. The damage assessment could wait – he had a fractional window in which to act, otherwise their chance was gone. "Fire - now, now, now!"

Shade reacted instantly, disabling the safeties on their torpedoes and snap-shooting them from the aft launchers. The viewscreen switched to a view of the pursuing

Skirmisher which, as Sterling had anticipated, had remained tight in on their tail. He cursed out loud as the first torpedo missed and snaked out into the darkness. The second one struck true and the Skirmisher detonated violently. The explosion was so close to the Invictus that the shockwave literally rattled Sterling's teeth. More alarms wailed and the damage control readout on his console went momentarily haywire. Then the alarms all steadily began to fall silent and the shimmies and vibrations through the deck subsided.

"All enemy vessels destroyed," Lieutenant Shade confirmed. "No more contacts on the scanner."

"Hull breaches secured," Banks added, looking down at her console. "Regenerative armor holding." Banks then sighed and flashed her eyes at Sterling. "We'll need to hammer a few more dings out of the hull, but we're okay. No critical systems were damaged."

Sterling nodded and pushed himself away from his console. "Stand down from battle stations," he said, staring out at the burning remains of the three Sa'Nerran Skirmishers.

The red alert lighting faded and the regular bridge lights switched back on. A melodious if chaotic howl then emanated from the direction of Banks' console and Sterling glanced down to see Jinx the Beagle wagging her tail. The hound appeared to be peering at the wreckage of the alien warships on the viewscreen.

"I think she approves of our victory," said Banks, bending down to pet the dog.

"You're going to have to figure out a more appropriate

station for Acting Ensign Jinx," said Sterling, frowning at the Beagle. "I'd forgot the damned thing was still on the bridge."

"It's a dog, not a thing, Captain," Banks hit back, sounding suddenly defensive. Sterling glowered at his first officer and she straightened to attention, realizing her slip. "But, yes sir, I'll make sure Jinx stays out of the way," she added, in a more professional tone.

"Captain, since we're low on supplies, might it be worth analyzing the wreckage for anything salvageable?" Lieutenant Shade asked, appropriately steering the conversation away from canine matters and back to the mission. "At the very least, there might be some tech or metals that we can adapt and use to fabricate spare components."

Sterling considered this then nodded. "While I don't relish the idea of eating salvaged Sa'Nerran meal trays, it's worth a shot," he replied to Shade. Then he glanced out through the viewscreen again, anxiously watching the pulsing beacons surrounding the aperture. "But before we commit to a salvage op, I want to be sure Fleet or the Sa'Nerra won't catch us with our cargo bay doors down, so to speak."

Banks raised an eyebrow. "That's a colorful metaphor," she replied while beginning an analysis of the aperture that led back to G-sector. "So far, I'm only detecting our residual surge energy. There's nothing to indicate that other Fleet ships are following us through," Banks added, while continuing to work through the readings.

"Captain Anders will be speaking to Griffin or one of

the other admirals in G-sector now," said Sterling, picturing the scene of havoc they had just left behind. "The top brass are likely still deciding whether to risk coming after us or not."

Banks' console chimed another update and her scowl deepened. "Wait one... I'm detecting a surge," Banks said, fingers flashing across her console to analyze the new readings.

"From the aperture to G-sector, or one of the others?" Sterling asked. He wasn't thrilled at the prospect of having to deal with any Fleet ships that had been sent after them. However, the alternative – more Sa'Nerran warships – wasn't particularly appealing to him either.

"It's from an aperture at the far side of the sector," Banks finally answered. "Correction, I'm picking up surge fields from four apertures, all of them vectoring into the Sa'Nerran half of the void." There was then a brief pause, during which time Banks' eyes grew wide. "Wow..." she said, taking a step back from the console and holding up her hands, as if the surface had suddenly become electrified.

"Is that a good 'wow' or a bad 'wow'?" Sterling asked, though, as always, he instinctively assumed the worst.

"Take a look for yourself," replied Banks, tapping a few quick commands into the console then peering up at the viewscreen.

Sterling frowned and adjusted his gaze to the screen. "Wow..." he said, parroting his first officer. Surge flashes were popping off in space like a fourth-of-July fireworks display.

"One hundred and fifty-eight, so far..." Banks said,

switching her focus between her console and the viewscreen. "Two forty... three hundred... Hell, they just keep on coming."

"Ensign Keller, set a course for the aperture to Colony Middle Star and engage at best possible speed," ordered Sterling, wasting no time in getting the Invictus moving again.

"Aye, Captain," replied Keller, snapping into action like a mousetrap. Moments later the thrum of the engines through the deck plating began to build and Sterling felt the ship accelerate hard.

"They've seen us," said Banks, who was still frantically working at her station. Sterling tapped his finger on the side of his console, waiting for Banks to announce whether any ships from the alien armada had splintered off to pursue them.

"There are now over four hundred Sa'Nerran warships in the sector, and the surge energy readings are not diminishing," Banks continued, still peering down at her console. "So far, there's no indication any of the vessels have adjusted course to intercept us."

Sterling let out the breath he realized he'd been holding for the last few seconds and nodded to Banks. "Let's not give them any reason to come after us," he said, turning his attention back to the viewscreen and the growing armada of alien warships. "Hopefully, a single ship isn't worth their time."

Banks' console them chimed again and Sterling felt his stomach knot.

"We've just monitored a massive spike in surge energy,"

said Banks, ramping up her rate of speech almost as rapidly as Sterling's pulse was climbing. "Something big is coming though..."

Sterling fixed his eyes on the viewscreen and waited. There was a flash, so bright that it could have been a supernova. Out of the corner of his eye, he could see Banks return her gaze to her console, working through the sensor data to figure out what had just arrived. However, the answer was already clear to see on the viewscreen. It was another Sa'Nerra warship. However, this vessel was unique and it was also not the first time Sterling had seen it.

"It's the super-weapon," said Banks, glancing up from her console to look at the ten-kilometer-long leviathan on the viewscreen.

"It's actually the Sa'Nerran Battle Titan," Sterling said, correcting his first officer. "That's what they've decided to call the thing," he added, tearing his eyes away from the screen to look at Banks.

"How the hell are we supposed to take that down?" wondered Banks, shaking her head at the image of the warship.

Sterling also turned back to the viewscreen and frowned at the vessel. "The bigger they come, the harder they fall, Commander," he said, as more surge flashes popped off behind the Battle Titan. "But right now, we have other concerns."

"Captain, I'm picking up another vessel near the aperture to Colony Middle Star," said Ensign Keller, spinning his chair to face the captain's console. "It's an old generation-one Fleet Destroyer, though it appears to be heavily modified."

"A Marshall?" wondered Banks, tapping her console and throwing an image of the new contact up onto the viewscreen.

"Monitor that destroyer closely, Ensign," said Sterling. He'd had the same thought as Banks and was taking no chances. "If it turns toward us or deviates from its course, I want to know immediately."

Keller uttered a brisk reply as Sterling turned his attention back to the Sa'Nerran armada. It was now approaching eight hundred vessels strong. However, despite the mass of warships that had already arrived, there was still one missing.

"Are you picking up MAUL in the Sa'Nerran aramada?" asked Sterling, glancing over to his first officer.

"Negative," Banks replied. Her response had been instantaneous, suggesting she'd spotted the curious anomaly too.

"Then where the hell is that devious bastard?" said Sterling, muttering the words under his breath.

"The gen-one destroyer has surged Captain," Ensign Keller called out. "From the vector of the residual surge energy, I'd say it was also heading to Colony Middle Star."

Sterling cursed then let out another long sigh. If it wasn't the Sa'Nerran trying to kill him, it was his own kind. He rubbed his eyes and the back of his neck, feeling suddenly dog-tired and weary.

"Maintain your course, Ensign," Sterling replied to his helmsman. "We'll worry about that old destroyer later."

Keller responded in his usual, snappy manner. However, despite what he'd just said, in truth the destroyer was already on Sterling's mind. The war fleet amassing in the Void was not his immediate concern, nor was it a threat to his mission to find Colicos. However, if the old Fleet Destroyer that had just surged ahead of them was a Marshall, he knew that he was merely leaving one problem behind and flying headlong into another.

CHAPTER 4
INTENSE DREAMS

STERLING AIMED his plasma pistol at the head of Commander Ariel Gunn, but kept his eyes fixed onto the Sa'Nerran warrior. The alien merely hissed back at him and tightened its grip around Gunn's throat. The creature's long, leathery fingers were slowly choking the life out of his friend's terrified eyes. The indicators on the neural control weapon attached to Gunn's head were blinking furiously as it worked to pervert her mind and turn her into a weapon of the Sa'Nerra. Sterling could already see the spidery trail of corruption leaking out from Gunn's neural implant. He knew it wouldn't be long before her mind was turned.

She's already gone... Sterling told himself. *She's not Ariel any longer. She's just another puppet with the Sa'Nerra pulling the strings.*

Sterling tightened his grip on his plasma pistol and retuned his gaze to the yellow eyes of the alien warrior. The Sa'Nerran had already killed or turned other members of the

Fleet Dreadnaught Hammer's crew and now it was trying to turn Ariel Gunn too. Anger surged through his veins and he gritted his teeth, ready to squeeze the trigger and put an end to the threat. Gunn was just a casualty of war, he told himself. She'd made her choices, and she'd made bad ones. She alone bore the blame for her death. Sterling was merely doing what he had to – what was necessary.

"You've killed her before, you can do it again," said the Sa'Nerran in a waspish perversion of the English language. Sterling froze and relaxed his grip on the trigger. The shock of hearing the alien speak to him had caught him off guard. "Go on, kill your so-called friend," the alien continued, goading Sterling while fixing him with its egg-shaped yellow eyes.

"Her blood is on your hands, not mine!" Sterling yelled back at the alien. "If you think I won't do it then you're sorely mistaken."

Sterling then straightened his arm and fired, blasting the head of Commander Ariel Gunn clean off her shoulders. The smell of charred and burned human flesh assaulted his senses, but he held firm and returned his focus to the alien.

"You can test me all you like, alien, but you'll never win," Sterling spat at the warrior. "I will do whatever it takes to bring you down."

The Sa'Nerran's yellow eyes grew even wider and the perverted smile on its hard, plasticky face grew wider, making the thing look like a grotesque caricature of itself.

"You could kill her easily, because you've done it

before," the alien hissed. "But will you be so ready to kill this one?" A freakish smile curled its thin, slug-like lips.

Sterling frowned and looked at Gunn, but instead of a headless body he was now staring into the eyes of Mercedes Banks. Sterling felt his stomach churn and his throat tighten. Then as the alien wrapped its leathery digits around his first officer's throat, Sterling's sick feeling was replaced with burning anger.

"Let her go, you bastard!" he yelled, trying to aim his pistol at the warrior, but the alien had expertly slipped behind Banks to use her as a shield. Suddenly, a neural control weapon appeared on the side of Banks' head, as if it had materialized out of thin air. However, this was not the original, cruder device, but the modified weapon that had been responsible for the creation of the Sa'Nerran Emissaries, Clinton Crow and Lana McQueen.

"You only have a few seconds left, Captain," the warrior hissed, peeking around the back of Banks' head. "Soon, she will be mine, just like all the others." A long, snake-like tongue slipped between the warrior's lips and lashed the side of Banks' head. The tongue slowly drew itself down across Banks' long neck, leaving a slimy trail in its wake.

"Get off her!" Sterling yelled at the alien, his entire body now trembling with rage. "I'll rip you apart with my bare hands, you alien piece of shit!"

Sterling adjusted his position to get a better angle, but it was as if the alien could read his mind. No matter what he did, he couldn't get a clean shot at the warrior. Sterling and the alien continued this abhorrent dance for several seconds, and all the while the warrior continued to lick Bank's face. Sterling couldn't stand it any longer and tightened his grip around the trigger. Then, finally, the alien retracted its tongue back into its mouth and curled its slug-like lips into another grotesque smile.

"You can end it now," the warrior said, slipping out of sight behind Banks' head. "Just shoot and it will all be over. Do what is necessary, Captain. Prove she means nothing to you."

Suddenly the indicators on the neural control weapon stopped blinking and the rageful expression on the face of his first officer became blank. There was no longer any anger or revulsion at what the alien had done. It was like a switch had been flipped in her brain.

"Look, she has turned," the warrior said. "You're already too late."

Sterling roared and thrust the plasma pistol at Mercedes Banks, forcing himself to meet her soulless, dead eyes. He added pressure to the trigger, but then Banks opened her mouth and spoke.

"Join me, Lucas," said Banks, stretching out a hand to Sterling. "We can be emissaries together, you and I. You want us to be together, don't you?"

Sterling gritted his teeth and shook his head. "You won't win," he spat. "You won't beat me. I've been tested before. I'll beat the test again."

Banks simply smiled back at him, as if Sterling's words had washed over her unheard. "You can be with me, Lucas," she said, with a sudden softness and tenderness. "You don't have to do this. You don't have to kill me," she continued, still holding her hand outstretched. "The rest of the fleet doesn't deserve your sacrifice. Humanity doesn't deserve your loyalty. They fear and despise you Lucas, the same as they fear and despise me. We're outsiders. Freaks. We belong together."

The alien's long fingers then released their hold on Banks' neck and she stepped off the command platform. Sterling jerked away and took a hurried pace back, still aiming the weapon at his first officer.

"Join me, Lucas," Banks continued, her words so soft and her eyes so adoring that Sterling could not help but be swayed. "They don't deserve you. They don't want you. But I do, Lucas. I want you. We deserve each other."

Sterling shook his head again and added pressure to the trigger, but he couldn't pull it, not while he still held Banks' eyes.

"Join me, Lucas," he heard Banks say again. "Love me, as I love you."

However, Sterling had already looked away and closed his ears to his first officer's pleas. A flash of plasma lit up the bridge like a bolt of lightning illuminating the night sky. It was followed a moment later by the thump of Mercedes Banks' headless body hitting the deck. Sterling lowered the pistol and raised his eyes to the Sa'Nerran warrior, avoiding looking at the corpse.

"You won't beat me," Sterling said as the alien continued to smile back at him, hissing slowly as it breathed in the cool air of the Hammer's bridge. "I'll do whatever it takes to beat you."

"We shall see..." the alien replied.

Sterling squeezed the trigger again and blasted the alien in the face, splattering its leathery skin and brains across the viewscreen behind it. He then drew in a deep breath, tasting the burned flesh of both Sa'Nerran and human, and tossed the weapon to the deck.

"Lucas..."

Sterling froze. *No, it's not possible...*

"Lucas!" the voice said again. A familiar voice. Then Sterling felt a neural link begin to form. He fought it, but the connection was too powerful.

"Lucas!" the voice of Mercedes Banks cried out in his mind, so loud and clear that it caused a shooting pain to race through his temples.

Sterling spun around to see Banks standing behind him. Her entire face was melted away. Sterling screamed, but his cries were strangled as Banks' hands closed around his throat and applied pressure. He fought back, but there was nothing Sterling could do against the super-human strength of his first officer.

"Lucas!"

Sterling shot up in bed and saw Mercedes Banks in front of him. She was squeezing his shoulders with her vice-like grip and staring into his eyes, with an expression of concern, confusion and sheer bewilderment.

"What the hell is going on with you?" Banks asked, as Sterling shuffled away from her, his heart beating so hard in his chest that he could hear it pounding in his ears. His t-shirt was soaked through and his skin was hot and clammy.

"It's nothing, it was just a dream," said Sterling, fighting hard to regain his composure. He then threw his legs over the side of the bed and stood up. Dizziness almost overcame him and he was forced to press his hand to the wall to keep from falling over.

"Like hell it was 'just' a dream," Banks hit back, pushing herself off the bed and facing Sterling. "I hit the door call button ten times before the computer let me in," Banks continued. She sounded angry at him, which only made Sterling react more defensively.

"Remind me to re-program that damned thing," said Sterling, glancing up at the ceiling. However, the cheerful voice of the ship's AI remained conspicuously absent.

"You were really zoned out there, Lucas," Banks said, refusing to let the matter drop, "and when I formed the neural link, it felt like you were dying."

Sterling sucked in a deep lungful of the ship's recycled air and let it out slowly. His heart-rate was returning to normal and he was already feeling more in control. These were techniques Sterling had honed over the last year in command of the Invictus in order to combat his frequent nightmares. He was again master of his own consciousness. The raw, primal emotions of his sleeping mind had been relegated to the depths of his psyche.

"I get intense dreams sometimes, there's nothing more to it than that, Mercedes," Sterling said, turning to meet his first officer's eyes. "Now can we drop it?"

Banks' frown deepened, but whatever questions or concerns were racing around her mind, she left them unspoken.

"Consider it dropped, Captain," Banks replied, straightening her back. She then raised her hands and waved them at Sterling. "Mind if I use your head, though?" she added, nodding in the direction of Sterling's compact shower room. "I still have your sweat on my hands."

Sterling raised an eyebrow at his first officer then extended a hand to his rest room. "Be my guest," he said, stepping over to his wardrobe and pulling out a clean uniform. "But be quick, I'm going to need a shower."

"Aren't you forgetting something?" Banks called out from the shower room. A plume of steam from the hot water tap was wisping out of the door.

"Unless you mean how I forgot to actually invite you in, I don't think so," Sterling replied, tossing a pair of pants and a tunic onto the foot of the bed.

Banks emerged from the rest-room, a thin smile curling her lips. "I mean your ritual fifty push-ups," she said, pointing to the floor. "I can sit on your back again, if you like? Unless that was too difficult for you?"

Sterling folded his arms and glared at his first officer. "I managed it just fine the first time, didn't I?" he said. A challenge had been made and he wasn't about to let it go unanswered.

"Drop and give me sixty then, sir," said Banks, inviting Sterling to assume the requisite position on the deck.

Sterling's scowl deepened. "I thought it was fifty?" he said, dropping to his knees in the middle of his compact captain's quarters.

"Well, seeing as you managed fifty 'just fine', I thought we could push it a little," Banks replied, standing behind Sterling. "Unless it's too tough for you, that is?"

Sterling laughed then sprang into a plank position. "Just plant your ass down on my back and count," he said.

Sterling was counting on the adrenalin that was still surging through his veins to spur him on. And he was also hoping that some hard exercise would help to shake the tension from his body and mind. Banks obliged then straddled Sterling and lowered herself into position. Sterling winced, forgetting that his first officer's incredible muscle density meant that she was significantly heavier than her athletic frame suggested.

"Lieutenant Razor has managed to narrow down our next destination from the data Admiral Griffin provided," Banks said, as Sterling began his set. "Based on her analysis of the shuttle's trajectory as it departed Far Deep Nine, she extrapolated that the vessel would have travelled through Thrace Colony."

Sterling pushed out a rep and sucked in another lungful of air before answering. "That's where James Colicos gathered some of his test subject from, right?" he said before continuing the push-ups.

"That's right," replied Banks, as Sterling continued to bob up and down, quickly reaching then surpassing the half-way mark. "He took them from the wreckage of a battle between Fleet and the Sa'Nerra, some years ago."

Sterling considered this for a moment, though his focus was distracted by the burning pain in his chest and shoulders and the tightness of his breath. "But if that was years ago then surely the chances of that shuttle still being at Thrace Colony are practically nil?" Sterling eventually said, though getting his words out was becoming a struggle.

"Most likely, but it's our only lead," said Banks. "Maybe someone at Thrace came into contact with them, or the Shuttle was forced to refuel and there's a record of it. Who knows?"

Sterling nodded, but he was too breathless to respond verbally. He then squeezed out the remaining few push-ups and held himself in plank. Banks, however, remained seated on his back.

"You can get off now," Sterling said, wondering why his first officer was still using him as a bench.

"That's only fifty-nine, Captain," Banks replied, dryly. Sterling couldn't see her face, but he guessed she was grinning.

"Are you sure? I definitely counted sixty." Sterling hit back.

"Come on, Captain, just one more," Banks said, oblivious to Sterling's protests. "Unless, you've had enough, of course?"

Sterling shook his head. He knew he shouldn't take the bait, but he wasn't about to let Banks win. Dropping his chest to the deck he then squeezed out a final push up. The effort was excruciating and it felt like his head was going to explode.

"There, sixty," said Sterling, triumphant. "Now can you get off?"

Banks stood up and stepped to the side. Sterling suddenly felt like he was about to float off the deck.

"Nice work, Captain," Banks said, giving him a sarcastic-looking hand clap. Sterling pushed himself upright, feeling a little light-headed. Then Banks sniffed the air. "Now you really do need a shower," she said, smiling.

"Thank you for that expert assessment, Commander," Sterling replied, metering out an appropriate amount of sarcasm. "Let me finish up here and I'll meet you in the wardroom in twenty." He headed towards his shower cubicle.

"Aye, Captain," Banks replied, moving up to the door and pressing the button to open it. She stepped into the threshold then stopped and turned back, looking a little perplexed.

"Was there something else, Mercedes?" asked Sterling, touching the stream of water from the shower to test if it had gotten hot.

"You're not the only one who gets 'intense' dreams, you know," Banks said, meeting Sterling's eyes.

Sterling frowned, but didn't answer. In truth, he didn't know what to say. However, as it turned out, no response was necessary. In his moment of delay, Banks had already stepped out into the corridor and the door had slid shut behind her.

COMMANDER MERCEDES BANKS slid two meal trays onto the table then planted herself firmly into the seat opposite Sterling. He paused, with the remaining half of his grilled ham and cheese in his mouth, staring down at the trays.

"We're low on supplies, remember?" Sterling said, after taking a bite of the sandwich. "Don't you think you can ration yourself to just one breakfast?"

Banks tore the foil off the first tray, allowing the steam to billow out above a course of sausage and fried potatoes. "I've implemented a quota system already," said Banks, tucking in to the food. "It comes into force tomorrow, though," she added, with a mouthful of food. "I thought I'd let the crew have one last meal, before they get stuck with commando bars and coffee for breakfast."

Sterling smiled. "I'm sensing a little bit of motivated self-interest in that decision, but okay, Commander," he replied, returning to his own food.

There was a strident "yip" from beneath the table and

Sterling leant over to see Jinx staring up at Commander Banks with big, brown eyes. Banks smiled at the dog then skewered a sausage on a fork and offered it to her. The animal snatched it and devoured it in a matter of seconds.

"Where the hell is that thing going to do its... you know?" said Sterling, hooking a thumb at the dog.

"No, I don't know," replied Banks, tearing the foil off her second tray and starting on the ham and eggs.

"You know, it's 'business'," replied Sterling. Then he threw his arms out wide. "Come on, I'm eating, don't make me be any more descriptive."

Banks shoveled some more eggs into her mouth and shrugged. "Well, pretty much wherever she needs to," she replied, drawing a horrified stare from Sterling. "Outside the door to your quarters is one of her favorite places."

Sterling folded his arms. "You know, I'm considering a no dogs policy on this ship," he said, as Banks fed Jinx a few pieces of bacon. "And also a 'no Mercedes' policy."

Banks laughed. "Relax, Lucas, Jinx is very well trained," she said, patting the hound on the head. "She's an Omega ship's dog, after all."

Sterling rolled his eyes then started grazing on the rest of the food on his tray. It was then he spotted Ensign Keller out of the corner of his eye. He was already holding a meal tray, but instead of sitting down he was standing in the middle of the wardroom, looking like he was lost.

"Put the kid out of his misery already," said Banks, wafting her fork, which had a piece of sausage on the end, in the direction of Keller.

Sterling snorted a laugh then kicked out a chair from

under the table. It screeched across the floor, causing Keller – and the other crew in the wardroom – to jerk around, looking for what made the noise.

"Take a pew, Ensign," said Sterling, tossing the crusts of his grilled ham and cheese back onto the tray.

Keller trotted over and slid his tray onto the table. "Thanks, Captain," the helmsman said, sliding into the chair that Sterling had kicked out. "I'm never sure whether I'm intruding," he added, while adjusting the position of his meal tray and tucking in his seat. "You know, you two could be discussing secret command-level secrets, for all I know." The ensign then spotted Jinx underneath the table and reached down to pat the hound on the head.

Banks dropped an elbow on the table and leant in closer to Ensign Keller, fork still in hand. The sudden closeness of the ship's first officer clearly made Keller nervous and he pushed himself flat against the back of his chair.

"Is this a private room, Ensign, or can any officer come in here?" Banks said, locking eyes with the helmsman.

"Well, all the Invictus' officers can come in here, right?" said Keller. He sounded uncertain, as if he was worried that Banks was trying to trick him.

"Don't answer a question with a question, mister," Banks replied, skewering another piece of sausage and slotting it into her mouth.

"Yes, Commander, any officer can come in here," Keller said, this time with conviction.

"So, what are the chances that me and the Captain are

discussing something that is for command ears only?" Banks continued, chewing on the sausage.

"Umm, none?" said Keller, again a little uncertain.

"Right again," replied Banks. She then lifted her elbow off the table and rested back in her chair. "So next time, just come over and ask to join us, rather than standing in the middle of the room like a kid on his first day at a new school."

"Aye, Commander, I'll do that," Ensign Keller replied, almost instantly becoming more at ease. The helmsman then tore the foil off his meal tray and grabbed his fork, ready to get stuck in. Banks peered down at his tray with interest. Sterling realized that it was a number thirty – a rarity on the Invictus.

"Damn it, I was going to have that for lunch," said Banks, eyeing up the pepperoni pizza slice on Keller's tray.

"I'm sure you'll find something else to eat," said Sterling, cutting in before Keller politely – and foolishly – offered to give the pizza to his first officer.

Lieutenant Katreena Razor then strolled over with a meal tray in hand. Her bright white hair and dazzling, augmented eyes were a stark contrast to the austere, military architecture of the wardroom

"Mind if I join you, Captain, Commander?" she said. Her question was asked with none of the timidity or self-consciousness of Ensign Keller.

Sterling kicked out another chair. "Be our guest, Lieutenant."

Razor scowled at the chair that Sterling had pushed out and navigated to the opposite side of the table. Choosing a different chair she then sat and slid her meal tray out in front of her.

"Something wrong with that chair, Lieutenant?" asked Sterling, regarding his engineer with a quizzical eye.

"I prefer to sit so that I can see the exit, Captain," Razor replied, peeling the foil off her tray. Banks glanced at the contents then shook her head.

"Let me guess, you were going to have that one for dinner?" Sterling said, nodding towards Razor's tray.

"Well, I was, actually," said Banks, huffily.

"Good choice, Commander," said Razor, tucking in to the duck cassoulet on the even-rarer number four meal tray. "I was surprised to see this in storage, since they haven't been available for about a year. I found it right at the bottom of the pile. It took some getting at, I can tell you."

Sterling took a sip of coffee then looked over the top of his cup at Banks. "I wonder how it found its way there?" he mused, flashing his eyes at Banks, who just scowled back at him.

"Since you're both here," Razor went on, tossing a piece of duck to Jinx, who caught it in her jaws and wolfed it down in an instant, "an analysis I was running overnight just completed, and I think I've figured out how Admiral Griffin intends for us to get back into Fleet space again."

Sterling sat up, awaiting Razor's findings with interest. Ever since they'd disobeyed orders and surged through the aperture in G-sector into the Void, he had been wracking his brains trying to work out how to return again. He knew that the Sa'Nerran invasion force would have already reached G-sector, which Fleet had abandoned, and started constructing its own forward operating base. Although each sector contained many apertures, each leading to new star systems within that same sector, there was only a single aperture that connected one sector to another. Fleet had intentionally engineered it that way precisely for the situation they now found themselves in. For the Sa'Nerra to progress deeper into Fleet space, the alien armada would have to go through F-COP and the Fleet Gatekeeper Odin, along with at least half of the entire war fleet. It also meant that in order for the Invictus to reach F-sector, it would have to go through space that was now occupied by nearly a thousand Sa'Nerran warships. In short, there wasn't a chance in hell of reaching Fleet space, unless another route could be found.

"I'm all ears, Lieutenant Razor," said Sterling, turning his body to face his engineer. "What is the Admiral's genius plan for getting us home?"

Razor scrunched up her nose then cocked her head to one side. "Well, technically, I haven't discovered exactly how to get back into Fleet space," the engineer said. Her statement deflated Sterling's excitement like a pin popping a balloon. "What I *have* found is an encrypted file labelled, 'Invictus – Return'," Razor then went on.

Sterling perked up again. "And that's what your program just cracked overnight?" he asked, hopefully.

Razor shook her head. "I'd need the computer resources of an entire COP to crack this file, a least in any reasonable amount of time," she answered, instantly deflating Sterling's mood again. "But there was a second file attached to it that was easy to break open. It simply said, 'Shade is the key'."

Sterling flopped back into his chair. "What the hell does that mean?" he said, sighing and rubbing the back of his neck.

"Does she mean Lieutenant Shade?" asked Keller, dropping the crust of his pizza slice onto his tray. Banks picked it up and began to feed chunks of it to Jinx.

"I did ask Lieutenant Shade if she had any idea what the message meant, but she said no," Razor replied, meeting the ensign's inquisitive eyes. "In fact, that one word is about as much as she's said to me since I joined, outside of formal communications that is."

"Don't take it personally," said Commander Banks, brushing the pizza crumbs off her hands. "Shade isn't really what you'd call a people person".

Razor shrugged. "I didn't take it personally, Commander," she replied, dryly. "Most of the time, I prefer to be alone too. Then at other times I don't."

Banks frowned back at the engineer, but Sterling understood exactly what she meant. Sometimes, the only place he ever wanted to be was on the bridge, surrounded by his crew in the thick of the action. Then sometimes he just wanted to be in quarters, by himself, shut off from the sights and sounds of the outside world.

"Thank you, Lieutenant Razor, I'll pick up the matter with Lieutenant Shade directly," Sterling said to his chief engineer.

"Aye, Captain," Razor replied, with a respectful nod of her head.

An alert chime then rang out in the wardroom and the computer's cheerful voice interrupted them.

"Captain, we are approaching Colony Middle Star," the ship's AI said, with its usual breezy charm. "Long-range sensors are detecting three vessels in orbit around the fourth planet. They appear to be adrift and derelict."

"Thank you, computer, I'll be on the bridge presently," Sterling replied, directing his answer towards the ceiling, where he always imagined the invisible presence of the computer to be located. He met Banks' eyes in order to gauge her reaction to the news.

"A possible salvage opportunity?" said Banks, with a slight eyebrow raise. "The fourth planet has been all but abandoned for years."

"Maybe," replied Sterling. "Or it could be a trap. We haven't seen any sign of that mysterious gen-one destroyer since arriving in the Middle Star system."

"If it is a trap then it's probably better that we deal with this new Marshall sooner rather than later," Banks said.

Sterling nodded and sighed before pushing his seat back and standing up. "Breakfast is over people," he announced. "Return to your stations."

Razor and Keller got up without protest and immediately headed out of the wardroom. Banks stood, but unlike the others she didn't also immediately head for the door. Instead, she leant over the table and picked up the crust of Sterling's grilled ham and cheese that he'd discarded onto his tray earlier.

"Waste not, want not," Banks said. She then pushed the crust into her mouth and dusted off her hands.

CHAPTER 6
JUSTICE VERSUS THE LAW

CAPTAIN STERLING PEERED out through the viewscreen at the three ships circling the fourth planet of Colony Middle Star. He glanced across to Commander Banks, tapping his finger on the side of his console while he waited for her analysis. The soft bleeps and chirps from her console as she worked were soothing, though he doubted the current serenity on the bridge would last for long.

"Two of the vessels are light freighters that were first registered decades ago," said Banks, her eyes still focused down at her console. "They're typical of the sort of trading vessel that operated in the outer colonies, before the Void was established." Banks then glanced over to Sterling and raised an eyebrow. "Except that they've been extensively modified with thicker armor and Sa'Nerran plasma weapons."

Sterling huffed a laugh. It was looking increasingly likely that the ships were merely playing possum, waiting for an unsuspecting ship to pass by and eye them up for salvage.

"What about the third ship?" Sterling asked, realizing that Banks hadn't yet mentioned the final vessel in the trio of derelicts.

Banks flashed her eyes at Sterling – a surefire tell that his first officer had uncovered something of note. "That's a generation one Fleet Destroyer," she said, a corner of her lips curling into a smile.

"Well, that settles it then," Sterling said, peering out at the ships on the viewscreen.

"The destroyer has also been extensively modified, so much so that's its barely recognizable as a Fleet design anymore," Banks went on, folding her powerful arms across her chest. "The ship's registry has been wiped, but the energy signature matches the vessel we saw surge ahead of us into this system."

Sterling stopped tapping the side of his console and straightened up. "Well, whoever it is has gone to an awful lot of trouble to lure us here," he said, scowling at the old destroyer on the viewscreen. "We should probably find out why."

"We could just as easily just fly on by," said Banks, with a shrug. "Those ships could never catch us. The Invictus is too fast."

Sterling shook his head. "No, that will only postpone the confrontation to another time," he said, resolute in his decision. "I'd rather have it out with them now and be done with it."

Banks nodded. "Aye, Captain. I'll order Lieutenant

Razor to make sure reserve power is allocated to our weapons and armor," she replied, reaching for her neural interface. The door to the bridge then swooshed open and Razor walked inside.

"Speak of the devil," said Sterling, hooking a thumb in the direction of their chief engineer.

"I've diverted all available power, including reserves, to the weapons and regenerative armor," said Razor. She stepped over to the row of consoles at the rear of the bridge and began to transfer her engineering readouts and controls to them. "We'll need to find a fuel source soon, though," she added, working on the new array of consoles. "Otherwise we'll be running on fumes pretty soon."

"That's strange, I was just about to ask you to do all the things you've already done," said Banks, scowling back at Razor. "I know we can read each other's minds, but typically we need a neural link to have formed first."

The white-haired officer turned to face the command area, pressing her hands to the small of her back.

"My apologies if my actions were presumptuous, Commander," Razor replied, though to Sterling's ear she didn't sound particularly apologetic.

"No apology necessary, Lieutenant, I appreciate you taking the initiative," replied Banks. "Next time, just square it with the bridge first, understood?"

"Aye, sir," Razor replied with a respectful nod. "I merely assumed that since we were about to enter into a combat situation it was the prudent course of action."

"A warship operates on orders not assumptions," Sterling chipped in, though secretly he appreciated Razor's initiative too. Then he thought more about his chief-engineer's justification and rested back on his console, peering at Razor with a quizzical eye. "What leads you to presume we're about to enter a combat situation, Lieutenant?" He was genuinely curious to understand how Razor had come to this conclusion when she hadn't been on the bridge during the tactical analysis.

Razor frowned then pointed to the three ships on the viewscreen. "Well, I monitored the ships from engineering and it's just about the most obvious setup for an ambush that I've ever seen," she said. The tone of her voice suggested she considered it so obvious that the question was unnecessary.

Sterling laughed. "Yes, I suppose it is," he replied, glancing back at the supposedly derelict trio of ships. "Carry on Lieutenant."

Sterling then turned to face his weapons officer. As usual, Shade had been quietly observing the crew interactions on the bridge, without getting involved.

"Target the weapons systems and engines of the destroyer only," Sterling said, his tone becoming firmer as the time for combat drew near. "If this is another Marshall, I'd rather try to reason with him or her than destroy them. We're going to be in the Void for some time and could do without making an enemy of every Marshall we run into."

"Aye captain," replied Shade, coolly. "What about the freighters?"

Sterling thought for a moment, weighing up the options, though on this occasion he felt a show of strength was merited. "If they power weapons and lock on, destroy them," Sterling said, meeting his weapons officer's intense, emotionless eyes. "These people need to learn not to cross us."

"Aye Captain," replied Shade, still with cool detachment, though also a touch more eagerness. "I have relayed an attack pattern to Ensign Keller, based on my assessment of their most-likely ambush strategy," the weapons officer added. She did not touch her console, Sterling noticed. Clearly, like Shade, she had also already taken the action she was proposing.

"And what ambush strategy is that, exactly?" asked Sterling. His crew appeared to be in the mood for taking presumptive action. Some Captains would find this annoying, but Sterling appreciated that his crew had the experience and intelligence to apply foresight to their duties.

"The destroyer is closest and positioned between to the two freighters," Shade replied, working at her console and sending her analysis to the viewscreen. "Once we close in, the freighters will power up and attempt to catch us in a crossfire. It's crude, much like their vessels, but effective."

Sterling nodded. "Then let's make sure we spoil their plans, Lieutenant," he replied, turning his attention to the viewscreen.

"Aye, Captain, I intend to," Shade replied. Her tone was still level, but Sterling could now detect an undercurrent of eager anticipation in her voice. There was nothing Opal Shade enjoyed more than acts of violence.

"Then let's spring the trap," said Sterling, again resting

forward on his console and allowing his fingers to slide into their familiar grooves. "Battle stations..."

The main lights on the bridge went out and his crew was bathed in the crimson hue of their low-level alert lighting. Sterling could feel the thrum of the Invictus' engines and reactor building, as energy was produced and redirected to the offensive and defensive systems. It was like the ship itself had received a shot of adrenaline directly into its heart.

"Coming up on the destroyer now, Captain," said Ensign Keller, who was primed and ready at the helm controls. "Combat maneuvers programmed in and standing by."

Sterling nodded, but kept his eyes focused on the old gen-one destroyer in the center of the viewscreen. The Sa'Nerran weapons that had been retrofitted to its vintage hull were also older designs, like the ship itself, but at point blank range they could still do serious damage to the Invictus. He knew they had to be precise in their actions and use the Marauder's superior capabilities to their full advantage. Banks console then chimed an alert and Sterling felt the hairs on the back of his neck stand on end.

"The freighters are powering up and locking weapons," said Banks, working her console. "And fast too. These crew are certainly not rookies, that's for sure."

Sterling then saw lights flicker on across the hull of the destroyer. Its plasma weapons began to glow brightly, like the tips of cigars being smoked in a dark room.

"Execute the combat maneuver, Ensign," said Sterling, gripping the side of his console tightly. His stomach had tightened into a knot, but he wasn't nervous – like the rest of the crew, he was eager to get into action.

Ensign Keller worked the console with his usual proficiency and the Invictus powered away from the destroyer, rising above it like a bird of prey. The freighters both fired, but their plasma blasts crossed harmlessly in space. Sterling detected a succession of small impacts on the hull as their ambushers opened fire with mass-turrets. However, these archaic conventional weapons posed no immediate threat to a powerful ship such as the Invictus. It was like trying to break through a bank vault door by firing a pistol at it. All three enemy ships tried to re-orient themselves in order to bring their main guns to bear, but it was already too late.

"Firing..." Lieutenant Shade called out.

Two flashes of plasma lit up the viewscreen as the Invictus' plasma turrets unloaded on the two freighters. A smile curled Sterling's lips as he saw explosions ripple across the hulls of the enemy vessels. Shade's precisely aimed shots had crippled their weapons systems and drilled into the command decks, opening the compartments to space. Sterling could already see the bodies of the freighter crews spiraling out into the Void. More explosions rippled across the freighters and both listed out of control, except this time they weren't merely playing dead.

"The destroyer is adjusting course," said Banks, peering down at her console. "It's turning to run."

Sterling glanced across to Shade, who had held fire, awaiting his confirmation. Another captain of another ship might have let the destroyer go. However, Sterling didn't care that the enemy vessel was fleeing. The captain of the ship had made his bed and now he'd have to lie in it.

"Open fire, Lieutenant," Sterling said with conviction.

The main plasma rail guns of the Invictus fired, but at the last moment the destroyer tried to evade. The blasts cut through the enemy vessel's port side engines, destroying them completely and sending the ship into an uncontrolled spin. More flashes lit up the screen as the Invictus' plasma turrets picked off the destroyer's weapons, leaving it crippled and defenseless.

"We're receiving an incoming transmission," said Banks, cocking an eyebrow at Sterling.

"I thought we might," replied Sterling, pushing himself away from his console and straightening his tunic in readiness to take the call. "Put them through."

Banks tapped her console and moments later the image of a man in a leather frock coat appeared on the viewscreen. He was older than Sterling, perhaps in his sixties, he reasoned, though the weather-beaten look to his skin could have aged the man beyond his years. Wispy grey hair protruded below the line of the man's black, pork-pie hat, creating a sharp contrasting line with the stiff brim of the old-fashioned-looking headwear.

"I see that your reputation is not unwarranted, Captain Sterling," the man said. However, the words were uttered with contempt, rather than admiration.

"Care to explain who the hell you are, and why you attacked my ship?" Sterling replied, getting straight the point. He wasn't interested in a prolonged conversation; he had more important matters to attend to.

"My name is Ed Masterson," the man replied, maintaining a remarkable level of composure, considering his ship was out of control and his escorts had been obliterated. "But most people know me as Marshall Masterson, senior."

Sterling sighed and nodded. The reason for the ambush was now clear. Revenge.

"Then I assume this is about your son, Marshall?" Sterling asked, again trying to railroad the older man into getting to the point.

"You admit that you killed him?" the Marshall replied, his eyes narrowing a fraction, which brought his silver-grey eyebrows below the rim of his hat.

"He double-crossed me then tried to kill me and kidnap a member of my crew," Sterling said, upholding his rigid posture and level tone. "For a lawman, he was remarkably unconcerned with the law."

Sterling saw the older man's jaw tighten. The Marshall chewed the inside of his mouth, as if shuffling gum or tobacco from one corner to another before finally answering.

"The law is set by the Marshalls, Captain Sterling," Masterson replied. "Fleet don't make the rules out here. What you consider fair, or a double-cross, or 'illegal' is beside the point." The Marshall leant in closer, making his lined face grow larger on the viewscreen. "Fact is you killed a Marshall, Captain Sterling," he said, anger now bleeding into the man's words. "That he was also my son don't matter a god-damned bit. You killed a lawman and you must be judged and punished for your crime."

Sterling shook his head. He'd hoped to be able to reason with the man, but it seemed clear that he could not. Commander Banks' console then chimed an alert and Sterling felt a neural connection form in his mind.

"The destroyer's engines are shot, Captain, and it's drifting rapidly toward the planet," Banks said, through the neural link. "Unless we grapple it, the Marshall's ship will start to fall through the atmosphere in the next few seconds."

Sterling glanced at his first officer. "He's not going to leave us alone, is he?" he asked through the link.

Banks shook her head. "No, he's not."

Sterling sighed again then tapped his neural interface to close the link before turning back to the viewscreen. He saw that the Marshall's destroyer had already hit the upper atmosphere and was shrouded in a corona of flames.

"Your son got what he deserved, Marshall," Sterling replied. "And now you will too."

Sterling then cut the transmission from the ship, leaving the image of the incensed older Marshall imprinted on his retinas.

"Shall I destroy it, Captain?" asked Lieutenant Shade, with her usual cold detachment.

Sterling shook his head. "They're already dead, Lieutenant," he replied. "Let them burn."

"Aye, sir," replied Shade. The weapons officer pressed her hands to the small of her back and joined Sterling and the others in watching the destroyer descend deeper into the atmosphere.

Sterling knew that allowing Shade to finish the

destroyer would have perhaps been the more merciful thing to do. However, he wasn't feeling merciful. He was angry. The older lawman and his crew hadn't needed to die. Only stubbornness and pride had prevented Masterson from saving his own skin. It was a pointless death. Yet, it was also necessary. Sterling was not about to allow one man's inconsequential vendetta to risk his crucial mission.

"I'm picking up what looks like an old Fleet outpost on the surface of the planet," said Commander Banks, this time speaking out loud. "We didn't detect it previously because we were too far from the planet."

"Do you think it could still contain some supplies?" Sterling asked.

Banks worked her console for a couple of seconds then shrugged. "I can't get a reading from up here, but the storage vaults in these places were shielded and below ground." She stopped working at her console then folded her arms and turned back to Sterling. "Assuming, no-one else has raided it, there's a good chance it has what we need."

Sterling considered this for a moment while continuing to watch the Marshall's ship fall faster through the atmosphere, burning up like a meteor.

"Lieutenant Razor, how are our fuel reserves looking?" Sterling asked, glancing back to his straight-talking engineer.

"They're looking empty, Captain," Razor replied, bluntly. "If there's a chance this planet has what we need, I'd recommend we take it," she added. "I can ration enough fuel for us to reach orbit again in case it's a bust, but after that we'll have to land at Bastion on the main colony planet and try to barter for what we need there."

Sterling glanced at Banks and his first officer's expression told him that she liked that idea even less than he did.

"We'd have more luck bartering with the Sa'Nerra than with the inhabitants of Bastion," Banks said, speaking her mind.

Sterling nodded and turned back to the viewscreen. Either option presented risk. However, if he could recover the supplies without having to visit a colony planet that was vehemently hostile to the Fleet, it was worth a shot.

"Ensign Keller, configure the ship for planetary entry," Sterling announced, making his decision. "Then take us down to the Fleet outpost."

CHAPTER 7
CLANGING BALLS OF STEEL

STERLING AND BANKS stood at the edge of the landing platform at the abandoned Fleet base and surveyed the lush forest that surrounded the former hilltop fort. The base was on the second of two habitable planets that existed inside Middle Star's goldilocks zone. The original name of the planet, before the start of the war relegated it to the Void, was buried somewhere in the recesses of Sterling's memory. Now it was simply known by Fleet's formal designation of, "Colony Two: Middle Star."

In the distance, Sterling could see the fires of primitive industry sending plumes of acrid smoke into the cool atmosphere. However, while the war had not driven humanity from the Void Worlds completely, the reality was that few human settlements remained on the planet. It was also true that many – though not all – of the towns and broken cities that had survived were now treacherous places. They were blessed with technology from the twenty-fourth century but cursed with the lawlessness and brutality of Europe's middle ages. Even so, Sterling still preferred setting down on Colony Two to their only other option of landing at Bastion. At least on Colony Two they would be left alone. On Bastion, they would be seen as being no better than murderers.

"You wouldn't think that the Sa'Nerra bombarded this planet only forty or so years ago," said Banks, standing with her hands on her hips. A fresh breeze was whipping through the valley and pushing back her shoulder-length chestnut hair so that it acted like a windsock.

Sterling drank in the breeze, grateful for the opportunity to taste real air, at least for a few hours. He then glanced to his right, towards the fractured remains of a once great city. Now, it was merely a blackened wasteland of rubble and death.

"This planet was one of the most developed United Governments outer colonies in existence at the start of the war," Sterling said, thinking back to his Fleet history lessons at the academy. Then he held out his arm and gestured to the broken city in the distance. "Now look at it."

"I remember reading about the Battle of Middle Star," said Banks, turning her head to look at the city. The wind lashed her hair across her face, forcing her to brush it away. "It was quite a story, though a little maudlin and over-dramatic for my liking."

Sterling turned back to his first officer and smiled. "You old romantic, you," he teased.

Banks folded her arms. "Don't tell me that a cold-hearted killer like you sympathizes with what Fletcher did?" she asked, sounding astounded by Sterling's comment.

"Not exactly," replied Sterling, still smiling. "If we all acted as selfishly at Lieutenant Fletcher did all those years ago, we'd have lost the war already."

"But..." pressed Banks, evidently still curious about exactly which part of Fletcher's story he empathized with.

"But I admire his determination and, quite honestly, his solid-steel balls," Sterling continued, drawing an even more astonished look from Banks. "In many ways, he's not all that unlike us."

"How exactly is a mutinous bastard like Christopher Fletcher like us?" Banks demanded. She'd now switched from being simply curious to downright offended.

"He made a hard call," Sterling retorted, undeterred by his first officer's ire toward his statements.

"He made the wrong damned call," Banks hit back. Sterling could see that the muscles in her arms and legs had tensed up. She wasn't just playing devil's advocate – she was genuinely riled up.

"Make no mistake, Mercedes, I disagree with his reasons and motivations," Sterling was quick to add, since Banks was now turning slightly red in the face. "He was selfish. He disobeyed orders and his actions cost the life of his captain."

"But..." Banks said again, sensing that Sterling still had more to say.

"But he *won*, Mercedes," Sterling said, throwing his arms out wide. "He commandeered the Bismarck then rallied twelve other ships to mutiny before surging back to

Middle Star and kicking the Sa'Nerra off their planet."
Banks' eyes narrowed. She still looked deeply skeptical, but
she didn't interrupt him. "That's the sort of grit the Fleet
will need if we're to win this war," Sterling sighed, peering
back toward the ravaged city. "Fleet ordered all ships to
withdraw from Middle Star," Sterling went on, his tone
turning wistful. "We abandoned these people to the
Sa'Nerra then ran away, just like Fleet is doing now by
retreating to F-sector. At least Fletcher stood his ground
and fought."

"Fat lot of good it did him," Banks replied, seemingly
unmoved by Sterling's speech. "He mutinied so that he
could go back and save his wife, the same as the others did
in order to save their own families or lovers. But Fletcher's
wife was already dead by the time he got back; killed in the
first wave of Sa'Nerran bombardments. So he did it for
nothing."

Sterling considered his first officer's argument and
could not fault her logic. It was true that Fletcher had made
a hard call that day, but it had been for self-serving reasons.
The whole point of the Omega Taskforce was to make the
hard calls, but only when it served the greater good. Every
life that Sterling took was in order to save more. Fletcher
and the other mutineers had acted in their own self-interest
and, in the case of Fletcher himself, he still lost. Yet in
defeat, he didn't crumble or run. He stayed at Middle Star
and fought the Sa'Nerra so hard that eventually they gave
up on the system and left. He showed that the enemy could
be beaten. It was a lesson that the Fleet admirals of today –
Griffin excluded – could stand to learn, Sterling thought.

"You're probably right," Sterling said, finally admitting defeat. "It's a shame though. If we had more captains with the grit that Fletcher showed at the Battle of Middle Star, we probably wouldn't be in this mess now."

"What would you have done?" Banks wondered, stirring Sterling from his musings. "Imagine if it was your wife on the planet, and you were ordered to leave her, knowing that she and the other colonists would be killed."

"I'm not married, Mercedes," said Sterling, defensively. He already didn't like his first officer's little thought experiment.

"Just imagine you are," Banks hit back, not letting him off the hook. "Or imagine it's me on that planet when the order comes in for you to withdraw. What would you do?"

Sterling scowled and folded his arms. "You know what I'd do, Mercedes. I'd leave," Sterling replied, a little huffily. "Middle Star had little tactical value and the Fleet ships were needed to reinforce more critical sectors."

"Then why defend what Fletcher did?" Banks said, sounding like a prosecution attorney grilling a witness.

"I'm not defending the reasons for his actions," replied Sterling. "I just think Fleet could use a bit of Fletcher's passion right now."

"Passion?" repeated Banks, again looking a little stunned. "Passion was his whole problem, if you ask me. He was thinking with his pecker and not his head."

"I didn't ask you, actually," Sterling hit back, a little peevishly. He was now growing annoyed by the conversation. "But if you want to get down to brass tacks, think of what's happening now." He took a step closer to

Banks. "Earth is Fletcher's wife, Mercedes, and we're being asked to let it go. The UG and war-weary Fleet admirals have lost the hunger for battle. They already think we've lost, that's why we have to fight for our home. We have to show them the Sa'Nerra can be beaten, even if that means flying in the face of orders."

Banks cocked her head to the side and studied Sterling for a few moments, though she still looked unconvinced.

"I know what you're trying to say, Lucas," his first officer eventually answered, "and I don't disagree that Fleet could do with growing a pair of clanging steel balls."

"But..." said Sterling, mimicking his first officer.

"But Fletcher isn't anything like you or me," Banks continued. "In fact, he's the opposite of us. He fought to save someone he cared about. We make the impossible decisions, even if it means killing the ones we love."

Sterling frowned, intrigued by the phrasing of Banks' last sentence. However, he didn't get a chance to quiz his first officer before Lieutenant Shade came jogging over from the entrance to the Fleet complex.

"Captain, Commander, we've found the entrance to the underground vaults," Shade said, sounding slightly breathless. "There are signs of several attempts to break into them, but nothing that appears recent, and nothing that was successful either."

Shade then sucked in another deep lungful of the cool hillside air and rested her hands on her hips. Sterling imagined that his weapons officer had just run the entire distance from the vaults back to the landing pad in order to relay her report.

"Thank you, Lieutenant, but why are you not using neural comms?" Sterling asked, curious as to the purpose of the weapon's officer's unexplained calisthenics.

"Neural comms can't penetrate below the surface, sir," Shade answered. She then gestured to the dark stone surface of the landing pad. The smooth rock glistened under the evening sun, as if it had been sprinkled with a wafer-thin coating of glitter. "There's something in these rocks. Lieutenant Razor says it scatters the signal. She's working on building some portable relays, in addition to modifying the relays on the ship to work with the new boosters."

Sterling then looked over at the Invictus and saw Lieutenant Razor standing on top of the hull. She had an equipment bag at her side and was working on one of the external transceiver antennae.

"What the hell is she doing up there?" said Banks, who had also spotted the engineer.

"Planning to fall to her death from the looks of it," Sterling replied. He tapped his neural interface then began pacing back toward the ship. The connection formed to Razor, but the signal was choppy and weak.

"Lieutenant, we have repair drones that can do that work," said Sterling through the link. He had opened it so that Banks could monitor.

"Aye, sir, but they can't do it as well as I can," replied Razor, while continuing to work on the antenna. "Besides, I like to be hands-on."

"And I like my engineer to be one piece, rather than pancaked onto the rocks below the ship," Sterling hit back.

"Finish what you're doing then get back to the bridge. That's an order."

There was a brief silence, during which time Sterling could see Razor wrestling with a wrench. If her foot slipped or she took even a single pace back, the engineer was liable to fall forty meters to her death.

"Aye, Captain," Razor finally replied, tossing the wrench back into her equipment bag. "I'm all done, anyway, though I'll still need to test and calibrate the system, so you'll be radio dark down in the vaults for a little while longer."

"Understood, Lieutenant," replied Sterling shaking his head. If it wasn't aliens, vengeful Marshalls or turned Fleet crew trying to kill them, it was their own eccentricities.

"Sir, I have a commando squad standing by with breach gear and cutting tools ready to break into the vaults," Lieutenant Shade announced, oblivious to the dressing down the ship's engineer had just received. "Commander Banks and I are ready to proceed on your order."

"Get them ready to move out at once, Lieutenant," said Sterling, turning to his weapon's officer. "But grab an extra set of body armor and a pistol for me too. I'm coming with you."

"Aye, Captain," Shade replied before briskly moving toward the lowered cargo ramp of the ship.

"I didn't have you down as a tomb raider," said Banks, with a wry smile. "Are you hoping to find some buried treasure?"

Sterling smiled. "In a manner of speaking," he answered, slapping Banks on the shoulder and setting off toward the steps that led down into the old Fleet complex. "There might be some vintage Fleet meal trays in storage down there. And knowing your tendency to hide away the good ones for yourself, there's no way I'm letting you inside those vaults without me."

A DROP of freezing cold water fell from the ceiling of the tunnel complex below the abandoned Fleet base and rolled down the back of Sterling's neck. A shiver ran down his spine and he slapped his hand to the spot, as if he'd just been stung by a wasp. Shining his torchlight up, he could see thousands more shimmering globules of water clinging to the ceiling, just waiting to drop more ice-cold bombs onto his head.

"Your earlier quip about tomb raiding seems oddly appropriate now," said Sterling, returning his torchlight to the corridor ahead. The beam of light illuminated the back of Commander Mercedes Banks, who was a short distance ahead of him. "It feels like no-one has been down here for thousands of years, never mind just a few decades."

Banks smiled, appearing far more at ease in the dank underground complex than Sterling was, then continued to survey ahead. She pushed through a door, which creaked like a coffin lid from an old horror movie, stepped over the threshold and peered inside.

"It looks like the crew left in a hurry," she said, shining her light inside the room.

Sterling followed Banks into the space and discovered that it was one of the crew quarters. "It looks like the place has been ransacked," he commented, sweeping his light across the rows of empty beds.

Sterling moved further inside, his boots clacking resonantly against the hard, sodden floor. An assortment of unidentifiable bric-a-brac and personal effects lay scattered across beds and bedside tables. He spotted a collection of old photographs that had been left on one of the chests of drawers. Curious, he walked over and picked one up, shining his torchlight onto the faded and moisture-damaged image. In the photo was a Fleet Crewman First-Class standing with a woman in typical civilian colony clothing. The man had his arm wrapped around the woman's waist and was holding her left hand, highlighting a ring on the fourth finger; an engagement band with a clear stone in the center. Out of the corner of his eye, Sterling caught the glint of something metallic on top of the drawer unit. Adjusting the angle of the torchlight, he saw that it was the same ring from the photograph. A simple silver band with a shimmering stone that, unlike everything else in the room, had not lost its luster. Together, the two items told a story, Sterling thought. Though he also had a feeling it was a story that did not end as happily as the two people captured in the photo appeared.

"Diamonds are forever," said Banks, appearing behind

Sterling's right shoulder and adding her torchlight to the ring on the drawer unit. "Unlike that happy couple, I suspect," she added with a darker, unfeeling tenor.

"I wonder how many of them mutinied and joined Fletcher's little rebel troupe," Sterling mused, tossing the photograph back onto the top of the drawer unit.

"I wonder how many are still alive," Banks replied. She had already moved away to the other side of the room. "This all happened more than forty years ago. That's a long time to survive in the Void."

A voice echoed along the corridor outside. Sterling instinctively placed his hand on the grip of his pistol and hustled back toward the corridor. Banks arrived moments later, weapon in hand. Sterling then saw the flicker of a torchlight moving toward him. He raised his hand to shield his eyes from the glare and saw that it was Lieutenant Shade. Sterling and Banks glanced at each other; the relief evident in one another's eyes.

"This place is beginning to creep me out," said Sterling as his weapon's officer approached. "The sooner we're done here the better."

"The cutting team has almost broken through, Captain," reported Shade, lowering the torchlight so that she was no longer blinding him.

"Are there any further indications that others have been down here recently, Lieutenant?" Sterling asked as Banks stepped out of the crew bunk room, holstering her weapon again.

"It's hard to say, sir," Shade replied. "The damp and constant drip of water from the ground above would mean that any recent tracks will have been obscured." Shade then shone her torch at the seam between the wall and the ceiling. "I'm afraid they didn't build this base to last."

Sterling followed the path of the beam and saw a crack running through the surface. He shone his own torch along other sections of the walls and ceilings, noting several other hairline cracks and larger fractures.

"Most of this base would have been 3D-printed on-site," commented Sterling. "There would have been plans to build a more permanent structure, but the outbreak of war put paid to that."

"Hopefully, the vaults have remained intact," said Banks, stepping further along the corridor and shining her light into the darkness. "We should get down there. There's nothing else in this base but ghosts."

Shade led the way through the maze of corridors until they reached a wide staircase that descended to the storage areas. Sterling was about to follow Shade down the flights of stairs when something caught his eye. He stopped and shone his light onto the landing area across the far side of the staircase.

"Lieutenant, have you or your team been along this corridor?" Sterling asked, frowning down at the marks in the grime on the floor.

"No, sir, my team went directly to the vaults," Shade replied, jogging back up the steps to Sterling's side. The weapon's officer added her torchlight to Sterling's, illuminating the area more clearly. With the extra light, Sterling could see that the grimy scuff marks on the floor extended down the opposite flight of stairs and into the storage level.

"We didn't go down this corridor, did we?" Sterling asked Banks, who had also moved back onto the landing. "This place all looks the same to me in the dark."

Banks shook her head. "No, we didn't get this far. Whoever made those marks, it wasn't us."

Sterling sighed and clipped his torch to the shoulder attachment on his body armor before drawing his pistol. "Then if it's not us, we're not alone down here, after all," he said, ominously.

Shade and Banks also attached their lights to their armor and held their weapons ready. The three officers then stood back-to-back on the landing, covering the three exits. The damp, cold air inside the complex felt suddenly colder, as if a malevolent spirit had just floated through the corridors and passed through their bodies. Sterling tapped his neural interface and tried to reach the squad of commandoes. However, his mind was merely swamped by a hazy white noise, like an old de-tuned radio. Cursing, he tried to reach out to Lieutenant Razor, but his attempts to form a link to his engineer were similarly ineffective.

"Damn it, Razor hasn't got the neural relays online yet," Sterling said, sweeping his weapon along the dark corridor.

"Do we go on or go back?" said Banks, who was covering the corridor behind Sterling.

Another drop of freezing cold water trickled down the back of Sterling's neck, but this time he didn't try to wipe it away. He welcomed the sudden, icy shock, which acted like a splash of water to his face, sharpening his senses.

"We go forward," he said, with determination. "I don't care if this place is plagued by the undead spirits of deceased Fleet crew. Nothing is stopping us from getting those supplies."

Sterling moved out first, cautiously stepping down the stairs to the storage level. Flicking his eyes between the steps and the route ahead, he following the swirling marks on the grime-covered floor that had been left behind by the unknown intruder.

"Straight ahead then second right," said Shade, as Sterling reached the foot of the staircase.

Sterling nodded then moved ahead, observing that the swirling marks on the ground had multiplied and appeared to spread in all directions. A scraping noise filtered along the corridor to their side and Sterling froze, holding up a clenched fist to the others. The clack of their boots on the hard floor stopped, and all that remained was the sound of their breathing, and the drip, drip of water from the fractured ceiling. The scratching sound then came again, sharp and frantic against the deathly stillness of the underground compound. Shade indicated ahead, pointing two fingers into the darkness like a pistol.

"Let's do this," whispered Sterling, glancing to Banks and Shade in turn. "A straight up power play, nothing fancy."

Shade and Banks both nodded then got ready to move. Sterling again led the way, creeping along the corridor and following the tracks left behind by whomever or whatever was stalking them. The scratching sounds came again, growing louder and clearer the further Sterling ventured into the belly of the complex. Shade then threw up a signal to stop before indicating that there were enemies ahead. Sterling pressed himself up against the wall beside the junction of the corridor where the noises were coming from. Heart thumping in his chest, he checked that Banks and Shade were in position then gave the signal to attack.

The trio of Omega officers burst out into the corridor in perfect synchronization. The combined effect of their torchlights shining along the passageway was dazzling and for a moment Sterling was blinded. Suddenly the scratching sounds rose to a piercing screech and Sterling saw the silvery eyeshine of an animal racing toward him.

"Fire!" Sterling called out, aiming as best he could and squeezing the trigger.

The fizz and flash of plasma weapons was followed by a shrill yowl as the unknown beast was hit and sent down. Then as the corridor again fell into partial darkness, Sterling could see the shine of yet more eyes ahead, like stars piercing the veil of night. He couldn't count them all, but he knew that the numbers were greater than he, Shade and Banks could handle alone.

"Fall back!" cried Sterling backing along the corridor and retracing his steps. Then he turned and saw more silver discs of light along the adjacent corridor. Cursing, he glanced back in the direction they had come and the same shining dots in the darkness peered back at him.

"We're surrounded," said Banks, opening fire to Sterling's rear. "They've been hunting us!"

"And we walked right into their trap," Sterling replied.

One of the beasts darted out of the shadows and

Sterling fired hitting the creature on its flank. The animal fell a few meters from his feet, writhing in agony. However, it also gave Sterling his first clear look at the beast. It resembled a wolf, but with a head that was more akin to a bear. Its skin was leathery and its limbs stocky with highly-developed shoulder muscles on its front legs that gave it a lopsided appearance. It was a powerful-looking animal that had clearly evolved to kill.

"Keep moving," Sterling called out as more flashes of plasma fire lit up the corridors.

The scratches of the beasts' claws on the floor were now matched only by the howls of pain as they fell. However, the creatures kept coming, undeterred by the deaths of the others in their pack. Banks reached the foot of the staircase and began to climb, but was then faced with two more of the creatures on the landing. She fired, but both creatures had already stalked away into the darkness and her shots flew wide.

"Reloading!" Banks called out, releasing the energy cell in her pistol and slapping in a new one.

Sterling turned to cover his first officer but was then pummeled in the back and knocked to the cold, wet floor. It felt like he'd just been tackled by a gorilla. A close-range blast from a plasma pistol blinded him, then the weight was lifted from his back. He spun over and saw Shade at his side, standing over the body of the dead creature. The rank odor of burned flesh assaulted Sterling's senses even more severely than the creature had done. It was a smell he seemed unable to escape from for long.

Replacing the cell in his own pistol, Sterling climbed to

a crouch and continued to fire, but the onslaught from the beasts seemed never-ending. Backing up the stairs, he glanced across to Banks, who was still trying to fight back the creatures that were amassing on the landing. Suddenly, one of the beasts made a move, launching itself at Banks like a cat pouncing at its prey. Sterling fired, trying to hit the creature in mid-flight, but missed. The beast collided with Banks, its powerful front legs clawing at her. Sterling could do nothing other than watch in horror and amazement as Banks caught the creature by its shins and wrestled it off her. The eyes of his first officer were almost as wild as those of the beast. Sterling continued to fire, driving back the other creatures on the landing as Banks roared and retaliated. The organic snap of muscle being torn from bone then echoed through the corridor. It was followed soon after by a nauseating howl, the likes of which only a medieval torturer might have heard before. Glancing across to Banks, he saw she had ripped the animal's legs out of its shoulder joints, leaving them splayed at ninety-degree angles. It had been as effortless as pulling a cooked chicken leg from the carcass of the roasted bird.

Suddenly, fire engulfed the landing at the top of the stairs, and more howls and scraping claws filled the air. Through the blaze, Sterling saw another figure, but unlike the beasts that had stalked them, this was human. Flaming torches sailed over Sterling's head, so close that the fire singed the short hairs on the top of his head. The torches landed at the foot of the staircase and immediately the beasts howled and scurried away. In the new light from the fires, Sterling could now see the figure at the top of the stairs more clearly. It was a woman dressed in a combination of furs and what looked like old Fleet survival gear. She was perhaps in her thirties, though Sterling found it difficult to judge considering that her mouth and nose were covered by a fabric bandana. The woman was then joined by another woman and two men.

"You can come up now," the woman who had first appeared called out. "They don't like fire. They won't come near us now."

Sterling turned back to Shade and handed her his pistol. "Cover our rear," he said, before turning back to the new arrivals and climbing the stairs to the landing.

Banks arrived at Sterling's side, her chest still heaving from the exertion and adrenalin of her struggle with the beast. Her eyes were no longer wild, but she still bristled with raw, nervous energy. If it were needed, Sterling felt sure that she could have punched her way through the walls of the complex to make an escape route.

"I've never seen anyone do that before," the woman said, peering down at the mutilated body of the beast, spread open like a spatchcocked hen. "Are you human or some sort of android?" she addressed Banks directly.

"I'm just someone it's best not to make angry," Banks replied, though her tone was surprisingly light and convivial.

"I can see that," replied the woman. She then pulled down her bandana to reveal her face and offered Banks her hand. "I'm Jana, by the way," she said. Banks took the woman's hand and shook it. "I'm guessing you guys are Fleet?" she added, this time looking at Sterling.

"Yes, we are," replied Sterling, offering Jana his hand, which she accepted. "Thanks for the assist. I don't think we'd have gotten out of here without you."

The woman nodded, accepting Sterling's thanks. "The question is, what are you doing here?" she said, releasing Sterling's hand. "I haven't seen anyone from Fleet on this world since..." she hesitated then shrugged. "Well, since forever. For as long as I've been alive, in any case."

"It's a long story," replied Sterling, with a wry smile.

"I'd like to hear it," Jana replied. "We don't get many visitors around here."

Sterling glanced down at the smoldering bodies of the wolf-like beasts. "Not friendly ones, anyway," he said, gesturing the creatures.

Jana laughed and wafted her hand at the creatures dismissively. "Oh, these things are puppy dogs compared to some of the genuine monsters that lurk down here," she replied, darkly.

Sterling remembered about the commando team and his pulse began to race again. "Can you come with us?" Sterling asked. "We have more people down here that might need your help, and your fire."

"I know," Jana said, with a breezy nonchalance. "I'll take you to them, and make sure the way back to your ship is kept clear of our furry friends," she added. As with his earlier conversation with Banks, Sterling could tell there was a but coming. "But if you want our help, you'll need to give us some of the contents of those vaults," Jana added. "We've been trying to get into them for years."

Sterling glanced at Banks, who just shrugged in

response. He then peered down at the still smoldering collection of beasts littering the stairwell and huffed a laugh.

"Under the circumstances, I think I'll accept your offer," he said to Jana, smiling. "It sounds like a fair deal."

BY THE TIME Sterling and the others had reached the vault rooms, accompanied by the colonists, two commandoes had already been killed. The beasts that inhabited the lower levels of the abandoned Fleet base had torn through their commando armor like it was paper, then ripped their flesh to shreds. The three remaining commandoes had managed to drive the creatures back, discovering only by accident the protective effects of fire. Incendiary grenades had not only served as an effective weapon against the creatures, but the burning remains of the dead beasts had ensured others kept clear. Now it was the flaming torches of the colonists that protected the group. Dozens had been set up outside the vault-room door, and lining the corridors back to the ship. Even so, the eyes of the predatory creatures that had attacked Sterling could be seen lurking in the areas of the base that were still shrouded in darkness. On the plus side, Sterling had managed to retrieve some old command access codes from the computer on the Invictus. These had successfully unlocked the vault door, without the need for a brute-force entry.

"Let's have your report, Lieutenant," Sterling asked Lieutenant Razor, who was interrogating the vault's inventory computer. "Is there anything of value in here or not?"

"Well, there's good news and bad news," said Razor, in a matter-of-fact tone.

"That's not exactly what I wanted to hear," replied Sterling, feeling his mood sink. "Give me the bad news first."

Razor turned from the computer interface on the wall and referred to the device on her wrist instead. She tapped the screen so that it expanded and solidified to provide a wider field of view.

"The bad news is that probably fifty percent of the stored meal trays have perished," Razor began, scanning down the list of items she'd highlighted. "That was down to the local vermin that the Fleet crew who managed these stores failed to deal with."

Sterling scowled then began to check the floor around his feet. "Vermin? What kind of vermin?" He said, sounding a little fretful. Given the beasts they'd just encountered, he was envisaging rat-like monsters the size of small dogs with three-inch fangs. Banks snorted a laugh as Sterling hopped around on the spot, causing him to scowl back at her instead.

"Long dead vermin, thankfully, Captain," Razor then answered. "They may have found food in here, but there was no oxygen or water. However, while they were alive, they did plenty of damage."

Sterling sighed then nodded. "How long will the food supplies last us?" he asked, returning his attention to the chief engineer.

"Three or four months, I'd say," replied Razor.

Sterling's brow wrinkled. "Three or four months? I don't plan on being in the Void for three weeks, never mind three months, Lieutenant," Sterling replied, feeling a sudden weight lift from his shoulders. "What about fuel stores and other components?"

Razor checked her computer while Sterling sifted through some of the intact meal trays that his engineer had uncovered.

"The official inventory reports that the fuel depot is at ten percent of capacity," Razor continued, while continuing to flick through the data. "That's more than enough for the Invictus, especially if we're not planning a protracted stay in the Void."

"Understood, Lieutenant," Sterling replied, smiling at one of the vacuum-sealed trays then handing it to Banks. His first officer took the tray then laughed, flipping it over and holding it up like a trophy.

"A vintage number four, duck cassoulet," Banks said, smiling sweetly at Sterling. "You sure know how to treat a girl, Captain."

Sterling picked up another tray and tapped his finger to the identification code on the packaging. "Even better, they have a stack of number twenty-sevens," he said, unable to hide his excitement.

Razor observed the curious exchange between the two most senior officers of the Invictus, appearing more awkward as the conversation developed.

"Are you sure those are safe to eat, Captain?" Razor chipped in, picking up one of the trays and examining it. "They are over forty years old, after all."

"They could be two hundred years old for all the difference it would make, Lieutenant," Sterling replied, dropping the number twenty-seven back onto the pile. "Just heat 'em and eat 'em, that's all there is to it." However, judging from the revolted expression on his engineer's face, Sterling didn't think Razor had been fully convinced by his assurances that the vintage meal trays were edible. "Transfer what we need to the Invictus, Lieutenant, but take only what we need, understood?"

"Aye, sir," replied Razor, though the engineer appeared perplexed. "Our hold is large enough to take it all, though, Captain, should you want to."

Sterling shook his head. "Leave the rest for the colonists. We would have been dinner for the creatures down here if it wasn't for them."

"Aye, sir," Razor replied, briskly. The engineer then headed off to continue her inventory and co-ordinate the teams from the Invictus who were standing ready to transfer the supplies to the ship.

"We should take it all, you know," said Banks, once Razor was out of earshot. "If we take damage and are forced to land to make repairs, it could easily be a couple of months before we get back to friendlier space."

"Perhaps," said Sterling, idly picking up an old Fleet

issue plasma pistol and toying with it. The energy cell design was now incompatible with the newer pistols they carried making it nothing more than a display piece. "But I made a deal," he added, meeting Banks' eyes. "I may be a cold-hearted killer, but at least I'm true to my word. The Omega Directive hasn't taken that from me yet."

Sterling then noticed that Jana, the colonist who had saved them from being mauled to death by alien hounds, had stepped inside the vault. Sterling and Banks turned to greet their savior as she approached with a smile on her face.

"I have a group of people waiting outside the perimeter fence of the base to carry the supplies back to our camp," said Jana, sifting through a selection of meal trays. "I must admit that you were far more generous in your allocation than I was expecting," she added.

"I imagine you have as much claim to these supplies as I do," Sterling replied. Jana frowned, apparently not understanding his meaning. Sterling pointed to the old Fleet-issue survival gear underneath the woman's furs. "I'm assuming you either took these from a base like this, or inherited them from their original owner?"

Jana looked down at the combat pants, which were patched up in so many places the DPM pattern was barely visible, then met Sterling's eyes again.

"They belonged to my grandmother," Jana said, lowering her eyes to the floor. It was obvious to Sterling that simply admitting that fact had been difficult for the colonist. "She was stationed here when the war broke out, but refused to leave when the evacuation was called," Jana continued. The colonist then picked up the old Fleet pistol that Sterling had been toying with earlier and turned it over in her hands. "My mother was ten at the time," she continued, tossing the pistol onto the pile. "This was their home. They didn't want to leave." Jana looked at Sterling again and he could see bitterness and sadness in her eyes. "Fleet tried to force them onto the transports, but my grandmother ran with my mom and a group of others who felt as she did. Fleet just left them behind."

Sterling nodded. "I guess you weren't thrilled to see a Fleet ship land here then?"

"I was more surprised than anything else," Jana replied. "Fleet forgot about us a long time ago."

"Not all of us," Sterling said, picking up the vintage Fleet pistol again. "These old weapons may have fired their last blast, but the fight isn't over. I still plan to kick the Sa'Nerra out of the Void and all the way back to the shithole planet they came from."

Jana laughed, which was not the reaction Sterling had expected in response to his audacious pledge. "Well, I hope I'm still around to see it, Captain," she said, a smile returning to her face.

Sterling felt a neural link form in his mind. He'd grown so used to the absence of neural communication that the sensation took him by surprise. Sterling tapped his neural implant and opened the connection to allow Banks to monitor.

"Captain, we've detected a ship entering the atmosphere a few hundred kilometers from our location," said Lieutenant Razor. "However, at ground level, the metals in these rocks are playing havoc with our scanners. We lost the ship in the noise, but if it's heading in this direction, we may only have minutes before it arrives."

Sterling tossed the pistol then clicked his fingers to get Lieutenant Shade's attention. The weapons officer responded without hesitation, tapping her link to join the neural conference call.

"Lieutenant, get everyone back on-board the ship and prepare to launch," Sterling said, hustling toward the door. "And arm the weapons and charge the regenerative armor. We'll be with you shortly."

Razor uttered a brisk acknowledgement then the link went dead. Sterling turned back to Jana, who was looking understandably puzzled by his actions. As a second-generation survivor, Jana lacked a neural implant.

"There's another ship incoming," Sterling explained to the perplexed colonist. "I suggest you get clear of the base until we're sure it's not a threat."

Jana nodded then followed Sterling and Banks out of the vault. Shade and the commandoes had already moved ahead, following the path laid out through the torch-lit corridors. From the darkness of the adjoining sections, Sterling could still make out the silvery eyes and hear the scrape of claws from the beasts that inhabited the underground space. Bursting out into open, Sterling was forced to shield his eyes from the sudden, intense brightness of natural light. The thrum of the Invictus' reactor filled the air with the sound of raw power and energy. Squinting his eyes across to his ship, Sterling peered up at the command level and tapped his neural interface.

"Lieutenant, we're clear of the underground levels. Tell Ensign Keller to take off as soon as we're on board," Sterling said.

"Aye, Captain, we're all set," Razor replied.

Sterling then closed the link and turned to Jana. "Anything left in those vaults is yours," he said, offering the colonist his hand.

"Thank you, Captain Sterling," Jana replied, shaking his hand firmly. "I hope one day you'll come back and make good on your promise to kick the Sa'Nerra out of the Void."

"I will, you can count on it," Sterling replied. It wasn't a lie or an exaggeration. To Sterling, winning the war didn't mean merely stopping the Sa'Nerra from invading the solar system. It meant beating them back to their own corner of the galaxy for good. And, if necessary, wiping them out completely. The War Council and Fleet admirals may not have had held true to his personal definition of success. However, to Sterling victory could never be claimed until the Sa'Nerra had been crushed and put in their place.

"You're not going anywhere!"

The shout came out of nowhere and took Sterling by surprise. He spun around to see Marshall Ed Masterson standing on the flat roof above the entrance to the lower levels. In his hands was an older model Fleet plasma rifle and he was aiming it directly at Sterling's chest.

STERLING PEERED up at the Marshall, at first unsure whether his eyes were playing tricks on him. The last time he'd seen the man, the Marshall's crippled ship was spiraling out of control into the atmosphere of the planet. Yet here the old lawman was, still looking remarkably alive. However, despite Masterson's miraculous escape, Sterling could see that the older man was badly injured. His face was cut and blooded and his clothes were scorched and torn.

Moments later, more armed men and women scurried out across the rooftops and from the overgrown flora that had grown up inside the base over the decades. Sterling watched as the Marshall lowered himself to a sitting position with his legs dangling over the side of the building, wincing in pain as he did so.

"My guess is that you're probably wondering how I'm still alive, Captain," the Marshall said, perceptively.

"It had crossed my mind," Sterling replied. He was

eager to get on with his mission, but at the same time curious to know how the lawman had escaped his fiery fate.

"That old gen-one destroyer wasn't the only ship I commandeered over the years," the Marshall replied, pulling a bent cigar from his jacket pocket and popping it into his mouth. "Sa'Nerran combat shuttles are a pig to fly, but they're tough as old boots." The Marshall lit the cigar from a lighter that had also been in his jacket pocket. The tip of the cigar burned brightly then a dark plume billowed out of the lawman's mouth, like the smoke from the factories on the horizon.

"I'm a busy man, Marshall, what do you want?" Sterling called up to the man. It was a pointless question, since it was clear what the lawman wanted. However, Sterling was keen to progress their encounter to its conclusion.

The Marshall laughed but his chest quickly began to spasm and the sound descended into a harsh, throaty cough. Masterson removed the cigar from between his lips and spat a globule of red spittle onto the rooftop beside his leg.

"What do I want?" the Marshall eventually managed to reply, coughing and laughing at the same time. "I want justice," he added, calmly. "It's judgement time, Captain."

This time it was Sterling who laughed. "This isn't your courtroom, Marshall, you have no jurisdiction here," He pointed over to the Invictus, parked on the landing pad only a hundred meters away. "One word to my ship and a dozen plasma turrets will reduce you and what's left of your deputies and mercs to ashes."

The Marshall shoved the cigar in his mouth then sucked in another lungful of black smoke before allowing it to slowly escape from between his lips. All the while he continued to watch Sterling closely. If the man had a plan for what he intended to do when he caught up with Sterling, he didn't appear to be following it.

"I lied to you earlier, Captain, when I said that it didn't matter that the lawman you killed was my son," the Marshall said, tapping the cigar against the wall to dislodge the ash. "I think I believed I was merely seeking justice at the time. But the truth of it is that I don't care about justice. Not in this case."

Sterling felt a neural link begin to form as the Marshall was speaking. The presence of Banks, Shade and Razor filled his mind.

"I have weapons locked on to the Marshall and his deputies, Captain, but the risk of hitting you is high," Razor said through the link.

"My commando team is standing by, ready to move out on your order, sir," Shade added.

"Understood," Sterling replied through the link, though he continued to focus on the Marshall. "Lieutenant Razor, get ready to take the shot on my command. The commandoes can then mop up what's left of them."

Both officers replied with brisk acknowledgements. Sterling then focused back in on the Marshall's voice, leaving the neural link open.

"The truth is, Captain, that you killed my son, and I can't let that go," the Marshall continued, unaware of Sterling's secret conversation. "I'm sure you're not bluffing when you say your fancy ship could take me down. But if that happens then my deputies are under orders to kill the other colonists we found waiting just outside the gate."

Jana bristled at the mention of her companions and took a step toward the Marshall's perch. The barrels of multiple pistols and rifles turned toward her as she did so.

"My people have nothing to do with this," Jana called up to the Marshall. "Leave then out of it, or you'll have more than just a pissed off Fleet Captain to deal with." The woman was not pleading with the Marshall – Jana was angry and sounded like she meant every word she'd said.

"I'm afraid that since you already buddied up with the Fleet, you made yourself a part of this, missy," the Marshall hit back. The lawman then returned his attention to Sterling. "I'll make you a deal, Captain," he said, popping the cigar back into the corner of his mouth. "You give yourself up to me for judgement, and I let the colonists and the rest of your crew go."

Sterling shook his head. "If you're looking for a noble sacrifice, Marshall, then you clearly don't know who the hell you're talking to," he hit back. "My life, your life, and especially the life of your double-crossing son don't matter. My mission is bigger than myself and it's bigger than my ship and my crew." Sterling pressed his hands to the small of his back and stood tall. "So, if you want a fight Marshall, you've got one."

The Marshall's eyes grew wide and wild and he raised his rifle. "Shoot!" the Marshall bellowed, the cigar falling from his mouth and he did so. "Shoot! Kill them all!"

Sterling had already relayed his order to fire through

the neural link before the Marshall had even opened his mouth. Plasma erupted from the turrets on the Invictus, thumping searing blasts of energy into the forest and undergrowth surrounding the base. Screams of agony followed soon after. Sterling grabbed Jana and pulled her down into cover, but not before the Marshall was able to get a shot off. Sterling felt the punch of the plasma blast hit his back, but his body armor protected him from the older-model weapon the Marshall was using. Turning back to the Marshall's perch, Sterling saw the Invictus' turrets reduce the front of the building to rubble. The Marshall had managed to scramble clear moments before being pulled down into the collapsing structure. Sterling aimed his pistol then a blast from the Invictus disintegrated the lawman's left arm like it was kindling in a camp fire. He heard the man scream, then lost sight of the Marshall in the clouds of dust rising from the destroyed buildings. Cursing, he turned his attention to the deputies and mercenaries surrounding the complex. Fires had sprung up all around them, but through the smoke he could see that the Marshall's remaining forces were fleeing.

"Lieutenant Shade, take your commandoes and pursue the Marshall and any survivors," Sterling called out through the neural link. "Eliminate them all. This time, we leave nothing to chance!"

"Aye, sir, moving out," Shade replied. Sterling could practically feel the adrenalin surging through his weapons officer's body as she spoke the words in his mind.

Moments later, Sterling saw Lieutenant Shade and the commandoes rush down the cargo ramp of the Invictus and head toward them. Sterling pushed himself up, quickly checking on Banks, who nodded to signify she was okay. Jana was also moving, though Sterling could see blood matting the hair around the back of her neck. He quickly checked her over, but her injuries were not serious, and seconds later they were both on their feet.

"Permission to join Lieutenant Shade to pursue those bastards," said Commander Banks, rising to her full height.

"Denied, Commander," replied Sterling, stepping beside his first officer and dusting himself down. "Let her do her job. We need to do ours and get back on-mission."

Suddenly, Lieutenant Razor's voice filled Sterling's mind from the bridge of the Invictus. "Captain, we have a second ship incoming!" the engineer bellowed. Her voice was so loud inside his head that it was like Razor had shouted the words directly into Sterling's ear.

"Why did we not detect it sooner?" Sterling replied, scanning the horizon.

"Unknown, Captain, but it's right on top of us," Razor replied. "What are your orders?"

The ground beneath their feet shook, then a Fleet Destroyer rose from the valley beneath them, like a phoenix from the ashes. The ship was old and battered, and barely larger than the Invictus, but the glowing tips of its plasma guns were no less threatening because of it.

"Stay where you are or I will open fire!" a voice bellowed out through an external PA.

Lieutenant Shade and the commandoes slid to a stop and took up positions, aiming their weapons at the destroyer, but Sterling held up a hand to stop them.

"Hold your fire," Sterling called out, directing the command to both Shade and Razor through the open neural link.

Shade and Razor acknowledged the command then Sterling turned back to the ship and scowled up at the scarred hull. There was something about the aged gen-one destroyer that he found familiar. Then he noticed the chipped and faded letters of the vessel's name, barely visible on the ship's belly. It was the Fleet Destroyer Bismarck. It was the mutineer ship commanded by Lieutenant Christopher Fletcher.

CHAPTER 11
BETWEEN DUTY AND HUMANITY

STERLING WAS STILL STARING into the glowing barrels of the destroyer's plasma cannons when Jana suddenly leapt out in front of him. The colonist thrust her hands skyward and waved to the vessel like a marshaller on an airport runway. The ventral turret beneath the nose of the old destroyer then swiveled and pointed down at Jana. Sterling felt his heart leap in his chest and was ready to bundle the colonist out of the line of fire. However, he reasoned that there had to be a motive for the woman's curious actions and decided to let it play out. Yet at the back of his mind was the worry that the charred and pulverized remains of Jana would soon be splattered across his face.

"Jana? Is that you?" the voice said over the PA.

"Yes, of course it's me!" Jana shouted back. "Get down here, already, I have someone you need to meet!". The colonist waved her hands madly toward the second landing pad on the base, again as if directing traffic.

The turret on the destroyer immediately stood down

and Sterling saw the glowing tips of its plasma rail guns fade. The veteran ship soared across the sky before dropping down gracefully onto the landing pad beside the Invictus. It was a skillful maneuver that demonstrated an intimate understanding of the old warship's capabilities. However, if the captain of the destroyer was indeed Christopher Fletcher, as Sterling suspected, the man's four decades of experience would explain his exceptional skills.

"It's okay, this ship is one of the good ones, not like those Marshalls," said Jana, walking toward the destroyer and indicating to Sterling to follow her.

"Lieutenant Shade, form a perimeter around the ship," Sterling said to his weapons officer through the still active neural link. "I don't want what's left of Masterson and his cronies trying to sneak back up on us."

"Aye, Captain," Shade replied. She hustled away, directing the commandoes that had abandoned pursuit of the Marshall due to the Bismarck's sudden arrival.

"What are the chances that the captain of this ship will also try to kill us?" wondered Banks, walking by Sterling's side. "We haven't had much luck with people in the Void so far."

Sterling huffed a laugh. He couldn't argue with Banks' assessment, yet he also had a good feeling about Jana.

"A local advocate could be exactly what we've been missing," Sterling replied, peering up at the Fleet Destroyer Bismarck. It may have been old and battle-scarred, but it was still a handsome ship, he mused.

"Assuming this Jana person actually does vouch for us,

and not double-cross us like everyone else," Banks replied, darkly.

Sterling snorted. "You're usually the mildly more optimistic one out of the two of us," he said, glancing over at his first officer. "What happened?"

"The Void happened," Banks replied, still in a dark mood. "This place sucks the optimism out of you like a black hole devours light."

"Perhaps, but maybe the universe finally owes us one," said Sterling, slapping Banks on the back. "Come on, let's meet our mutinous new friend."

The old warship's cargo ramp was already in the process of lowering as Sterling drew near. If the vessel's external appearance hadn't already implied its advanced years, the groans and creaks of the gears and hinges did. Hot plumes of steam were then ejected from vents all around the hull, making the vessel appear to be floating on a cloud. A few moments later a man in scuffed Fleet commando armor that had been rendered obsolete decades ago appeared through the haze. He was tall and walked with the confidence of a righteous crusader. The man's neatly-trimmed full-face silver beard and isolated, turned up moustache only added to his regal sense of authority.

"Jana, glad to see you're okay," said the man, nodding and smiling at the colonist.

"Glad to see you're still looking out for me," Jana replied, returning a nod and a smile at the warship captain.

The commander of the destroyer then turned to Sterling and studied him attentively, like a father might scrutinize his daughter's prom date. However, the expression the older man was wearing suggested he was more curious than was suspicious.

"So, who are your new friends?" the man asked. The question had been directed at Jana, though the commander's eyes remained locked onto Sterling's.

"This is Captain Sterling and his first officer, Commander Banks," Jana said. "They're from Fleet," the colonist added, making it sound like she'd just uttered a dirty word.

"Yes, I can see that," replied the man, who was now studying Sterling's distinctive uniform. "The silver stripe is a new one to me though. Is there now a fifth fleet or are you something special?" The man smiled. "My guess is that you're the latter."

"Oh, it's definitely the latter," Sterling replied, returning a knowing smile to the commander of the destroyer. "Though it will take a little time to explain why," he added, mysteriously. Sterling then offered his hand to the man. "I presume that you're Lieutenant Christopher Fletcher?"

The older man peered down at Sterling's hand but did not take it. Instead he made a show of slowly folding his arms across his chest, causing his vintage armor to creak and groan like the gears of his ship.

"If you know who I am then you know that I'm no fan of Fleet," the man replied. "You'll also know that Fleet are not a fan of me, either."

Sterling withdrew his hand, but refrained from making a similarly defensive gesture. Instead, he simply pressed his hands together at the small of his back.

"We're not like the rest of the fleet, Mr. Fletcher," Sterling said. He had assumed that the man's earlier response was as close to an admission of his identity as he was going to get.

"Forgive me Captain, but I find that hard to believe," Fletcher hit back. "Hundreds of Fleet captains have come and gone in the years I've been flying around Middle Star and not one has ever extended a hand of friendship, as you just did. So you'll forgive me for being a tad suspicious."

For the first time since the man had arrived, there was a more aggressive bite to his words. However, Sterling could see that it wasn't anger directed at him personally, but at the Fleet as an entity.

"In your position, I'm sure I'd feel the same way," Sterling replied, truthfully. "If you'd rather we just leave then I'll be on my way."

"Give them a chance, Fletch," Jana cut in. She had been quietly observing the exchange and appeared to be enjoying how the two men were sparring with words. "They opened the vaults and left me way more than they've taken. From the stories you and your mother used to tell me about Fleet, that's not normal."

"Indeed, it's not," said Fletcher, smiling over at the colonist. The man sounded more than a little intrigued by Jana's revelation. "Has Fleet finally developed a conscience about how they treated those they abandoned in the Void?" he wondered, again locking eyes with Sterling.

"I'm afraid not," Sterling replied. "In fact, the Sa'Nerra are pushing Fleet further back toward Earth. We're the only ship out beyond G-sector, and officially we're not even supposed to be here."

This seemed to intrigue Fletcher further, though it was clear he was also confused. "So what are you then? Some kind of humanitarian mission?"

Banks laughed, drawing a wrathful glower from Fletcher. Sterling held up a hand to draw the older man's focus back to him.

"Forgive Commander Banks, she means no disrespect," Sterling said, glancing across to his first officer.

It was then he noticed that Banks appeared just as defensive and standoffish at Fletcher did. In fact, she looked ready for a fight.

"Isn't that right, Commander?" Sterling added more insistently in an attempt to prompt Banks into practicing a bit of Fleet diplomacy.

Banks glowered at Sterling then met Fletcher's eyes. Her powerful arms were still folded across her chest, just as Fletcher's were.

"I meant no offence, Lieutenant Fletcher," Banks finally replied, stressing the older man's former Fleet rank. "Though I don't know why you're so interested in our mission," she went on, maintaining a passive-aggressive tone. "It seems to me that you stopped caring about Fleet orders a long time ago."

Sterling turned his attention back to Fletcher. His prickly first officer had failed the test of diplomacy, though he was curious to see how the disgraced former Fleet officer reacted to her accusation.

"It was just the one order in particular that I took issue

with, Commander Banks," Fletcher hit back, giving as good as he got. "I was proud to serve Fleet and my captain, just as I imagine you are," Fletcher went on, still with his arms folded. "I bled for the cause, lost more friends than I care to count and sent men and women to their deaths, all in support of the war. I had no issue with any of it. I wanted to beat the Sa'Nerra and kick their assess back where they came from, just as you do." Fletcher then leant in a little closer to Banks, fixing her with even greater intensity. "Make no mistake, Commander, the part of me that hungers for war has never gone away. It never will."

Sterling could see that the older man's muscles were tensing up as he spoke. The scuffed armor creaked more loudly as Fletcher hugged his arms tighter around his chest. Sterling imagined that it was all the old warrior could do to stop himself from striking out at Banks. The man's capacity for self-restraint was fortunate, Sterling told himself. Banks was far less likely to hold back.

"But after all we'd fought and died for, to simply abandon the people of Middle Star to the Sa'Nerra was a crime," Fletcher went on, the anger now flowing freely through his words. "I stand by what I did, Commander Banks, and I'd do it again, in a heartbeat, despite what it cost me." The man took a breath, though his eyes did not leave Banks' for a second. "Pray that you do not ever have to make a choice like I did. Pray that Fleet does not force you to choose between your duty and your humanity."

Sterling could see that Banks was burning to respond and to hit back with some truths of her own. His first officer glanced across to him, her eyes imploring Sterling for permission to speak. However, he simply shook his head and Banks reluctantly bit her tongue. It wasn't that Sterling didn't sympathize with his first officer's desire to speak up. He too felt like setting the sermonizing old warrior straight and explaining to him just how wrong the man's condescending assumptions about them had been. However, to do so would have meant revealing the true nature of their mission. And while he admired the former officer, he didn't yet trust him.

"We've all had to make hard choices, Lieutenant," Banks eventually replied, forcing the words through gritted teeth. "The difference is that the choices that we make affect the outcome of the entire war, not just the lives on a couple of backwater planets a long way from home."

"These two 'backwater planets' are my home, Commander," Fletcher replied, though he too had reined in his anger. "If I don't fight for them, no-one will. That's the truth of it."

The group fell silent for a moment. Their exchange felt oddly cathartic, despite the requirement for Sterling to remain guarded about his mission. Though he wasn't ready to trust Fletcher, their chance meeting had only reinforced the feeling in his bones that the older man had a lot of fight left in him. Despite the ignominious manner in which Fletcher was dismissed from Fleet, the man had retained a sense of honor too.

"Well, I'm glad you all got that off your chests," said Jana, stepping in and breaking the wall of ice that had frosted up between the current and former Fleet officers. "Now how about you military bulldogs stop barking at

each other and get along? We have enough enemies as
it is."

Fletcher glanced at Jana then looked at Sterling.
Sterling glanced to Banks then back to Fletcher. It was like
a Mexican standoff, but instead of waiting to see who
would be the first to shoot, it was a case of who backed
down first. Fletcher then let out a boisterous laugh, which
struck Sterling with such force that he almost fell
backwards.

"Trust Jana to act as peacemaker," Fletcher said,
hugging the colonist. "Fine, if Jana likes you then I'll get off
your asses too," the old soldier went on.

Fletcher's mood had changed so quickly it was like a
switch had been flipped. Sterling quietly observed the
interactions between Jana and the commander of the
Bismarck for a few seconds. It was clear there was a
connection between the two of them. However, he didn't
feel like it was an appropriate time to ask what that
connection was and, if he was honest, he had little interest
for such matters of small-talk, anyway.

"I haven't seen a ship like that before," Fletcher then
said, glancing across to the Invictus with admiring eyes.
"Then again, I haven't seen a Fleet ship in Middle Star for
many years."

Sterling smiled. Showing appreciation for the Invictus
was an easy way to get into his good graces. It was also a
suitable ice breaker. Even a hard-ass like Mercedes Banks
could be swayed by someone offering compliments about
their ship.

"She's called the Invictus," Sterling replied, also

admiring his ship. "It's a Marauder Class Destroyer, just over a year in service." Next to the boxy and utilitarian design of the generation-one destroyer, the Marauder looked alien and otherworldly. "It was designed for long-range strike missions," Sterling went on. "It's compact and lean, but packs the offensive power of a third-generation heavy destroyer. It also has regenerative armor, which essentially repairs itself."

"You're on the third-generation now?" said Fletcher, raising an eyebrow. "I'll bet you haven't seen an antique like the Bismarck in quite some time then?" He hooked a thumb in the direction of his ship.

Sterling huffed a laugh. "You'd be surprised. It seems that these old gen-ones are the favored mode of transportation for many of the Void Marshalls."

The mention of the Void Marshalls seemed to stir something inside Fletcher.

"The Marshalls..." Fletcher said, almost spitting out the word. "Those crooks make the lawmen of the Old West look like saints in comparison." He cocked an eyebrow at Sterling. "I heard Marshall Masterson Junior got killed recently. Word is that a Fleet crew was involved."

"Masterson got what he deserved," Sterling replied, though his answer didn't appear to shock or perturb Fletcher. "But he's not why we're out here. Now, I'm afraid we really do have to be on our way."

Fletcher nodded, respectfully. "Very well, Captain Sterling," he said, affably. "I'll inform the rest of my squadron that you're not a threat. They'll allow you to pass through Middle Star without any further trouble." The older man then shrugged. "Well, without any trouble from us, anyway. I can't vouch for the Marshalls or the Void Pirates, though the latter stay away, knowing that we're still out here."

"How many of you are left?" Sterling asked, curious to dig deeper into the status of the other mutineer ships from the Battle of Middle Star.

"All of us," Fletcher replied, with a palpable sense of pride. "All thirteen ships from the Battle of Middle Star still protect this system, and occasionally others too. We've even added a few more to our ranks since then."

"How many is a few?" Sterling asked, growing even more curious.

Fletcher smiled. "Not enough to match one of your fancy gen-three fleets," he replied, evasively. "But enough to keep the Sa'Nerra at bay, and that's all that matters."

Sterling nodded. He had held back information from Fletcher, so could hardly feel aggrieved that the older man had done so with him. However, there was a piece of information he felt he could reveal and, in doing so, he hoped it might reveal something about the former officer too.

"Between us, Mr. Fletcher, we could use all the ships we can get," Sterling said, taking a suddenly graver tone. "The war is going badly. The Sa'Nerra have a new weapon. A ship that can potentially destroy an entire COP in one shot, and perhaps even a small moon." Fletcher's expression hardened as Sterling spoke, but he did not interrupt and instead listened with keen interest. "Together with their neural control weapon, the United Governments are contemplating offering terms."

"*What?*" Fletcher replied. The man barked the word so harshly that a bystander might have thought Sterling had just insulted the man's mother. "They can't be serious?"

Sterling nodded. "I'm afraid so," he replied, calmly. "We're out here to try to change things, but the Sa'Nerra have the advantage. The truth is you may not be able to stay out of this war for much longer."

Fletcher drew in a long, deep breath then let it out slowly. "My war ended a long time ago, Captain," he replied with a steadier and wiser tone that more closely suited his regal appearance. Then Fletcher offered his hand to Sterling. "But I wish you good fortune in your war."

Sterling accepted Fletcher's hand and finally they shook. Fletcher turned to Jana and gave her another brief hug.

"Any chance I can convince you to come with me and get off this old rock?" Fletcher said to the colonist.

Jana shook her head. "My home is here, uncle," she replied, warmly. "But don't be a stranger. You know where I am."

Fletcher nodded then turned to Commander Banks' and nodded again, though a little more reticently. Sterling's first officer returned a similarly awkward and guarded gesture. Fletcher then again met Sterling's eyes.

"Good hunting, Captain," Fletcher said, offering a lazy salute, which Sterling returned with more practiced professionalism.

The man then turned on his heels and marched back

toward his ship. Sterling smiled. Even after all the years that had passed, Fletcher still possessed the unmistakable, regimental gait of someone who had trained and served in the military.

"See you around, Captain and Commander," Jana said. "Thanks again for the food."

Sterling and Banks said their goodbyes, then the colonist moved away, leaving the two of them alone, standing between the old Fleet Destroyer and the state-of-the-art Invictus.

"I don't think that's the last we've seen of Christopher Fletcher," commented Sterling, as the cargo ramp of the Bismarck began to grind shut.

"Nor do I," Banks replied, also regarding the old ship as it prepared to leave. She then sighed and finally unfurled her arms from around her chest. "Thing is, I'm not sure if that's a good thing or a bad thing."

ENSIGN KELLER MADE another slow pass around Thrace Colony, while Commander Banks and Lieutenant Shade examined their scanner readings of the settlement. However, even from the aerial image on the viewscreen, it was clear to Sterling that the colony had been attacked. Half of the buildings were either completely or partially destroyed, and those that weren't appeared to be without power. Windows were smashed and the walls of the intact buildings displayed the obvious scars of plasma weapons' fire.

"This place is as bleak as they come," commented Banks as a flash of lighting streaked past the viewscreen. "It looks more like a prison gulag than a settlement."

The desolate appearance of the settlement wasn't helped by the fact they'd arrived in the dead of night, during a heavy thunderstorm.

"According to the meteorological readings this weather

is mild by Thrace Colony standards," Sterling replied as several more flashes lit up the horizon.

"I'm picking up readings that suggests there may be life or at least a weak source of power down there," said Banks, glancing over to Sterling from her station. "But honestly, it looks like whatever happened here went down a long time ago. I'm not sure what we can hope to find."

Sterling sighed and nodded. He'd come to the same conclusion as Banks had. However, Thrace Colony was their only lead to the whereabouts of James Colicos. If there was even a small chance that they could find something in the colony that might direct them to where they needed to go next, they had to take it.

"I don't see that we have a choice," Sterling replied, pushing himself away from his console. He looked over to Ensign Keller, who was still maneuvering the Invictus around the colony, like a hawk surveying its hunting grounds. "Land on the outskirts of the main settlement, Ensign. I'm going to take a closer look."

"Aye, Captain," Keller replied, immediately adjusting course and swooping down toward a section of hard ground at the edge of the ramshackle colony.

Any other helmsman would have flown further out from the settlement in order to make a more gradual approach. Keller simply turned the Marauder on a dime and began the landing cycle with a fluidity that made the ship seem organic in nature, rather than technological. Sterling likened the comfort with which Keller performed the maneuver to the way Fletcher had navigated the old destroyer, Bismarck. Despite decades separating the two pilots, Keller was easily a match for the veteran spacefarer when it came to flying a warship. Sterling felt a distant thud through the deck as the landing struts made contact with the ground. He could even detect the gradually descending whine of the engines through the vibrations in his console. In all, he knew that the Invictus had completed its landing cycle even before Keller had informed him of this fact.

"Down and secure, Captain," said Ensign Keller, spinning his chair to face the command platform. "Shall I open the cargo bay door?"

"Not yet, Ensign," Sterling replied. He turned to Shade at the weapons console. "Order the commandoes to set up a secure perimeter around the ship. I don't want to be caught out again, like we were in Middle Star," he said, remembering how easily Marshall Masterson had snuck up on them. "Then meet the commander and me outside. The three of us will check out the main settlement administration block on foot."

"Aye, sir," Shade answered. "I'd recommend full commando armor, Captain. It's forty degrees outside and the storm doesn't appear to be letting up."

"Agreed, Lieutenant, we'll get kitted out while you organize the perimeter," Sterling said.

Shade nodded then hustled off the bridge, tapping her neural interface en route in order to relay her orders to the commando units.

"I hate the rain," Banks commented, securing her station and stepping beside Sterling with her arms folded across her chest. "Why can't this trail lead us to some tropical planets for a change? You know, azure water and long, golden beaches..."

"Where's the fun in that?" replied Sterling, smiling. "Give me an inhospitable hellhole any day."

Sterling invited Banks to take the lead and tapped his neural interface to connect with his chief engineer.

"Lieutenant Razor, the ship is yours while I'm gone," Sterling said through the neural link. "But if so much as a gnat buzzes past this planet, I want to know about it."

"Understood, Captain," Razor replied, smartly. "I'm on my way to the bridge now."

Sterling wasn't a fan of wearing commando armor. He found it to be too bulky and restrictive compared to his regular uniform. However, as he and Banks stepped onto the deck of the cargo area, and heard the rain hammering down onto the lowered ramp, he was glad of the extra protection it offered. Lieutenant Shade appeared at the top of the ramp, rifle slung over her shoulder, and waited for Sterling and Banks to arrive. Rain streamed off her armor like water off a car windshield. The wetness caused the dull-grey, composite material to shimmer with a soft luster, reflecting what little light the planet's twin moons offered.

"The commando units are in position and I've placed sensor beacons around the ship," said Lieutenant Shade as all three began to step down the ramp. "If anything tries to creep up on us this time, we'll know about it." Shade then raised her left arm. The computer screen was showing a rough, wireframed schematic of Thrace Colony. "This appears to the be the main administrative building for the colony," Shade went on, highlighting the building in red.

She scrolled the display to the right and highlighted a larger, multi-story structure. "This appears to be a standard colony accommodation block. The energy readings we picked up from the ship are concentrated in these two areas."

Sterling nodded then unslung his plasma rifle. "We check out the administration building first," he said, dialing the power level of the weapon to a medium setting. "If any of the colony's scanners were active during the time Colicos' shuttle passed through here, we might be able to retrieve some information from their logs."

"With power out, we might need to force entry," Banks added. She then jogged to the side of the hangar bay and lifted a hefty-looking, reinforced backpack off the wall. "This pack includes some basic tools and equipment, along with some portable power cells," she said, slinging the pack on as she returned.

"I didn't have you down as a cat burglar, Commander," teased Sterling. "I might have to check the ship's stores to make sure there are no missing meal trays."

"If I wanted to break into the stores, I wouldn't need the gear in the backpack," Banks replied, tightening the strap. "I'd just rip the door open."

"Noted," replied Sterling with a smile. He then looked up at the dark sky and driving rain and the smile fell away. "Okay, let's move out," he said, stepping out into the elements and instantly regretting it as rain hammered down on his helmet. It sounded like someone was playing a drumroll on his head.

"Let's make this quick, before the weather takes a turn

for the worse," Banks said, appearing at Sterling's side. She was scowling up at the swirling black clouds, blinking rainwater out of her eyes.

"Can it really get any worse than this?" Sterling replied, stepping off the ramp and into the mud. His boot sank into the ground then made a sickening organic squelch as he pulled it out again. "On second thoughts, don't answer that," he said, not wanting to tempt fate.

Lieutenant Shade took the lead and soon they had reached the sensor perimeter the commandoes had set up around the ship. The computer on Sterling's left arm bleeped an alert as Shade stepped across the threshold, followed by two more alerts as he and Banks followed soon after. The mud made progress slow and laborious, but eventually the sludge retreated and gave way to the synthetic road surfaces that most outer-world colonies used. Even so, some of the structures on the outskirts of the colony town had still been built on elevated footings over coarse gravel surfaces. Over time, Sterling knew that these temporary structures would have been replaced with permanent buildings as the colony developed. However, it was clear that the Sa'Nerran attack had spoiled those plans a long time ago.

"I think I preferred the mud," said Sterling, pausing for a moment to survey the colony, which looked even bleaker up-close than it had from the air.

Wind howled through the streets, whistling through smashed windows and slamming doors that were already partly broken off their hinges against the walls. However, while Sterling counted weapons and even the odd boot amongst the litter lining the streets, the absence of one thing in particular was beginning to concern him.

"Where are all the bodies?" said Sterling, kicking one of the boots across the hard floor. "The Sa'Nerra just leave the dead to rot, but if the Sa'Nerra did this then we should be seeing some evidence of human remains."

"And Sa'Nerran remains," Banks added, kneeling down to pick up a satchel that was strewn across the street. "Those alien bastards don't care about their own causalities either," she added, unzipping the bag.

"Animals could have eaten the bodies, though I'd still expect to see sections of warrior armor scattered across the ground," Lieutenant Shade pointed out.

Shade was scouring the area like a hunter, though unlike himself and Banks the rain did not appear to faze the weapons officer in the slightest. Banks finished rummaging through the bag she'd found, pulling out a broken personal data assistant, a half-drunk plastic bottle of water and a wallet. She flipped open the wallet, the contents of which had largely perished under the continual, driving rain that afflicted Thrace Colony, and scowled down at an ID card.

"Anything useful?" asked Sterling.

Banks tossed the Satchel away then moved over to Sterling, holding the ID card up so that he could read it.

"It's just a standard outer-colony ID card and founder's rights claim," she said, allowing Sterling time to scan the card before tossing it into the mud. "This place is a graveyard. If the Sa'Nerran warrior did bring Colicos here, all they would have found was a whole lot of nothing, just like we have."

Sterling cursed and peered up into the sky again. The rain was now coming down so hard that each drop felt like a ball-bearing being shot into his face. The wind had also picked up and the distant rumble of thunder was growing less distant with each passing minute. Shade's computer then bleeped an update and the weapons' officer raised her arm to check it. Sterling observed a hint of quiet concern on Shade's usually unreadable expression.

"Is there a problem, Lieutenant?" said Sterling, stepping closer to the weapons officer so he could be heard. The howling wind was stealing his voice and carrying it away into the darkness.

"I'm detecting movement, Captain," replied Shade, getting straight to the point. "The storm is interfering with the readings, but it looks like it's from inside the administration building up ahead."

Sterling checked his own computer then updated the weather report. The storm was worsening and it had also changed direction. The worst of it was now going to roll straight through Thrace Colony, rather than skirt around the edge.

"Let's give it another thirty minutes, then head back," Sterling said, lowering his arm and raising his rifle. "If we don't find anything by then, we'll come back after the storm has passed."

"We might be here a while in that case," said Banks, who was also studying her computer. "Based on these projections, the colony is going to be hit worse over the next few days than it is now. Believe it or not, this may be the calmest spell of weather we're going to get for some time."

Sterling cursed again then glanced ahead to the administration building. He hated having decisions forced on him by circumstances out of his control, but even an Omega Captain couldn't bend the elements to his will.

"Okay, let's check out the administration building," he said, taking the lead this time. "Everyone switch to neural communications. I can't hear anything over the sound of rain drilling into my head."

Sterling pushed on, reaching a narrow flight of stairs that led up to the administration building. Sections of the structure had been smashed open, allowing him into the foyer without needing to employ the equipment in Banks' backpack. The relief from the driving rain was instant and welcome. However, the damage to the structure was so severe that water cascaded down the walls and streamed in through holes in the ceiling.

"The computer console on the reception desk looks intact," said Banks, moving over to the machine. She tried to activate the computer, but the screen remained blank. "The power is out, I'll try to connect an external source," she added. Banks then unslung her pack, removed a portable power cell and a toolkit, and set to work.

Sterling left his first officer to the task at hand. Then another alert chimed out from his and Shade's computers.

"Movement again," said Shade, who was quicker on the draw than Sterling and had already assessed the reading.

"Where?" said Sterling, holding his rifle ready.

"West side," said Shade, indicating the direction with her hand.

"Commander, hurry it up, we have company," Sterling said to Banks.

"I've got this thing live," Banks replied. "Give me two minutes to interface my computer with it."

Sterling saw that Banks' face was now illuminated by the cool glow of the administration computer's screen. The opportunity to retrieve valuable information from the console was worth the risk, he judged.

"Two minutes, Commander, but look alive," Sterling replied as the sound of glass smashing and heavy blocks crashing to the deck reached his ears. This was followed by a series of reverberant thuds through the building's concrete floor. "Weapons ready, take cover," Sterling called out, upturning a steel table then ducking behind it. Lieutenant Shade had slipped behind a support pillar; weapon also held ready. However, Banks was still exposed.

Hard thuds continued to hammer through the floor, then suddenly stopped. Sterling concentrated, trying to filter out the near constant white noise of running water. Then a deep bass rumble cascaded through the floor, like the sound of percussionist beating a timpani drum. However, this time it was not thunder that had rattled Sterling's chest. This was something else, and it was coming closer.

SUDDENLY A SECTION of the west wall exploded as if a bomb had gone off, sending breeze blocks and rubble soaring across the room. Shade narrowly missed being struck by one of the missiles and was then consumed by dust and smoke. Sterling instinctively ducked behind the table, which was then peppered with flying debris and glass. Coughing dust from his mouth and lungs, Sterling recovered then aimed his rifle over the top of the table, looking for the source of the blast. What he saw was enough to chill the bones of even the coldest killer. Red eyes the size of tennis balls stared back at Sterling from what remained of the west wall. The creature had rough grey skin with a head like a rhinoceros, but a body that more closely resembled a gorilla. It rested forward on claw-tipped knuckles, attached to arms that looked like they could have supported the weight of a combat shuttle. The creature roared and the rumble of its voice almost bowled

Sterling over. It then hammered its fist into the deck, cracking the concrete, and charged directly at him.

Sterling opened fire with his rifle, striking the creature three times before it bundled through the table like a bulldozer. The blow sent him crashing against the far wall and left him in a heap on the floor. He was dazed and winded; the protection of his commando armor saved him from what otherwise would have been a fatal impact. Plasma blasts then cut through the clouds of dust, striking the massive animal in the chest. Sterling saw Shade advancing on the creature until she was blasting it at near point-blank range. The beast's skin was now blackened and burned in places, but incredibly it was still alive. Shade's onslaught would have been enough to kill a whole squad of Sa'Nerran warriors, but the creature refused to die.

There was another roar from the beast then a swipe of the animal's claw hammered Shade across the room. She skidded over the smooth concrete like a hockey puck then Sterling lost her in a cloud of dust and rubble. Pushing himself up, Sterling saw his rifle on the ground and threw himself at it. The creature spotted him and advanced, but was then hit by more plasma blasts, this time from Commander Banks. One of the beast's enormous claw-tipped arms now hung limp at its side, burned in a dozen places. The animal roared again then raised its good arm to shield its face before charging at Banks. Due to the injuries it had sustained, the creature's movements were less explosive than before, but the impact of its charge was still like a grenade detonating at close range. Sterling saw Banks' dive over the counter moments before the beast piled through it, wrecking it and the computer system that she had been working on. Sterling's first officer was back on her feet in a flash, but the creature reacted just as swiftly, stabbing at her with its claw. Banks managed to deflect the attack with her rifle, but the impact smashed the weapon in half. The creature then drew back its claw and thrust it at her again, but Banks caught the beast's talon and pushed back with all her strength. The sheer mass of the creature was too much for Banks to overcome and she was driven back against the wall. Sterling saw the claw begin to penetrate through the chest armor of his first officer. It was only because of her inhuman strength that she was able to resist the beast at all.

Knowing he had mere seconds to act, Sterling grabbed his rifle, turned the power setting to maximum, then ran at the creature. The beast's red eyes saw him approach and the creature tried to kick out at him with its shorter, but still stocky rear legs. Sterling evaded the kick then ducked under the beast's massive arm, which was still crushing Banks hard against the wall. With its other arm still limp and useless, the creature was unable to intervene as Sterling thrust the barrel of the plasma rifle underneath the beast's head and fired. Even at point-blank range the creature's impossibly tough shell repelled the blast, but Sterling fired again and again and again. Finally, the creature's head exploded, splattering Sterling with chunks of hot flesh that were harder than lumps of coal. He fell back and slid down against the wall alongside his first officer, who had prized the dead creature's claw away from her body. Turning to her, Sterling held the back of Banks head and peered into her eyes. She was breathless and too exhausted to speak, either with spoken words or through their neural link. Then she raised her own hand, grasped Sterling's wrist and nodded to him. This was all the reassurance Sterling needed to know that she was okay.

"Lieutenant Shade, come in," Sterling called out through the link. He released his hold on Banks and pushed himself to his feet. "Lieutenant, report!" Sterling called out again. Sterling then saw his weapons' officer through the cloud of dust that was still billowing inside the building.

"I'm here, sir," Shade replied, moving close. Sterling could see that she was walking with a limp. "But we have to move out now. There are more," she added in between bitter bouts of coughing.

"How many more?" Sterling replied, helping Banks to her feet.

"Unknown," Shade replied while slapping a fresh power cell into her rifle. "There are at least two between us and the ship," she added, meeting Sterling's eyes. He could see that she was clearly in pain, but Shade's expression was otherwise as calm and businesslike as ever. "And I estimate another one or two out west of this structure."

Sterling released the power cell in his rifle and reloaded. "We only have two weapons left," he said, keeping the power setting of the rifle dialed to maximum. "That will barely be enough to take out one more of these things, never mind four."

"This building is on the verge of collapse, so if we're cut off from the ship, we should shelter in the accommodation block," said Banks. She then spotted the backpack of equipment amongst the rubble and slung it back on. "We can get to the higher levels and block off the stairwell until reinforcements arrive. These beasts are powerful, but they don't look especially agile."

Sterling nodded, "Okay, let's move," he said. Then he saw blood leaking from a crack in the armor on Shade's thigh. "Assuming you can make it, Lieutenant?" he asked.

"Sir, even if that thing had torn my leg off, I'd crawl through the mud to get there if I had to," Shade replied. As usual from his weapons officer, this was not mere hyperbole. Shade was being completely serious.

"Then you set the pace," Sterling said, inviting Shade to take point. "And make it brisk."

Shade led the group back into the driving wind and rain and pushed on toward the accommodation block. Sterling checked his computer, studying the markers that Shade had highlighted as other possible beasts. The positions of the markers shifted constantly as he watched. The accuracy of the data feed was still being affected by the storm, which meant the true locations of the creatures was unknown.

"Lieutenant Razor, do you copy?" Sterling reached out to his engineer through the neural link.

"Barely, Captain," Razor replied. Her voice was thin and distant, as if she was speaking to him through a dividing wall.

"Recall the commando squads and seal the cargo bay," Sterling continued as rain stung his face and neck. "Arm the point defense guns and calibrate your scanners to look for lifeforms. This planet has a few surprises up its sleeve."

"Aye Captain," Razor replied. "Am I looking for Sa'Nerran life, sir?"

"No, think bigger, Lieutenant," Sterling answered. "You'll know it when you see them."

"Understood, scanning now," said Razor. "Should I send a squad to reinforce you?"

"No, in this weather they'll just get ripped apart by the things out here," Sterling replied. "We're aiming to reach the roof level of an accommodation block in the main colony," he continued, willing his body to push on harder through the rain and mud. "Once the storm has died down enough for the shuttle to take off, I'll let you know when it's safe to extract us."

"Aye, Captain, I'll be standing by," said Razor. The engineer's composed, no-nonsense reaction was both calming and reassuring. It was good to know that amidst the chaos and carnage, his crew had held their nerve. Sterling closed the link, confident that the Invictus was in safe hands. He then squinted ahead through the rain toward the accommodation block. Lieutenant Shade had already made it to the door.

"It's locked," Shade called back. The sky then trembled with the growls of the creatures that had attacked them.

"Let me try," said Banks, taking Shade's place.

Banks grabbed the handle and heaved back on it with all her unnatural strength, but the handle merely snapped off in her hand. Cursing, she tossed the handle aside then tried to manually force the door open, but it wouldn't budge.

"It's no use, it looks like the door and the ground level walls have been heavily reinforced," Banks added, hammering the door with her fist out of frustration. "It would take a blast from the Invictus plasma cannons to punch a hole in this."

More rumbles and roars then penetrated the veil of darkness, and Sterling could tell they were coming closer. They were running out of time.

"Cover me while I run a bypass," Sterling said, unslinging his rifle and handing it to his first officer. "This is an old Fleet colony, so there's a chance my command codes can still override the lock."

Sterling connected the computer on his left wrist to the door's keypad then began running the bypass program. Suddenly the rumble of the beasts' roars filled the air again, harmonizing with the ripples of thunder from the dark sky above them. Then a creature stepped out from the shadows and turned its red eyes toward them. This time, the monster appeared to be in no hurry to attack. It was taking the time to study its quarry more closely. *The beast knows it has us cornered*, Sterling thought.

"Hold your fire until it's closer," Sterling said, willing the computer to work faster. "And aim for the head or neck, otherwise you'll just piss it off."

The creature snorted, ejecting a plume of hot breath into the air from its long, horn-tipped nose. Then the beast advanced, but was quickly met with plasma blasts from both Shade's and Banks' rifles. Plasma energy thudded into the creature's head and neck, but its skin was as tough as starship armor and still it came on.

"Keeping firing, I'm almost there!" Sterling called out loud. His mind was too frantic for neural communications, though he doubted Banks or Shade could hear him over the fizz of their plasma rifles. Then there was a resonant thud followed by a dozen more like it in quick succession. A hiss of air slipped out from the seam of the door then it crept open, but only by a crack.

"It's unlocked!" Sterling called out, shouting at the top of his voice to be heard over the storm. Sterling then pressed his fingers into the gap between the door and the frame and hauled back, but the door wouldn't move. "Mercedes, I need you!" Sterling shouted, while still trying to pull the door open. The roar of his effort was almost as primal as the beast that stalked them.

"Take my place," Banks called back, handing the rifle to Sterling then wrapping her fingers around the side of the door instead. "Keep that thing busy!"

Sterling moved beside Lieutenant Shade and both continued to batter the creature with plasma fire. Energy flashed through the darkness, each blast striking true. However, the beast just raised its thick, claw tipped arm to shield its face and continued to stalk toward them.

"Hurry!" Sterling called back, as the door began to slowly creak open.

A second creature then appeared out of the darkness and Shade adjusted her aim, striking it cleanly between the eyes. The beast howled, drowning out of the sound of the thunder with its anguished cry. Enraged, the monster charged.

"Get inside, go!" Banks shouted.

Sterling turned and darted through the opening, closely followed by Shade, but the beast was only seconds behind her. Banks swung herself through the opening moments before the beast collided with the door, slamming it shut like a trap. Banks was propelled into the corridor as if she'd been shot from a cannon. The lock system engaged, hammering thick bolts into the foundational walls of the accommodation block and trapping the creatures outside. Sterling rushed to Banks' side and quickly checked her over. Her commando armor was cracked like the shell of an egg, but other than appearing dazed she was unhurt. Together, the three Omega officers collapsed against the wall, muscles tingling and chests heavy. Then a voice cut through the stillness like the flash of lighting through a midnight sky.

"Drop your weapons..."

STERLING TURNED to see a man and a woman in the hallway, both aiming old-fashioned firearms at Sterling's chest. The weapons, while clearly antiques, still looked powerful enough to penetrate his armor at close range. However, the colonists holding the weapons did not look like pirates or mercenaries. They appeared more terrified of Sterling and his crew than Sterling had been of the beasts outside.

"I said raise your goddam hands!" the man barked again. The colonist's voice quivered with fright, despite obvious attempts to disguise his fear in the barked command.

Sterling raised his hands, but kept hold of the plasma rifle, ensuring that the barrel of the weapon was pointed to the ceiling. Shade and Banks also raised their hands and turned to face the colonists.

"Take it easy, we're not your enemy," said Sterling,

keeping his voice calm and level, despite the fact his heart was pounding in his chest.

Behind them, the beast continued to hammer its fist into the massive, vault-like door that was protecting them. Each thud made the colonists jerk with fright.

"How about you slip your fingers off the triggers of those weapons?" Sterling said, fearing that the next thud against the door would cause one of the strangers to accidently shoot him.

"Last chance, Fleet," the man spat, ignoring Sterling's request. "Drop that gun or I blow your head off."

Sterling held his ground, though made sure not to make any sudden, provocative moments. "Are you sure you want me to put this down?" he asked, nodding toward the plasma rifle. "I don't think those two antiques you're holding will be much use if that thing outside breaks down this door."

"I built that door myself and it's held for the last ten years," the man hit back. "It'll survive another ten." Another thud vibrated through the walls and every muscle in the man's body tensed up. Sterling also flinched, but only because he expected to eat a bullet at any moment. "But you won't survive another ten seconds, unless you put that goddam rifle down!" the colonist barked, switching the aim of the weapon so that the barrel was now aimed at Sterling's head. The tremors shaking the man's body had become more obvious, despite the colonist's firm words. Ironically, Sterling realized it was more of a risk to drop his weapon than it was to keep possession of it.

"Fine, I'm putting it down," said Sterling, slowly crouching then placing the rifle on the ground. "You too,

Lieutenant," Sterling added, glancing back to Shade. Sterling knew Shade's subtle tells well enough to understand that his weapons officer did not agree with the command. However, she complied without complaint.

"My name is Captain Lucas Sterling," Sterling said, still showing the two colonists his hands. "This is Commander Mercedes Banks and Lieutenant Opal Shade. We're here looking for information, that's all."

"I don't give a damn what you're looking for, you're not welcome here," the man barked back. "How the hell did you get inside, anyway? That door was locked."

Sterling scowled at the man. It had suddenly dawned on him that these two colonists had been waiting on the other side of the door the whole time they'd been trapped outside.

"I managed to unlock it, no thanks to you," Sterling hit back. "Were you just going to leave us out there to get torn to shreds by those creatures?"

"If you were dumb enough to go walking around outside in the storm then you deserve what you get," the man replied, with a coldness worthy of an Omega officer. "Besides, you're Fleet. Gettin' mauled to death by those things is no more than you deserve."

Banks glowered at the man then balled her hands into fists. However, Sterling was quick to bar his first officer from going any further. They'd just survived a confrontation with alien beasts that could soak up plasma blasts like they were BB gun pellets. He wasn't about to lose his first officer to the nervous trigger finger of an irate colonist.

"I don't care if you like us or not," Sterling said, turning his attention back to the male colonist. "All I want is information. Once I get it, my officers and I will leave without any trouble."

The man frowned then glanced over at his companion. To Sterling, it looked like the man was seeking her approval, rather than her opinion, and guessed that she was the leader.

"Well, they're inside now, anyway, so we may as well make the best of it," the female colonist said.

The man sighed then pulled the rifle back, aiming the barrel at the ceiling. The woman behind him also lowered her weapon, but only aimed it fractionally off to one side.

"What the hell are you doing here, anyway, Fleet?" the man asked. "We haven't seen your kind around here for longer than I can remember."

"We're looking for someone," Sterling replied. "A scientist. We think he may have stopped by here in a shuttle, before heading deeper into the Void."

The woman cursed then flipped on the safety and shoved her pistol down the waistband of her pants.

"I told you that damned shuttle would only bring more trouble," the woman said, stepping to the side and glaring at Sterling.

"He was here?" Sterling said, feeling a rush of excitement race through his body. "It's imperative that we find him. The success of the entire war could depend on it."

The woman laughed openly and scornfully. "The war ended for us a long time ago, Fleet," she snapped back.

"No-one here cares about what happens to Earth or the inner colonies. Why the hell should we?"

"If Fleet loses then we all lose," Sterling replied, still managing to keep a lid on his own emotions. "The Sa'Nerra won't be content with Earth. Once they're done, they'll clean out the Void too."

The woman laughed again then gestured to the walls of the corridor around them. "Look around, Captain," she said, picking a strip of peeling paint off the wall. "Some of us lost already."

Sterling empathized with the colonist's anger and he knew their bitterness was justified. However, he was also rapidly losing his patience with their two reluctant saviors.

"How about we make this simple?" Sterling said, shaking off some of the excess water that had pooled on his armor. "You let us in, so we stop turning this corridor into a swimming pool, and we trade you for any information you have on that shuttle."

The mention of trade seemed to pique the man's interest. "What exactly are you offering?" he said.

"We need energy cells, a replacement type-seven generator and a whole heap of medicines," the woman interrupted, stepping forward and taking charge. "There are a hundred of us in this block alone, and many more spread out across what's left of Thrace. Some are sick, many are injured, and our supplies ran out years ago."

Sterling nodded. "If your information is good then you'll get what you need," he replied, calmly.

The woman scowled at Sterling then glanced across to her companion, who simply raised his eyebrows.

"Okay, Captain, you have a deal," said the woman. She then turned on her heels and marched back along the corridor. "The living areas are on the top floors," she called back as she walked. "I'm afraid you'll have to take the stairs. Like I said, the generator is out."

The man then slung his rifle and looked at Sterling. "The name's Bradshaw, by the way," he said, turning down the corridor. "She's Landry," he added, setting off in pursuit of his companion.

"Are those your first names or last names?" Sterling called after the man.

"Either or both, it don't matter, anymore," the man called back without stopping. "There ain't enough of us left here to need more than one name."

Sterling collected his rifle from floor then set off in pursuit of the two colonists. The adrenalin flowing through his veins was wearing off and he was suddenly conscious of a dozen new aches and pains resulting from the fight with the alien creatures. Banks and Shade followed, water pouring out of their armor like a leaky gutter. Both looked as weary as Sterling felt.

"We should be cautious," said Banks, stepping alongside Sterling and shaking the excess water from her armor. "Those assholes were willing to let us die out there."

"You'll get no argument from me," Sterling replied, activating the safety on his rifle then slinging it. "Lieutenant, make sure you watch our backs while we're up there," he added, glancing behind to his weapons officer. "We have no idea what to expect, and Bradshaw and Landry have already made it clear we're not welcome. They're not to be trusted."

"I don't trust anyone, Captain," Shade replied. Like

Sterling, she had also slung her rifle. "Well, almost no-one, sir."

Sterling smiled, grateful for Shade's quick correction, though he still couldn't be sure whether it was himself that his weapons officer trusted, or someone else entirely.

"At least we know that Colicos was here," Sterling continued, also shaking water from the joints of his armor. "That's a lot more than we knew a few minutes ago."

"Assuming it was Colicos' shuttle and not some other random transport," Banks replied.

"That's a possibility," Sterling admitted, while inspecting the dilapidated corridor of the accommodation block more closely. "But I don't think anyone would ever come here unless they didn't have a choice."

Sterling continued to lead the way, following the two colonists up the steep flights of stairs to the upper levels of the accommodation block. Due to their various bumps and bruises, plus the extra bulk of their armor, progress was slow. Eventually, they reached the seventh floor of the building and Sterling saw that a door had been left propped open for them. He pushed through it, feeling breathless and exhausted and was greeted with the smell of food. Moving further inside, Sterling was amazed to see that the entire floor had been transformed. Instead of multiple apartment blocks, the colonists had knocked through walls and created a number of larger communal areas, including a large kitchen and dining space. Sterling headed toward it, noticing that the colonists were using solid-fuel burners and actually cooking food on stoves that looked custom built. Sterling had spent most of his life eating Fleet meal trays.

The sight of an actual kitchen was as compelling to him as he imaged the sight of a starship would be to someone who had never been to space.

"Captain, might I suggest I hang back and cover you from the communal area?" said Lieutenant Shade stopping beside Sterling. The long climb up the narrow flights of stairs had opened the wound in her leg and blood was again trickling through the cracked armor. "It will also allow me to tend to my injuries."

Sterling could see that Shade was hurt, though neither her expression nor her voice gave away the fact she must have been in pain.

"Understood, Lieutenant," replied Sterling. "Co-ordinate with the ship and see when they'll be able to land a shuttle on the roof of this building. I have no intention of walking back to the ship with those things prowling outside."

"Aye, sir," Shade replied. She then began to limp toward the communal area, though she didn't take her eyes off Sterling and Banks for a moment.

Shade dropped into a seat then rested her rifle across her lap before removing the med kit from her armor. Sterling watched as a group of children went up to her, curious to learn what she was doing, but then quickly scattered as his weapons officer stared at them with her unflinching eyes. However, none of the children went far and simply hid behind various items of furniture, continuing to observe the surly-looking officer with intense interest.

"I must admit, this setup is pretty impressive," said

Banks, peering around the space. "They've modified the ducting system to vent the fumes from the cooking and heating stoves, as well as distribute heat around the floors. And it looks like they've engineered a rainwater tap over by the wall there," she added, pointing across to the cooking area. "They've adapted this entire building into a survival shelter. I doubt they'd ever need to leave it, other than to gather supplies."

Sterling nodded. In an age where everything he ever touched was made by a machine, he couldn't deny that the colonist's ingenuity was remarkable. He then noticed that Banks was smiling and frowned back at her.

"What are you plotting in that head of yours, Commander?" Sterling said, starting to feel a little self-conscious.

Banks nodded over to the kitchen area. "I thought I might sample the local cuisine," she said, still smiling. "I might be able to gather some intel from the other diners while I'm over there."

Sterling huffed a laugh. "You want to go eat just so you can gather intel, is that what you're telling me?" he said, shaking his head. However, Banks just smiled innocently and shrugged in reply. Sterling then saw Landry - the woman who had met them on the ground floor - approaching from out of one the enclosed rooms further into the space. "Hold that thought," Sterling said to Banks, as the woman came closer, holding out a thin sheet of material.

"Here, I made a list while you were taking a lifetime to make your way up here," said Landry. Sterling took the thin sheet, but the material just flopped around his glove, like a piece of fabric. "Our PDAs stopped working years ago too, like most things electronic in this place," the woman said, scowling at Sterling. "We make parchment from the pulp of a tree that grows locally. One of the other colonists managed to get a recipe for ink from our offline database, before the computers also lost power."

"Let me guess, because your generator packed in, right?" said Sterling, straightening out the piece of parchment with his other hand and ripping it in the process. The woman tutted loudly then folded her arms and waited for Sterling to read the items on the list. The menu of requests was extensive and unreasonable, but Sterling was careful not to show his concern. He needed to keep the colonist on-side.

"Commander Banks will make arrangements to have these items shipped over, once the storm lifts in a few hours," Sterling added, folding the note in half and handing it to his first officer. Banks took the parchment and read the items on it, her eyebrows rising further up her forehead as she progressed through the list. However, she had the wherewithal not to openly balk at its content. "Now, what can you tell me about the shuttle and the information concerning James Colicos?" he added, getting to the crux of why he was there.

The woman scowled then pointed toward the corner of the room, where the dining area had been laid out. An old man was sitting alone at one of the smaller tables, eating a bowl of stew.

"This shuttle you're so interested in landed by the

generator house," the woman went on. "Whoever was flying it broke in and stole all the goddam fuel, which is why we're living like cavemen." The anger and bitterness flowed out of Landry without restraint. "Four of my people were killed trying to stop those filthy, no-good thieves."

Sterling frowned. "So, how does he fit in to this?" he asked, nodding over to the old man.

"He was on his way back from the hills and passed near the generator house when it happened," Landry replied, scowling at the man. "He was supposed to be out foraging, but that old fool hasn't done a day of honest work for years. He just sits in the corner, eating our food." Then the woman took a couple of deeper breaths, presumably to calm the anger that the older colonist inspired in her. "Since that shuttle arrived, he just talks crazy about a speaking alien and a man with a secret mission," the woman went on, now meeting Sterling's eyes. "I don't think you'll get much sense of out him, but he's the only one still alive who saw that shuttle up close. It was gone before anyone else arrived."

Sterling nodded then the woman departed, joining a group of people in the communal area. Sterling noticed that all eyes were on them and realized that their sudden arrival and armor-clad appearance was probably quite unsettling. He noticed that Lieutenant Shade had casually moved her chair into a darker corner of the room. She was stitching up the wound to her leg, but the rifle was still resting across her lap and Sterling could see her eyes frequently flick over to his location.

"We're not really giving them all this, right?" asked Banks, holding up the parchment.

"Unless this old coot has something revelatory to say, I'm not giving them a damn thing," Sterling replied, in a manner that left Banks in no doubt as to his sincerity. Sterling hooked a thumb over to the man. "I'll talk to him alone. It will be less intimidating that way."

"Good idea, I'll get some supper while I'm waiting," his first officer replied, smiling again.

"Just make sure you leave some for everyone else," Sterling said to Banks as she departed. "And watch my back..."

Sterling set off in the direction of the old man, who had been watching him carefully out of the corner of his eye as he approached the dining area. Then, as it became clear that Sterling was heading toward him specifically, the man became suddenly excited.

"You've come looking for the others, haven't you?" the man said. He was perhaps in his late seventies, but still appeared active and unencumbered by his advanced years. "I told them others would come," the man continued, his voice growing louder as his excitement built. "I told them, but they wouldn't listen."

"Shut up, you crazy old bastard," a younger man from a nearby table called over. Four others on the table with him laughed then one of them flicked a crumb from the table, which struck the older man on the face.

"You'll see, Lars!" the man yelled back, shaking his fist at the younger man as he laughed, cruelly. "You'll see that I was right!"

Sterling held up his hand to get the older man's attention then glowered at the table of troublemakers. Despite his armor and the plasma rifle slung over his shoulder, the younger colonists did not appear intimidated by him.

"Tell me about this shuttle," Sterling said, managing to grab the attention of the older man again. "Did you speak to whoever was on board?"

"Yes, yes!" the man replied, the excitement again causing the volume of his voice to increase. "There were two of them. An impressive older gentleman and a Sa'Nerran warrior," the man went on.

"There was no goddam Sa'Nerran, you crazy old fool," the man who had been identified as Lars yelled from the table next to them. "How long are you going to keep this crap up? It was just one man that you were too chicken-shit to stop from stealing our stuff."

The older man's chair screeched back across the floor and he shot up, stabbing his finger at Lars. "Lies, lies!" the older man yelled at the table. "I was there! Where were you? Where!? You're the chicken shit here, not me!"

Enraged, Lars shot out of his chair and shoved the older colonist in the chest, knocking him back into his chair. Moments later the other four diners at the table also pushed back their chairs and stood behind Lars.

"Hey, take it easy, this doesn't concern you," said Sterling, looking up at Lars and the other colonists from his seat.

"This doesn't concern *us*?" Lars spat back, jabbing a finger into his chest. "You don't belong here, Fleet," the man continued, now pointing his finger at Sterling like it were the barrel of a gun. "Nothing that happens here concerns *you*. So, why don't you get lost before I feed you and your friends to those things outside?"

Shade and Banks both rose from their seats. Banks had been mid-way through a bowl of stew, but now had her hand clasped around the handle of a cutlery knife. Shade had finished stitching up her leg and had her rifle back in her hands. However, the weapons officer had exercised enough restraint to avoid aiming it at the colonist.

"Lars, sit your ass down and let the man talk," Landry called over from the communal area. She was still seated and appeared unconcerned by the younger man's actions.

Lars' eyes narrowed at the older woman, but he did as he was asked. The rest of the group followed, though all of them turned their seats to face the old man. Sterling now had an audience.

"Go on then, old man," Lars said, reclining back in his seat with his legs pushed out in front of him. "Tell him your crazy story. I could do with a good laugh."

The rest of the group again joined in with a round of jeers, but the old man was undeterred. Sterling imagined that it wasn't the first time the story had inspired ire and derision from the inhabitants of Thrace Colony. Ignoring the others as best he could, Sterling turned back to the older man and waited patiently for him to continue.

"The man, the human, he was the alien's prisoner," the old colonist continued. "The warrior killed the people from the colony who came to investigate then forced the man to carry supplies from the warehouse." He wet his lips and leant in closer to Sterling. "The alien, it actually spoke to the man." There was a ripple of laughter from the table next to them, but this time Lars did not interrupt.

"The Sa'Nerran warrior spoke to the guy in the shuttle?" said Sterling, checking to make sure he'd heard the old man correctly. "In words you could understand?"

The old man nodded excitedly. "It was difficult to make out at first, like a whisper from someone with a lisp, but it was definitely talking to him."

Suddenly, a crumb of bread hit the old man in the face, eliciting another ripple of laughter from the group to Sterling's side.

"See, I told you the old fool was crazy," Lars said, casting a sideways glance to Sterling. "Not one alien bastard has a said a single word that made sense since Fleet stirred up their hornets' nest fifty years ago," the young man continued, his eyes looking at Sterling accusingly as he said this. "Yet old man Hubbard here just so happens to find the first talking alien in the galaxy."

There was another ripple of laughter and this time the old man retaliated, tossing his bowl of food at Lars. The stew coated the young man's pants in thick, brown gravy. Lars shot out of his chair and struck Hubbard across the face, knocking him to the floor. Lars then pushed the table out of the way and surged forward, but Sterling caught the younger man's arm and twisted it into a lock. Lars yelped in pain as Sterling steered him away from the older man and placed himself between them.

"Let go of me, goddam it!" Lars yelled. "I'll kill you, you Fleet bastard! Let me go!"

Sterling released his hold on Lars and pushed him away. The younger man instantly took a step toward him, fists clenched, but reconsidered his attack as Shade moved into view, rifle held ready. The clomp of heavy boots then caused Lars and his group of sycophants to spin around. Banks was standing behind them, her eyes fixed on the ringleader, knife still in hand. Considering her immense strength, even the dull kitchen utensil was a lethal weapon.

"So, what? Are you three are going to stop all of us?" Lars scoffed.

"I don't have any quarrel with the rest of the people in here," replied Sterling, calmly, but with enough volume to ensure the anxious onlookers could hear. "It seems to me that it's only the five of you idiots that have a problem," he added, gesturing to Lars and the rest of his quintet.

"It's still five on three," Lars hit back. "The lady over there ain't gonna shoot us all before I stick a knife in your throat." The young man then hooked a thumb toward Banks. "And what's she gonna do? Swear at us?"

Banks gritted her teeth and swung her arm down at the table to her side, smashing it in half like a rotten twig. Lars jerked back as the broken ends of the four-inch-thick wooden beams slammed into the deck.

"Okay, that's enough goddam it!" yelled Landry, rushing into the middle of the fray. "Lars, get out of here, now!' she barked at the younger man.

Lars was still staring at the broken table in awe and disbelief, but then flicked his eyes across to Banks. The armor covering her forearm was cracked and smashed in a hundred places, but Banks herself showed no signs of pain.

She simply glowered back at the ringleader, willing him to make a move.

"Whatever, we're done here, anyway," said Lars, pushing through the rows of other tables and chairs to make his way out of the dining area. "Listen to that guy talk crazy all you want." The man aimed a finger at Sterling. "But you best be gone by sunrise. You ain't welcome here."

Sterling waited for Lars and the four others to move out of view then turned to Landry. She was staring at the table that Banks had split in half.

"Just how the hell did you manage that?" Landry demanded, turning her narrowed eyes to Banks. "That's the local hardwood. It's tougher than the composites they used to build this damned accommodation block with."

Banks just shrugged. "Adrenalin, I guess," she replied, casually, while trying squeeze her fractured forearm plating back into shape.

Landry's scowl deepened, but she didn't press Banks for a more detailed explanation. It seemed clear that they'd outstayed their welcome.

"I think under the circumstances, you'd probably better leave," Landry said, with the same hostility that she'd shown toward them earlier. "I trust you'll honor our bargain, though?"

Sterling considered telling the woman where she could stick her bargain, but mustered enough restraint to continue speaking in a calm and measured tone.

"There will be a window in the storm in about four hours, after which we'll get a crew to fix your generator," Sterling said. "There's a fuel processing plant on the west side of the colony. It was damaged in the attacks, but we can repair it easily enough. Then you'll be back up and running."

Landry considered this then shrugged. "Okay, and what about the other supplies?"

"Our chief engineer is working through the list now," Sterling lied. He didn't like lying, but they were heavily outnumbered and he didn't want a lynch mob bearing down on him.

Landry held Banks' eyes for a few moments then glanced down at the table. "You gonna fix that too?" she said, petulantly.

"I'm sure it can be arranged," Banks replied, with matching bite.

"Under the circumstances, you can't wait in here," Landry went on, returning her attention to Sterling. "I can't have you riling up the residents any more than you already have. You've caused enough trouble as it is." Banks looked ready to hit back at the accusation that it was them that had caused the trouble, but the firebrand first officer managed to bite her tongue. "There's a shelter on the roof," Landry continued. "We use it as a lookout. It might be a bit breezy, but it'll keep the rain off your faces at least."

Banks then nodded toward the kitchen. "Can you pot that up to go?" she said.

"This ain't a damn takeout, lady," Landry snapped back. She then wafted her hand despairingly at Banks. "But if it means you'll leave then I don't give a damn. Just make sure you're gone before Lars comes back with more guys. I won't be responsible for what he does when that happens."

The colonist then headed off, shaking her head and muttering under her breath.

"Glad to see you have your priorities straight," said Sterling, cocking an eye at Banks.

"We're leaving here empty-handed as it is," Banks replied, stepping toward the kitchen. "Since we're stuck here for the next four hours, the least we can do is get fed."

CHAPTER 16
A MOMENT OF WEAKNESS

STERLING SOON DISCOVERED that the rooftop shelter was as basic as Landry's description had made it sound. Nevertheless, it was adequate for their needs. The shelter provided protection from the rain and offered some respite from the lashing winds. It also had the advantage of not being populated by bitter and irate colonists, eager to slit their throats.

Seemingly more concerned about her rumbling belly than the prospect of being murdered, Commander Banks had carried up three pots of the stew from the kitchen. To Sterling's surprise it was delicious. Contained within its unappetizing-looking, murky brown contents were a variety of root vegetables and a dark meat that was so tender Sterling imagined it must have been cooked for days. What the meat was, Sterling had no idea and frankly didn't want to know.

After their meal, there was nothing more to do than wait. Sterling rested back on the hay-filled sacks that passed for furniture in the shelter and found himself drifting off to sleep, lulled by the sound of the wind and rain. Suddenly, he woke with a start to find that Banks and Shade were no longer in the shelter. The darkness had lifted and the storm was rolling away into the distance, leaving only a light pattering of rain behind, like an afterthought. Sterling rubbed his eyes and pushed himself up, but then heard a scratching noise. He froze and looked for his rifle, but it wasn't there. Cursing under his breath he looked around the shelter for anything he could use as a weapon then grabbed a fork from the empty bowl of stew he'd eaten earlier. Creeping toward the source of the noise, he was about to tap his neural interface to reach out to Banks and Shade when a hooded figure flickered through the shadows toward him. Springing forward, Sterling grabbed the figure and pressed the fork to their throat. Moments later the barrels of two plasma rifles were pressed to the sides of the intruder's head and Sterling saw Banks and Shade appear.

"Please, it's just me!" a voice said. Sterling pushed back the hood and found himself staring into the terrified eyes of the old man, Hubbard. "I came to find you. I have more to say!"

Sterling removed the fork from the man's neck, leaving three tiny pin-pricks of blood behind.

"Damn it, Hubbard, you were nearly skewered and blasted into a dozen pieces," Sterling said, shuffling back inside the shelter.

"I know, I'm sorry, but I had to sneak out," Hubbard said as Banks and Shade lowered their weapons. "Landry doesn't want me to speak to you anymore. They don't trust you. And you should be wary of Lars and his friends. They mean you harm."

Sterling snorted a laugh. "Harm is our specialty, old man," he replied, causing Hubbard to shrink away slightly. "I'd suggest you advise Lars to stay the hell away from us."

The man then reached inside his coat and Shade again thrust the barrel of the rifle at him.

"Not so fast, old man," Shade snarled.

Hubbard obeyed and continued at a far more unhurried pace, like he was moving in slow motion. A few seconds later the man opened his hand and held out a data chip.

"The human male who was in the shuttle, he gave me this," said Hubbard, offering the chip to Sterling. "He said it would help others to find him. He promised me that if I got it to Fleet, he would make sure I was taken care of. He said he'd pay to have me taken from this world to somewhere better."

Sterling took the chip and briefly examined it, though from its external appearance it was unremarkable. He pocketed the device and returned his attention to Hubbard.

"When did he give you that?" Sterling asked, regarding the older man with cold suspicion. "You said the Sa'Nerran warrior killed the other colonists who came to investigate the shuttle. Why didn't it kill you too?"

Hubbard's head dropped and he turned his eyes away from Sterling. "I... I hid," the old man replied. "In the warehouse, when I saw the others get shot. I took their weapons, but I..." he then held his head with shaking hands. "But I couldn't do it. I couldn't kill it."

Sterling could hear the shame and regret in the man's voice, but he felt no pity for him. This man had been given an opportunity to kill an enemy and stop Colicos from falling into the hands of the Sa'Nerra. All Hubbard had to do was shoot a single Sa'Nerran warrior. Instead, the man had cowered in the darkness. Had Hubbard stopped the alien then and there, perhaps the neural weapon would never have been developed at all, Sterling considered. He knew that not everyone was a fighter. And he knew that Hubbard was not the first to falter in the face of the enemy, nor would he be the last. It was unfair to lay the blame on the old man's shoulders, as in truth there were many who shouldered far greater responsibility for the current state of the war than Hubbard. However, Sterling couldn't help but wonder how many lives had been lost because of the old man's one act of weakness.

"Did he say anything else or do you remember anything else?" Sterling asked, burying the anger that the man's story had caused to swell inside him. "His name, the ID of his shuttle? Anything?"

The old man shook his head. "No, he only said that he was important and that Fleet would come for him if they knew he'd been taken."

Sterling sighed and nodded then stood up, feeling suddenly deflated again. The mission was the worst roller-coaster ride of emotions that he'd experienced yet. He preferred a straight fight to sneaking around on what was increasingly looking like a wild-goose chase.

A rumble of sound rolled across the horizon, but this time it wasn't thunder. Sterling peered into the brightening sky and saw the Invictus' Combat Shuttle heading toward them from the outskirts of Thrace Colony.

"If you find him and rescue him, do you think he will get me off this world?" Hubbard asked.

There was a glimmer of hope in the old man's voice, but mostly Sterling sensed desperation. "Honestly, I have no idea," Sterling replied, truthfully. "I doubt it."

Hubbard's head fell low and Sterling returned to watching the shuttle, which circled the apartment block and began to set down on the far side of the roof.

"Can you take me instead?" the old man pleaded, stammering the words. "I want to leave. I don't want to die in this place."

Sterling shook his head. "The Invictus is a ship of war," he said, peering down at the old man, who was still on his knees. "There's no place for you there."

The door of the shuttlecraft then hissed, releasing the processed air inside and allowing the cold, wet air of the planet to replace it. Ensign Keller was inside, silhouetted by the bright lights from the cabin. Sterling turned away from Hubbard, whose head hung low, shoulders shaking gently as he wept, then began walking over to the shuttle.

"What about the supplies?" said Banks, who had remained in her customary place by Sterling's side.

"Landry gave us nothing and we owe her nothing," Sterling replied. "Besides, they don't deserve our help. They'd have let us die on this forsaken rock."

"And what about him?" Banks added, nodding toward Hubbard, who was still weeping on his knees.

"He's not our problem either," said Sterling, frostily.

Banks nodded then glanced at Sterling out of the corner of her eye. "I feel like I should have at least fixed their table, though," she said.

Sterling frowned at her, unsure whether she was being serious or just making another one of her ill-timed jokes. This time, he really couldn't tell.

"We'll drop a disaster pod when we leave," Sterling said, reasoning that this was a fair exchange for the information they'd received, and the damage they'd left in their wake. "After that, these people are on their own."

STERLING ENTERED the compact science lab where Lieutenant Razor had been analyzing the data chip they had recovered from the old man on Thrace Colony. Pausing just inside the door, he realized that he'd perhaps only been inside the room maybe half a dozen times in the entire time he'd been in command of the Invictus. Considering the compact size of the vessel, he mostly spent his time moving between his quarters, the wardroom and the bridge. However, his decision to visit his chief engineer in the lab, rather than pull her away from her work, had the unexpected side-effect of making the ship feel strangely bigger.

"What have you discovered so far, Lieutenant?" asked Sterling moving beside Razor, who was working at one of the benches. Her skin, which had been augmented to provide UV protection on account of her albinism, sparkled more lustrously under the harsh lights of the lab. "We're just burning fuel, idling in orbit until you give us a heading," Sterling added, trying to subtly jockey the engineer into working faster.

Razor glanced up from the computer console she was working at and frowned at Sterling. "Surely, Ensign Keller has just put us into a geosynchronous orbit around the planet?" the engineer asked. "Besides the need for a little station-keeping, we shouldn't be burning any excess fuel."

"It was a figure of speech, Lieutenant," Sterling replied. He sometimes wondered whether his analogies were simply too subtle and clever for the rest of the crew, or if they were just plain bad. "I just mean that we're stuck here unless you can find a clue as to where Colicos went," he added, spelling it out for the engineer.

"Of course, sir," said Razor, politely. "Fortunately, I believe I have found something."

Razor then turned the screen of the console toward Sterling so that he could better see the contents. He frowned at the information flowing across the display, quickly realizing that none of it made any sense to him.

"I just see a lot of gibberish, Lieutenant," said Sterling, squinting at the pages and pages of code. "What am I looking at here?"

"Mostly, gibberish," admitted Razor. "The chip contains a hastily processed, raw data dump from a shuttlecraft's main computer core." She then began working on the console and a star map appeared on one of the larger wall screens. "The data on the chip is quite badly corrupted, likely as a result of age and poor storage conditions, but I believe I've pieced together a section of the vessels' journey from its navigational logs."

Razor tapped a button on the console and the computer began to trace a line through the star map. It passed through Thrace Colony and extended out toward the edge of the star system, where it abruptly stopped.

"So, where did it go from there?" asked Sterling, trying to contain his disappointment. The amount of information the data chip had provided was barely more than they already knew.

"Computer, add the locations of all known apertures that lead toward Sa'Nerran space to the display," Razor said. Moments later, three markers appeared on the map. "Project the course of the shuttle based on its last known course and speed."

Sterling watched as the computer extrapolated the shuttle's course, accounting for the gravity well of the planets and other stellar phenomenon it passed by on the way. The line on the map continued to grow until it neatly bisected two of the three aperture markers.

Sterling raised an eyebrow at his engineer. "This is the part where you impress me, isn't it, Lieutenant?" he said. "Because I see two possible routes where that shuttle could have gone, and only one Invictus."

Sterling was impatient for Razor's answer. He sincerely hoped that the engineer wasn't about to conclude that they had a fifty-fifty chance of guessing which aperture Colicos had gone through.

"Then prepare to be impressed, Captain," Razor replied, with just the right amount of swagger. "Because these two aren't the only apertures that lead into Sa'Nerran space from Thrace Colony."

Sterling frowned as Razor again worked on the console. A few seconds later, a fourth marker appeared on the map, way beyond the edge of the system's outermost planet.

"How have we not detected that aperture before?" Sterling asked, accessing one of the other consoles and zooming in on the location.

"It's something Fleet has never seen before," Razor replied. "In fact, were it not for me focusing scans along the line of the shuttle's projected course, I would never have discovered it either," she went on. "It would have been like looking for the proverbial needle in a haystack, except without even knowing that it was a needle you were looking for."

Sterling felt a tingle of excitement run down his spine. Like any good spacefarer, he loved a good mystery, and he loved discovering something new.

"Okay, I'm impressed," said Sterling. "Now impress me some more..."

"The signature of this aperture is uniquely different to every other aperture on record," Razor continued. The engineer's voice was also laced with energy and excitement. "However, it appears to be built on the same core principles as the known Fleet and Sa'Nerran apertures," Razor went on.

Sterling rubbed the back of his neck and stared at the new aperture on the wall screen. The data chip had provided as many questions as it had delivered answers.

"Can we extrapolate where it leads to?" Sterling then asked, turning back to Razor.

"It's guesswork at this point," the engineer replied,

shaking her head. "In principle, an aperture with this energy signature could have a surge radius many times larger than existing apertures. Perhaps, it could even lead directly into Sa'Nerran space."

"Can we surge through it?" asked Sterling. There were a dozen more prudent queries he could have – and perhaps should have - asked first, but the one he'd chosen was the only question that really mattered. Razor, however, appeared uncertain.

"For Colicos' shuttle to have successfully entered that aperture it would need to have radically modified its surge field," Razor answered. "It would take a genius to do it."

"I think it's fair to say that Colicos has the relevant qualifications," Sterling replied, though he was conscious that his engineer had not answered the question he'd actually asked. "But let's assume Colicos has the chops to make the surge. What I'm asking is can the Invictus follow?" Then he paused and rephrased his question. "In other words, Lieutenant Razor, do you have the chops?"

Razor raised one of her snow-white eyebrows at Sterling. "I believe I do, sir," she said, confidently.

Sterling nodded and smiled. "Well, you once told me you were looking to gain as many Fleet commendations as possible, so you can muster out early. Here's your chance to chalk up another one."

Razor nodded and smiled, something he'd rarely seen the Omega officer do. "Challenge accepted, Captain," she said. "Prepare to be impressed again."

"Keep me apprised, Lieutenant," said Sterling,

preparing to leave the engineer to her work. However, Razor was quick to stop him.

"There is one other thing, though, sir," Razor added, resuming a more stoical expression. "I managed to matched the energy signature of this portal to something already in the Fleet database."

Sterling stopped and returned to the engineer's side. "That sounds ominous," he said, impatient to hear what Razor had to say next.

"The aperture array that the Titan, the Sa'Nerran super-weapon, used to disintegrate the moon has a near-identical signature."

Sterling frowned. "What does that mean?"

"I don't know, yet, but I'll continue to analyze the data and see what I can find out," the engineer replied. "However, it may suggest that these apertures are dangerous. Perhaps even unstable."

Sterling sighed. As usual it was two steps forward and one step back. "Understood, Lieutenant, stay on it," he said, again turning to leave.

The door to the science lab swooshed open and Commander Banks walked in. She took several paces inside the lab then stopped and peered around the space. She wore the expression of a person who had entered a room then immediately forgotten the reason why they'd done so.

"Are you lost, Commander?" asked Sterling, as Banks continued to gaze around the lab with a look of deep consternation on her face.

"Has this facility always been on the ship?" Banks

asked, pressing her hands to her hips and frowning at Sterling.

"Yes, Commander, it's always been here," Sterling replied, shaking his head at his first officer. However, he didn't want to admit that he'd had similar doubts after first walking into the science lab.

"Well, I'll be damned," Banks said. "I'm sure I've never been in here before."

Sterling rested back against the workbench and folded his arms. "Is there a particular reason why you're here now, Commander?" he said, trying to jog his first officer's memory.

Commander Graves then walked in. He was holding a complicated-looking contraption in his hand that was a mass of spidery wires and smaller components. The medical officer frowned, realizing that three of the Invictus' other senior officers were also in the room.

"I hope I am not interrupting, Captain?" Graves began in his usual, polite and anemic manner. "I have some new information regarding the neural interface I reclaimed from the colonist on Far Deep Nine."

"No, the more the merrier, Commander," Sterling said, waving Graves over.

As the medical officer approached, Sterling realized that the main component in the device Graves was holding was a neural interface. Sterling could see that there were still lumps of brain attached to the device in various places. He grimaced at the contraption as Graves dangled it, along with the lumps of brain matter, in front of his nose.

"Let's hear it," replied Sterling, gently pushing the device away from his face with the back of his hand.

"As James Colicos hinted at in the logs we recovered from Far Deep Nine, this device is a neural translation matrix," Graves began. "I believe that Doctor Colicos used a similar device to map the brains of the Sa'Nerran hosts he captured, examining the neural activity of the alien species in infinitesimal detail."

Sterling frowned. "So, you're saying that Colicos figured out how the Sa'Nerran brain responds when the things hiss 'hello', then mapped that across to humans?"

"Essentially, yes," Graves replied. "However, the fundamental problem is that we have never been able to know when a Sa'Nerran is saying 'hello' or even if they say 'hello' at all."

Sterling massaged the bridge of his nose with his fingers and thumb. He wasn't particularly interested in the technicalities of how things worked or didn't work. His head was already hurting trying to understand what Graves was telling him.

"My theory is that Colicos found a sort of neural 'Rosetta stone'," Graves went on, unperturbed by the apparent mental suffering of his captain.

"The only stones I'm getting are kidney stones, Commander," Sterling replied, a little grouchily. "What does that mean in layman's terms?"

"Essentially, Colicos discovered a key that enabled him to map the corresponding brain activity of humans and Sa'Nerra," Graves continued, showing no sign of offence at his captain's crabbiness. "It would be fascinating to learn what this key was, but it is a mystery for a more peaceful time."

Sterling nodded. He was grateful that, despite his macabre personality, Graves did not possess the insufferable inquisitiveness of his former chief engineer, Emissary Clinton Crow.

"It goes beyond language, however," Graves went on. "Thoughts, actions, desires, wants, needs... it can all be captured and translated."

"And manipulated?" Sterling wondered, still pinching the bridge of his nose.

"I believe so," Graves replied. "We are looking at the basis of the Sa'Nerran neural control weapon."

Banks stepped forward; her brow also scrunched up into a painfully-confused frown. "But the old man on Thrace Colony said that the Sa'Nerran warrior he saw spoke," she cut in. "Didn't Colicos say that neural education was a bust? If that's the case, how was the alien managing to speak in English?"

Commander Graves shrugged. "I'm afraid I have no concrete answers to give you, Commander," the medical officer replied. "We will need to find Colicos to learn more. Alternatively, you will need to find me some live human and Sa'Nerran test subjects to conduct my own experiments on."

Razor laughed, believing Graves' statement to be a joke. Then she noticed that Sterling and Banks had remained straight faced and fell silent again.

"Let's hope it doesn't come to that, Commander," Sterling replied. "But keep that idea on the back burner, just in case." Razor's white eyebrows rose up her forehead, but she continued to remain silent. "I'll leave the science to you scientists," Sterling continued, pushing away from the workbench. He turned and pointed to the newly-discovered aperture on the wall screen then glanced over at Razor. "Relay the co-ordinates to Ensign Keller then figure out how we can surge through that new aperture."

"Aye, Captain, but realistically that could take days," Razor replied, sounding a little put out. "This is an entirely new aperture configuration. I'd need to study it more closely then adapt our surge field generator. Ideally, we should send some test probes through first, to make sure we don't end up in another galaxy, or another universe entirely."

Sterling knew that his engineer's reply was entirely reasonable. However, they didn't have time for reasonable. He needed, and demanded, only the exceptional.

"Computer, how long will it take us to reach that aperture at maximum speed?" Sterling said, casting his eyes toward the ceiling.

"By 'that aperture' I presume you mean the one that Lieutenant Shade recently discovered, Captain?" the quirky gen-fourteen AI replied. Its cheerful tenor was at odds with the facetious tone of the question.

"Yes, computer, obviously that one," Sterling replied, shaking his head.

"Four hours, twelve minutes and thirty-two seconds from the point at which I finish this sentence, Captain," the computer replied, breezily.

"You have four hours, Lieutenant," Sterling said, fixing

his chief engineer with a determined stare. Razor was new, but she had already learned that when her captain was open to input and when he just wanted the job done, even if it he was asking the impossible.

"Aye, Captain, I'll get right on it," Razor answered, straightening to attention.

"Pull this off and there's a commendation in it for you," Sterling added, as he headed toward the door. "Though I'm going to have to start rationing them, otherwise I'll soon be without a ship's engineer."

Sterling then set off along the narrow corridor outside the science lab with Banks at his side. "We've got some time to kill, so how about grabbing a coffee?" he said, returning a salute from a crew member that passed them by.

"Sure, and I might try out one of those new vintage meal trays from Middle Star too," Banks replied, with the same breezy nonchalance as the computer.

Sterling scowled at her. "You must have eaten at least three pots of stew on that flea-ridden world. How the hell can you still be hungry?" He then realized the stupidity of his own question and raised a hand to cut off Banks' unnecessary response. "Never mind, I already know the answer. You're always hungry, right?"

Banks smiled then shrugged and hit the call button for the elevator. The doors opened and Sterling found himself staring down at Jinx the beagle hound.

"Jinx, how did you get out?" Banks said, kneeling down and vigorously petting the dog, who appeared to enjoy the attention immensely. "She must have snuck out after me before the doors closed."

Sterling frowned as he stepped inside the elevator. "I hope that animal hasn't left any deposits in the ship," he said, grouchily. "I waded through enough crap on that planet."

Banks stood up and slapped Sterling on the arm with the back of her hand. As usual, it hurt like hell. "Don't be so miserable, Captain," Banks replied. "A ship's dog is good for morale

The beagle sat down and placed a paw on Sterling's boot, peering up at him with large brown eyes. He scowled down at the dog then pressed the button for deck two.

"Just don't feed it any number twenty-sevens," Sterling said, as the elevator doors began to close. "Or Acting-Ensign Jinx will end up as the first dog ever to make a home in Sa'Nerran space..."

Captain Sterling rested forward on his console, tapping his finger against the metal plating on the side in the usual place. In front of him on the viewscreen was an empty starscape at the fringe of the Thrace Colony system. Yet if Lieutenant Razor's analysis was correct, the emptiness hid a unique, undiscovered aperture.

"Are you sure this is the spot, Lieutenant?" Sterling glanced over to where Razor was working on the consoles at the rear of the bridge. "I'm so used to seeing aperture beacons flashing in my face, I'm struggling to believe there's anything there."

Razor continued working for a couple of seconds then turned to face her captain. "Aye, sir, it's definitely there," the engineer replied. "Whether we can surge through it is another matter, though."

Sterling glanced down at the readings on his console, continuing to drum his fingers as he absorbed the information. Rising to the challenge, Lieutenant Razor had spent the last four hours re-writing the book on interstellar surge mechanics. Rallying anyone on the ship with the ability to hold a spanner to her aid, she'd then reconfigured the Invictus' surge field generator to speak the same language as the aperture. Razor had explained that, in principle, the Invictus should be able to traverse the portal. However, his engineer had also been at pains to point out the many risks and variables involved.

"I wonder how many of these secret alien apertures there are throughout the Void," said Banks, frowning at the viewscreen, "and why we have never seen them being used before."

Sterling had spent some of the four-hour journey time considering this question and had come to an unfortunate conclusion. It was a conclusion that had already been postulated by his brilliant engineer.

"Given the tactical advantage they offer, my guess is that they're unstable," Sterling replied.

The right eyebrow of his first officer lifted by half an inch as he said this. "Sounds like fun," Banks replied, sarcastically.

"Captain, I'd still strongly recommend sending an aperture relay probe through first," Razor said, snatching back Sterling's attention. "I have taken the liberty of modifying one for this purpose. The data it records and hopefully transmits back to us should help to iron out the kinks in my surge calculations."

"What sort of kinks are we talking about, Lieutenant?" Banks asked, beating Sterling to the punch.

"The sort of kinks that could mean we exit the aperture in a billion pieces. Or not at all," Razor said, flatly.

Banks glanced over to Sterling, eyebrow raised even higher. It seemed clear that his first officer was in favor of a trial run. However, time was also of the essence. Every second they wasted, the Sa'Nerran armada made their way deeper into Fleet space. Yet, he also couldn't argue that their impact on the war effort would be radically diminished should their atoms end up dispersed across a thousand light years.

"Okay, Lieutenant, send a relay probe, but make it quick," Sterling said, turning back to his engineer. "Program the thing to power down once it has transmitted the data. We don't want to tip-off anyone on the other side that we're coming."

"Aye, sir," Razor replied before setting to work configuring the relay probe.

"And perhaps load that stowaway hound inside the probe while you're at it," Sterling added, with a little more volume for effect. "We can study this new aperture's effects on biology at the same time."

Banks shot him another look, but Sterling judged it to be considerably less friendly than the last one he'd received. "You know what happened to the Ancient Mariner when he shot his lucky charm," Banks said, still giving Sterling the evil eye.

"Probe ready, Captain," Razor called out from the rear of the bridge.

"Launch it, Lieutenant," Sterling said, returning to tapping his finger impatiently against his console.

The probe shot out ahead on the viewscreen and moments later it was consumed by the invisible interstellar gateway.

"The probe has entered aperture space. Telemetry lost," Razor said, giving a running commentary. An anxious few seconds followed while they waited for the probe to rematerialize on the other side of the aperture and begin transmitting.

"Probe reacquired," Razor announced, finally breaking the tension. "I'm receiving data."

"Well, at least it's still in one piece," said Banks, returning to her more optimistic outlook.

"It sustained some structural damage during transit, Captain," Razor added, while continuing to flit between the various consoles at the rear of the bridge. "The internal power core failed. It's running on reserve cells only..."

"So, where does that leave us, Lieutenant?" said Sterling, glancing back at his officer. "Can we surge or not?"

Razor continued to work, hopping between stations like an orchestral percussionist. She then finally stopped and stood tall, hands pressed to the small of her back. Her chest was heaving slightly as she regained her breath.

"Aye, Captain, we can surge," Razor replied. "I've made some adjustments to our surge field parameters, though I'd still expect a bumpy ride."

"What else is new?" said Banks.

Sterling nodded then turned to Ensign Keller, who was keenly awaiting his order.

"Take us in Lieutenant," he said before turning to

Lieutenant Shade. "Set condition battle stations. Let's be prepared for anything."

The general alert tone sounded then the lights reduced, giving way to the low-level red strips that encircled the bridge.

"Thirty seconds to aperture perimeter," Keller called out.

Sterling found his grip on the side of his console tightening.

"Weapons and regenerative armor at full power," Shade called out, adding to the chorus. "The ship is at battle stations."

"Ten seconds to aperture perimeter," Keller said, continuing his truncated countdown.

Sterling counted down the remaining seconds in his head. However, before his count had reached zero, the ship and his body were consumed inside the aperture. The unsettling feeling of disembodied thought seemed to persist for longer than usual. However, even judging time while inside the sub-dimension between apertures was like trying to guess the passage of time while asleep and dreaming. Suddenly, he exploded back into reality and was instantly hit with an intense wave of nausea and vertigo. Sterling thrust his hands out in front of him, trying to use his console to steady himself, but his arms just flailed helplessly in front of his body. The next thing he knew he was on the ground, his legs still on the command platform, but his head and back on the main deck. He saw Banks to his left. She was trying to push herself up, but even the muscles in her powerful arms and legs refused to obey her commands.

"Report!" Sterling called out, though the words sounded slurred and muddled in his own ears. "Report!" he tried again, managing to sound more coherent the second time. However, there was no reply from any station.

Finding that his coordination was beginning to return, Sterling pushed himself up to a crouch before his head again began to spin. Grasping hold of the stem of his captain's console, Sterling hugged it like a sailor hugging the mast of a ship in the midst of a violent storm. Slowly, he climbed hand-over-hand up the stem, dragging his disorientated body back to its feet.

"Helm control is down," Ensign Keller called out. The pilot was back in his chair, though was grasping onto the sides as if his life depended on it.

"Weapons down," Shade reported next. "Armor buckling..."

Sterling tried his own console. It was still responding, but his hands were still too unsteady to operate it. After several fumbled attempts to bring up a damage control panel, he saw that their reactor core was destabilizing.

"Lieutenant!" Sterling called out, forcing his body to turn and look for his engineer. "Initiate emergency reactor shut down, now, before it's too late!"

Razor was also clawing herself back to her feet. "I'm on it," she cried back, though Sterling could barely make out the words.

"Contact ahead!" Banks called out.

The warning cry was like a bucket of ice water over his

head. Sterling compelled his body to turn again then saw a Sa'Nerran Heavy Cruiser on the viewscreen. His head was still spinning, but even through his blurry eyes, he could tell it wasn't a design he recognized. Gritting his teeth, he stared down at his console, trying to make sense of the flashing lights and jumble of words that made up the status updates. He knew they couldn't fight, which meant fleeing was their only option. However, considering the battering the ship and the crew had taken from the first surge, he held out little hope they'd survive a second.

"Wait..." Banks then called out, filling Sterling with the faintest flicker of hope. "The cruiser appears to be powered down." Banks frowned at her console. She had recovered her senses far more quickly than Sterling had managed to. "I don't understand. Maybe it's a derelict or another ship that was damaged during a surge."

Sterling didn't care why the Sa'Nerran ship was inactive – only that it was. He glanced behind to Razor, who was tottering from console to console.

"Full reactor shutdown and restart initiated," Razor said before slipping and dropping to one knee.

"What the hell happened, Lieutenant?" said Sterling. "You said the probe sustained some structural damage. The transition damned near tore us apart!"

Razor pushed herself back to her feet. She looked embarrassed and angry, though Sterling knew the look well – he'd seen it in the mirror many times during his own career. She was angry with herself for dropping the ball, not for being admonished.

"I'm sorry, sir," Razor replied. "It appears that the

damaging effects of the surge increase according to the mass and energy of the object making the transition."

Sterling understood what his engineer was saying. It was like a leaf falling from a tree compared to a coconut. They both travelled the same distance, but due to the effects of gravity and air resistance, one hit a lot harder when it reached the end of its journey.

"I should have seen it, Captain," Razor went on. "I take full responsibility."

"This is my ship, and my responsibility alone, Lieutenant," Sterling hit back. He then aimed at finger at his engineer. "Your responsibility is getting our systems back online. Right now, we're in enemy territory with our pants around our ankles."

"Aye, sir, I'm on it," Razor replied, turning back to her console. "Reactor shutdown and restart in thirty..."

"Captain, we have another problem," Banks said, from her station next to Sterling's. "The cruiser is powering up. It appears that it was only dormant."

Sterling closed his eyes and muttered a curse under his breath before turning to his first officer. "How long do we have?" he asked.

Banks worked her console then met Sterling's eyes. "Sixty seconds until its core systems are online. Maybe double that before it can fire."

Suddenly the reassuring thrum of the reactor and engine systems vanished and a deathly silence washed over the bridge.

"Reactor down. Life support on reserve cells." Razor called out from the rear of the bridge.

"Get us back online as fast as you can, Lieutenant," said Sterling, as lights all across the hull of the alien heavy cruiser flickered on. "I don't care if we have crew floating through the halls. I need engines and weapons before that thing out there has a chance to fire."

"Aye, Captain," Razor replied.

Sterling could see that the engineer had resumed most of her fluidity, though she still wasn't operating at full capacity. No-one on the bridge was, least of all himself.

"Based on the scanner data we acquired before the reactor cycled, that Sa'Nerran warship is a variant of a phase one heavy cruiser, Captain," said Lieutenant Shade from the weapons console. "But it's something we've not seen before. Maneuvering capability is severely limited, but it has twice the firepower a ship of that era and class should have."

Sterling continued to study the alien vessel, watching as its thrusters started to flash into life. Questions were whizzing around his mind. *Why was the ship there? Why had it been powered down? Why was it so old as to be obsolete?* As usual, however, he had more questions than answers.

"It's a gatekeeper," said Banks, cutting through the confusion like a shark swimming through calm waters. "It's guarding the aperture. But maybe the shuttle was the last thing to come through here in a long while, so it went into a sort of hibernation mode to reserve power."

Sterling nodded. It was as good a theory as any. However, he also then realized that the "why" questions were unimportant. All he needed to know was how to stop it.

"Lieutenant, I need a weakness," Sterling said to his weapons officer. "If it's similar to a phase one design, we should know everything about it, including where to hit it to do the most damage."

"I know exactly where to hit it, Captain," replied Shade, with a cold, clinical certainly. "But we need to get close."

The familiar thrum of the deck plating then began to vibrate through Sterling's boots. He could literally feel the ship's vitality returning.

"Reactor restart complete," Razor called over. "It will be several minutes before we're at full capacity, but I've given everything we have to weapons and engines."

The Sa'Nerran gatekeeper had begun to turn toward them as Razor was speaking. Sterling peered down at his console and saw that the aged but powerful warship was charging weapons.

"One shot from its forward battery and we're finished," said Banks. Her report was given without undue alarm. It was simply a statement of the facts. Sterling knew she was right.

"Ensign, keep us out of reach of that ship's main guns," Sterling called out. He saw an attack pattern flash up on his console. He scowled at it then turned to Shade. "I know you said we had to get close, but does it need to be that close?" he asked, hoping that the woozy weapons officer had made a miscalculation.

"Our weapons are at reduced power," Shade replied,

calmly. "If we want to take it down in one shot, this is the only way."

Sterling nodded then sent the pattern to Ensign Keller. "Time to impress me with your fancy flying, Ensign," Sterling called over to his pilot. He then saw the forward plasma cannons of the alien gatekeeper begin to glow. "You can start by evading those guns!" he added, gripping his captain's console tightly again.

The kick of the Invictus' engines made Sterling glad he had held on. With the rest of the ship on minimal power, the inertial negation systems barely compensated for the ship's trust. Moments later the alien cruiser's guns flashed and four massive blasts of plasma raced across their bow and disappeared into the Void.

"That was damned close, Ensign," said Banks, glancing across to Sterling. "Less than ten meters."

Sterling flashed his eyes at his first officer. "I don't give a damn if it misses by ten meters or ten centimeters. A miss is a miss," he replied before turning his attention back to the viewscreen.

Under the expert control of Ensign Keller, the Invictus was now approaching the alien cruiser like a cannonball. Turrets flashed across the three-kilometer-long hull of the old alien warship and Sterling felt the impact of each blast as if the strikes had landed on his own body.

"Regenerative armor at twenty-seven percent, and holding," Shade called out. "Hull integrity stable."

Sterling's grip on his console continued to tighten as the Invictus powered toward the cruiser on a collision course.

"Impact in ten seconds, get ready to pull up," Shade called out. Her body was as steady and immovable as a marble statue, finger poised over her console, ready to fire. "Now!" she yelled.

Keller pulled the nose up and at the same time Shade unleashed the Invictus' forward plasma cannons at the cruiser at point-blank range. Explosions rippled across the hull of the cruiser and the Invictus rode the blast, like a surfer on the crest of a wave. Lights and consoles flickered on and off on the bridge and power relays blew out, but seconds later they were clear. Sterling allowed himself to take a breath – the first he'd managed since starting the attack run – and pushed away from his console. Keller slowed the ship and looped around, bringing the alien gatekeeper back into view. Shade had hit the alien beast exactly where she'd intended to, Sterling realized, disabling its main reactor and leaving it powerless to respond. The cruiser was now simply listing in space, crippled and defeated.

"No other contacts on the scanners, sir," said Banks, maneuvering her console back into position, having inadvertently torn it away from the deck during the battle.

"We're going to need to get you a stronger station," Sterling said. He then let out a long, loud sigh. "Good work, people," he said, casting his eyes first to Keller then to Shade. Then he turned to Lieutenant Razor and waited for the engineer to reluctantly meet his gaze. "Good work, everyone," Sterling said, holding Razor's gaze long enough for her to accept his sincerity. "Remain at battle stations and begin repairs. Weapons and armor are the priority, people. This is enemy space and we could be back in a fight before we know it."

There was a chorus of 'aye, sir,' from around the bridge and the crew of the Invictus immediately got to work.

"I have an idea for how we can discover where that shuttle went next," said Commander Banks, casting a sideways glance at Sterling.

"Is it an idea I'm going to like?" Sterling replied.

Banks shrugged then pointed to the Sa'Nerran Heavy Cruiser on the viewscreen. "That ship would have monitored Colicos' shuttle arriving through the aperture, so it stands to reason it probably also knows where it went."

Sterling smiled. "Are you suggesting we board that thing and interrogate its computer?" he asked.

"Yes," replied Banks, firmly. Then she shrugged again. "Along with whoever else we find alive over there."

Sterling nodded then looked out at the alien vessel on the viewscreen, bleeding smoke into space.

"Awaiting your orders, Captain," Banks asked. Sterling could sense that she was eager to flex her muscles once again. "Shall I plan a little expedition?"

Sterling clenched his fists and stood tall. "Suit up, Commander, we have a ship to board."

STERLING PEERED out at the crippled Sa'Nerran Heavy Cruiser from the cockpit of the shuttle, while Commander Banks piloted the craft toward the stricken vessel. Due to the devastating close-range assault by the Invictus, more than half of the cruiser had been rendered uninhabitable. However, even though the cruiser was dead in space, with its weapon systems and engines disabled, it still clung to life like a battle-scarred old shark. Several sections of the three-kilometer-long behemoth remained intact and pressurized, including its bridge and command deck.

Sterling's plan was to land the combat shuttle near the command center of the alien vessel then breach through an emergency escape hatch. Once the assault team had fought their way to the alien bridge, they would hack into the ship's command computer and download the data from the central memory core. Contained somewhere in the archives was the information that would point them to James Colicos. It was their only chance to pick up the trail of breadcrumbs that they'd lost at the entrance to the newly discovered Sa'Nerran aperture. If they failed then their mission was just as dead in the water as the heavy cruiser. Without Colicos, any chance of counteracting the alien neural control weapon would be lost.

Based on scans of the Sa'Nerran cruiser, Sterling had concluded that the bulk of the alien forces on board were either already dead, or cut off from the command deck. Nevertheless, Sterling was planning to go in hard. Seated in the rear of the shuttle was Lieutenant Razor and Lieutenant Shade along with the Invictus' four best commandoes. Shade's forces would secure a route to the bridge, where Lieutenant Razor would then hack the computer and recover the data.

Sterling glanced back at his engineer from the second seat of the combat shuttle. There was a hunger in her eyes that he'd not seen before. The talented engineer appeared eager to earn back the trust and respect she believed she had lost from her commander. The reality was that Sterling was not angry or disappointed with Razor over what happened to the Invictus after surging through the new aperture. Razor couldn't have known what would happen; none of them could. This was uncharted territory and risk was part of the game. However, the fact that Razor had not allowed the incident to rattle her confidence was encouraging. And the hungrier his unique engineer was to prove herself the more Sterling was sure that she would succeed.

"Thirty seconds to hard dock," said Commander Banks.

Despite this announcement, his first officer was still accelerating so hard toward the cruiser that it looked like she planned to ram the massive vessel. However, the element of surprise was crucial to the success of their plan. As such, hot-rodding through space like a cadet trying to impress his classmates was a necessary risk.

"Assault team, get ready to breach," Shade called out to the row of four commandoes seated opposite her. Each of them wore a helmet with a full cover face mask, giving them an anonymous, almost robotic-appearance.

"Breaking thrusters firing in five," Banks added from the pilot's seat, her voice now betraying her own unease at their rapid approach.

The shuttle spun around and decelerated hard, pressing Sterling into the back of his seat as if an invisible sumo wrestler had just sat on his lap. The roar of the engines was deafening and the whole shuttle shook like it was being buffeted by a tropical storm. Suddenly the weight pressing down on Sterling vanished and there was a solid thud against the hull. It sounded like someone had just pounded it with a sledgehammer.

"We're down and locked," Banks called out, appearing physically unaffected by the pressures that had just ravaged Sterling's body. "Hatch seal intact, cutting beams activated."

Shade punched the buckle on her chest to release her harness then sprang up and grabbed her plasma rifle from its stow to her side. The four commandoes were on their feet moments later, but these soldiers were packing far more devastating firepower. Two of the commandoes grabbed plasma hand-cannons from the rack; the twenty-fourth century equivalent of a sawn-off shotgun. The remaining two commandoes drew down heavy plasma rifles and moved to the side of the docking hatch. These heavier weapons were rarely used due to their propensity to blow holes through walls and even the sides of ships. They had earned the nickname, 'Homewreckers' on account of this. However, on this occasion, Sterling was willing to throw caution to the wind. The Sa'Nerra's armor, combined with the alien species' exceptional resilience to injury, meant that sometimes two or three shots from regular weapons were needed to put them down. In contrast, the Homewreckers could one-shot-kill even the toughest alien warrior.

"I haven't seen those used in a while," said Banks, sliding out of her seat and drawing her pistol. "I just hope those commandoes can shoot straight, otherwise we'll all end up being blown out into space."

Sterling might ordinarily have laughed, though on this occasion, Banks' joke was a little too close to the truth for comfort.

"Breaching in thirty," Shade called out as Sterling, Banks and Razor gathered their gear and got ready to move.

Razor pulled on a backpack containing the hardware she needed to hack the alien computer system. However, also tucked away inside the bag was another piece of equipment that Sterling was hoping they'd not have to use.

"Remember, we need to take one of the warriors alive," Sterling called out to Shade and the commando squad.

"Someone on the bridge or close to it. We may need an alien commander for this to work."

Shade acknowledged Sterling, but kept her eyes locked ahead. Her expression had hardened like granite and the weapons officer did not show a flicker of fear. This was Opal Shade in her element. Violence fueled her and Sterling knew the assault would be like injecting nitrous oxide into her veins.

Seconds later the cutting beams shut down and a commando kicked the hatch open. Immediately, plasma blasts flashed through the opening from inside the Sa'Nerran cruiser, illuminating the lusterless armor that Shade and the commandoes wore. Undeterred, the two lead heavy riflemen leaned out and fired. The sound of the over-powered Homewrecker weapons was more akin to the pulse of a rail gun blast than a hand-held weapon. Sterling imagined the rifles could probably take down an alien Wasp fighter as easily as a warrior.

"Moving out!" one of the commandoes cried before pushing through the hatch and into the alien ship. Shade and the remaining three soldiers followed right behind the helmeted commando. Sterling moved up to the hatch and peeked inside the alien ship. The Homewreckers had already left devastation in their wake. Walls had been blown through, metal panels were melted and the remains of five warriors with missing limbs lay scattered across the deck.

"This armor looks old," said Banks, moving through and taking cover behind a melted support column. "And look at their skin."

Sterling dropped to a crouch beside his first officer, keeping his plasma pistol held ready. He pressed a hand to the dead alien's leathery face and discovered it was clammy and slightly sticky.

"Hibernation," said Sterling, meeting Banks eyes. "These warriors have recently been thawed, and quickly too. I'm amazed they survived the process."

Banks nodded. "Something tells me they don't get much trade through that hidden aperture. They likely abandoned it because of the havoc it wreaks to ships passing through." Banks rapped her knuckles on the partially-melted chest plate of the dead alien. "These poor bastards were probably left to guard it, just in case. They could have been here for decades, for all we know."

Sterling felt a neural link form in his mind. It was Lieutenant Shade.

"The section is clear, Captain, you can move up," Shade called out. Sterling could feel the unadulterated thrill of his weapons officer's bloodlust through the link. It was intoxicating, like a sudden hit from a powerful narcotic. "Scans are showing at least another dozen warriors between us and the bridge."

"Understood, Lieutenant, proceed as planned," Sterling replied through the neural link. "Leave this channel open."

Sterling stood up and proceeded to walk through the corridors of the old warship. He checked the adjacent corridors as he moved, just to be sure that the commando squad hadn't left any of the warriors alive. However,

Shade's team had been as brutal in their work as Shade herself had been.

"Be advised that these aliens are recently out of hibernation stasis," Sterling added, allowing the entire assault squad to listen in. "That means there could be more of them in freezers, still waiting to thaw out."

Sterling, Banks and Razor caught up with Shade, who then moved into an adjacent section of the ship. It wasn't long before a thick blast door blocked their access to the next intersection. Shade ordered a commando to run a bypass, then they all took cover, expecting to meet resistance on the other side. Moments later the door swooshed open and plasma blasts flashed through, slamming into the ceiling and walls, causing showers of sparks to rain down on Sterling's crew. One of the heavy riflemen was hit in the neck and went down. It was a lucky shot to one of the only weak points in the combat armor. Cursing, Sterling darted over to the wounded soldier, picked up the powerful weapon and returned fire. The kick of the Homewrecker was ferocious, as was the effect of its blast. Plasma tore through the advancing alien warriors like bullets through paper, splattering their remains across the walls.

"Move out!" Shade ordered.

The three remaining commandoes advanced, blasting aliens, walls and decks to pieces as they pressed on.

"He's dead," said Banks. She had knelt down to check on the commando who had fallen.

"Here, you can probably use this one-handed," said Sterling, passing the Homewrecker rifle to his first officer.

Banks shifted the pistol to her left hand and took the weapon from Sterling. As expected, she wielded it like it was no more substantial than a plastic toy ray-gun.

"We're meeting more resistance than I anticipated," Sterling added, as the sound of more blasts filtered along the corridor. "We need to pick up the pace before more of these bastards thaw out."

He ushered Banks and Razor ahead then followed a few steps behind, checking their rear to make sure no more aliens had defrosted and come after them. Suddenly, a door thudded open to Sterling's side and he found himself staring into the yellow eyes of a Sa'Nerran warrior. Reacting on instinct, Sterling shot the alien at point-blank range. With his pistol set to full power, the blast burned straight though the warrior's gut, leaving a hole as wide as his arm, but to his astonishment the warrior didn't die. Hissing madly, the Sa'Nerran grabbed Sterling around the throat, seeming unaware that a chunk of its flesh had been melted away. The alien's clammy fingers dug deeper into Sterling's skin as he fought against the warrior's grip. Moments later the effect of the critical injury hit in full force and the warrior's strength faded. It released its hold on Sterling and dropped to its knees, revealing five more Sa'Nerran fighters in the room behind it. Opened hibernation chambers surrounded the aliens and Sterling could see a dozen more chambers inside the room that still remained sealed.

"On me!" Sterling called out, as the first of the alien warriors charged.

The warrior had already donned its armor, but was

equipped only with the serrated, half-moon blade that the belligerent aliens used for close-quarters fighting. Still struggling for air, Sterling aimed and shot the warrior in the chest, but its armor absorbed the blow. His second shot took the warrior down, but by then the other aliens were on him like a pack of wolves. One of the warriors grabbed his wrist and pushed his weapon hand away, while another drove him against the far wall of the corridor. A blade was raised, its sharp metal edge glinting under the ship's subdued lighting. Sterling edged away but then the alien's head exploded, covering him in hot flesh, some of which flew into his mouth. The taste was vile and he gagged before taking a hard shot to the body from another warrior. More plasma blasts raced along the corridor, striking two other aliens as they advanced on Banks and Razor. That only left a single warrior for Sterling to deal with, and he relished his task. The alien's assault on him had pissed him off and made him hungry for a fight.

Sterling spat the charred alien flesh in his mouth onto the deck then squared off against the warrior. The alien had only recently thawed and stood before Sterling entirely naked, with only the serrated blade in its hand. The Sa'Nerran's grotesque features were only made worse by its lack of clothes and armor. Sterling waved the warrior on and the alien advanced, but Sterling quickly snapped a kick toward its knee. The alien buckled under its own weight allowing Sterling to hammer a crushing elbow strike to its leathery face. Stripping the blade from the warrior's hand, Sterling then drove it into the back of the alien's neck. This was the second weak-spot in the otherwise robust

Sa'Nerran anatomy. The warrior hissed wildly as blood gushed from the wound, but Sterling pressed harder, digging the razor-sharp blade further into its flesh, severing arteries and bone until finally it was dead.

Banks then appeared at Sterling's side, aiming the Homewrecker rifle into the room from which the aliens had emerged.

"Are you okay, Captain?" Banks asked, after ensuring the room was clear.

"Let's just say this fight left a nasty taste in my mouth," Sterling replied before spitting more alien flesh onto the deck. He recovered his pistol, but retained the alien blade. He imagined he might need it again, before the day was out. "Destroy those other hibernation pods," he ordered, wiping blood from his face. "It's time we started to even the odds."

Banks nodded then blasted the power distribution hub that was feeding the hibernation pods. The hub exploded, sending sparks and fiery debris flying out into the room. Moments later the pods shut down and the yellow eyes of the alien occupants sprang open. Sterling could hear the sound of the warriors thudding against the insides of the chambers, their yellow eyes wide and wild-looking. However, the aliens were trapped, buried alive, and Sterling had no intention of releasing them from their tombs.

"Let's go, I have a feeling those aren't the last sleeping warriors on this ship," said Sterling.

Sterling took the lead, following the sound of plasma weapons fire, while Banks covered their rear. Soon they had caught up with Shade, Razor and the remaining three commandoes. They were at the door to the main bridge, but it was sealed tight. One of the commandoes was attempting to run a bypass, but Sterling could see that it wasn't working.

"Let me try," said Lieutenant Razor, hurrying alongside the commando, then dropping her backpack of gear onto the deck. The engineer pulled out a collection of wires from a device inside the pack and hooked them up to the locking mechanism on the door.

"How long will this take, Lieutenant?" asked Sterling, anxiously checking their rear.

"I almost have it, sir," Razor replied, working at her usual, frantic speed.

"Remember, I need one of these things alive, as insurance in case we can't crack the computer," Sterling called out to the assault team while they waited. "And check your aim in there. If we blast through the windows then we'll all get blown out into space."

"Got it!" Razor called out.

Shade ordered the commandoes to stand by and they each took up position behind the door.

"On three, Lieutenant," Sterling said to his chief engineer. He then began the countdown on his fingers, tightening his grip on the pistol in his other hand.

The door slid open and straight away the commandoes and Sa'Nerra on the bridge began trading blasts of plasma. A commando went down, hit in the gut, but Shade and the other two pushed through onto the bridge. Hisses and shouts filled the air along with the fizz of the weapons.

Sterling then moved through, shooting an injured warrior in the head before it could raise its pistol at him. He spotted a warrior in the center of the bridge, hiding behind what appeared to be the primary command consoles. The memory of his Omega Directive test suddenly rushed into his mind. Instead of the cruiser's leader, he saw the warrior on the bridge of the Hammer, with its fingers around the throat of Ariel Gunn. He physically shook his head to clear the image from his mind then gritted his teeth and advanced. Blasts flashed past him, missing by inches, but Sterling was relentless and fearless. Returning fire, the alien commander was struck in the shoulder and went down.

"Lucas!"

Sterling tried to shut out the voice of Ariel Gunn in his mind. She was dead and this warrior, like the one who had forced Sterling to kill his friend, would also die by his hand.

"Lucas, stop!"

Sterling fired again, pummeling blasts of plasma into the alien command console. Soon it provided no cover at all for the alien commander, who was struck to the thigh, then the wrist as it raised its arm in an effort to block the blasts. The next shot blew its hand off completely.

"Lucas, it's Mercedes! Stop!"

The neural link from his first officer felt like an eagle claw clamping down on his brain. He staggered back, lowering his weapon and pressing his hand to his temple.

"Lucas, it's me. Ease down, we got them..." Banks continued, though this time her voice was soothing and reassuring.

Sterling shook his head then turned to see Commander Banks beside him. She had taken a hit and was bleeding, but she still looked strong. Shade was by the door, which Razor had closed behind them after they'd all entered. The devices in her backpack were flashing as she worked on the locking mechanism. The two other commandoes were dead, as were six of the alien bridge crew. Sterling turned to the smoldering command console and saw the alien leader, cowering beneath the vessel's viewscreen. The warrior cradled what remained of its arm and hissed quietly as Sterling approached. He had no idea what the alien was saying, but he guessed it wasn't complimentary.

"Glad you're back with us, Captain," said Banks, raising her eyebrows at Sterling. "That creature over there is the only one we haven't killed," she added, pointing to the Sa'Nerran officer. "Wasn't it you that kept telling us to keep one alive?" she added, with a smile.

"It was," said Sterling, truthfully. Then he shrugged. "And I only said alive. I didn't say in one piece."

Banks laughed, causing the alien's hiss to grow louder. However, it soon fell silent again as Banks aimed the barrel of the Homewrecker at its head.

Sterling silently cursed himself for losing control, and he cursed his own mind for subjecting him to the memories of his Omega Directive test at such a crucial moment. There was a time when thoughts of Ariel Gunn would only recur during his sleep. Now they were encroaching on his waking life too. He didn't like it, and resolved to do something about it, but what that was he didn't know.

Turning to Banks, Sterling rested a hand on her

shoulder and met her eyes. "Thanks, Mercedes. Thank for bringing me out of... whatever that was I was in."

"Just doing my job, Captain," Banks replied with a heartfelt smile. She then playfully rapped her knuckles on Sterling's chest plate. As usual, his first officer struggled to moderate the strength of her blow and it hurt like hell, even through the armor.

Sterling then became aware that their intimate neural link was still active. Banks' emotions and echoes of her thoughts suddenly came through strongly. Sterling could feel that duty was not the only reason for his first officer's actions. There was something more, but it was new and unfamiliar. It felt like something secret; something Banks didn't want him to know. He quickly tapped his interface and closed the link. He didn't need any more distractions, nor did he want to invade the thoughts of his first officer, any more than he wanted others to know what lurked in the darkest recesses of his own mind.

The awkward moment was then interrupted by Lieutenant Razor, who approached with her backpack and set it down next to one of the consoles that hadn't already been blown apart.

"Is that our backup plan, sir?" Razor asked, pointing to the wounded alien commander.

"What's left of him, yes," Sterling replied. "Hopefully, we won't need it, but I'll keep it alive just in case."

Razor nodded then set to work, unpacking the gear from her backpack and attaching devices to the alien command console. Sterling then felt another link form in his mind. This time it was from Commander Graves on the Invictus.

"Captain, we have three gen-two Sa'Nerran Destroyers incoming," Graves said, in his usual unruffled, surgeon's voice. "They are less than an hour out."

"Understood, Commander," Sterling replied. He had expected company sooner or later, though he was surprised that the aliens had only sent three aging warships. "Standby, we're on the bridge now."

Sterling closed the link and peered out of the window of the old alien cruiser. Unlike the newer Sa'Nerran ships, the phase-one vessel still had viewing portholes in addition to its viewscreen. The space outside the ship looked the same as it did in every other system Sterling had visited. However, the stars he was looking at now had never been seen by human eyes before. They'd come further than any vessel in history and fought against odds that seemed unassailable. They should be dead, he realized, but the Invictus and the Omega Taskforce fought on.

"Penny for your thoughts?" said Banks, stepping up to Sterling's side.

Sterling reflected for a moment then glanced across to his first officer. "I think we're going to do this, Mercedes," he said, feeling electricity run down his spine. Then he glanced again at the alien, which recoiled from Sterling as he did so. "I think it's payback time."

CHAPTER 20
A TASTE OF ITS OWN MEDICINE

STERLING GLANCED down at the computer on his left arm for the third time that minute, following a group of markers that were steadily moving through the pressurized sections of the alien ship. Each marker represented an individual Sa'Nerran warrior that was heading their way. By his current count, ten aliens were already advancing on their location, outnumbering them by more than two to one. The longer they remained on the alien cruiser, the more warriors would come, and Sterling wasn't about to go down on the bridge of any ship, let alone an enemy one. The growing number of enemy forces wasn't Sterling's only concern, though. Their route back to the combat shuttle had already been cut off. Escape now required more innovative – and desperate – tactics.

Sterling switched to the remote piloting screen for their combat shuttle and recalled it to his current location. Their situation was growing more precarious by the second, but Sterling was determined to see the mission through to the end. They had to recover the data or all was lost, and the closer they came to failure, the more Sterling realized he'd rather die than return to Fleet space in disgrace with his tail between his legs.

Lowering his wrist again, Sterling glanced across to Lieutenant Razor, who was still working frantically to crack the Sa'Nerran command computer and retrieve the data that could lead them to James Colicos. However, it was becoming clear that the process was going to take too long. A more drastic solution was needed, but it was a contingency that they'd planned for.

"We're out of time, Lieutenant," Sterling said, stepping over to his engineer. "Can you crack this computer or not?"

Razor downed tools then shook her head. "Not in the time we have available, sir," she replied. "It will probably take me another thirty minutes to break through." Razor then rummaged inside her satchel and pulled out the neural translation matrix that Commander Graves had extracted from the colonist on Far Deep Nine. Sterling was pleased to see that there were no longer chunks of human brain attached to it. "I think we have to 'plan B' this, Captain," Razor went on, holding up the device. "I volunteer to try."

Sterling took the device from his engineer and examined it. Their plan B was highly theoretical, but Commander Graves and Lieutenant Razor both believed it could work. The principal was simple – adapt the neural interface so that it latched onto a Sa'Nerran rather than human brain, then reverse the flow of information. As the precursor to the neural control weapon, Graves believed the device could be used to coerce the Sa'Nerran brain into receiving instructions from another neural interface - a human interface. However, considering that the device had driven the colonist on Far Deep Nine mad, using it was not without risk. Consequently, Razor had explained to Sterling that she'd devised a "firewall" in order to prevent her from being turned or simply driven mad.

"Are you sure this thing isn't going to fry you brain, Lieutenant?" asked Sterling, handing the device back to Razor.

"No, sir, I'm not sure," the engineer replied, flatly. "But I don't see that we have a choice."

Sterling's computer on his forearm bleeped and he checked the update, noting that the number of Sa'Nerran warriors heading to the bridge had risen to fourteen. He cursed then met his engineer's eyes again.

"Do it, Lieutenant," Sterling said with conviction. He pointed to their Sa'Nerran prisoner. "If we can get that thing to unlock the computer for us, we can be out of here before this place becomes overrun with warriors."

"Aye, Captain," Razor answered. She then took a step toward the Sa'Nerran commander, which was now bound and under guard by Lieutenant Shade. The alien hissed at Razor as she approached and bore its jagged teeth. Razor hesitated, as if the thing were an angry rattlesnake.

"Make our guest more compliant, Commander," Sterling ordered.

"My pleasure, Captain," the Invictus' first officer replied, clearly relishing the opportunity to get hands-on with their prisoner.

Banks cracked her knuckles and paced over to the alien, showing none of the timidity that Razor had displayed. The warrior hissed again as Banks grabbed the alien commander and hauled it up. Unable to strike out with its leathery hands the warrior sunk its teeth into her armor. Banks grimaced and Sterling saw blood leak out from the puncture wounds, but the alien's desperate attack had only seemed to piss his first officer off. Grabbing the alien around the neck Banks pulled the warrior clear of her armor then held it tightly against the command computer. The alien struggled and hissed, but it was no match for the super-human strength of Commander Mercedes Banks.

"Make it quick," said Sterling, again anxiously peering down at his computer. The markers on the screen were still growing in number and getting closer.

Razor pulled the spidery network of wires over the alien's head then pressed the interface to the warrior's leathery temple. The neural interface powered up and dug itself into the side of the alien's head, like a python sinking its fangs into its prey. The alien hissed wildly and fought to free itself from Banks, but she was too strong. The warrior remained helpless as the device buried its tendrils deeper into the alien's brain.

Sterling watched the process with interest. Normally, neural interfaces were installed during infanthood and grew with their host, no different to any other sensory organ. Beyond a certain age, though, it became dangerous to integrate the technology. The process was simply too invasive; too painful. To an adult being, such as the Sa'Nerran commander, it was nothing short of torture.

However, Sterling felt no sympathy for the alien. It was merely a taste of its own bitter medicine. Lieutenant Razor then tapped her own neural interface and began working at a portable computer that she'd removed from her backpack.

"We're connected," Razor said, her fingers flashing across the screen of the console. "Firewalls established. There is now only a direct link between me and the alien."

Suddenly, Razor's muscles tensed up as if she'd just jabbed a fork into an electrical outlet. The alien's hisses became more labored and raucous. Its yellow eyes bulged and its own muscles spasmed wildly, causing Banks to tighten her hold even further.

"Lieutenant?" Sterling called out, kneeling at his engineer's side. "Lieutenant!" he called out again, but still Razor was unable to respond. He cursed and grabbed the neural device on the side of the alien's head, preparing it to tear it free. Then he felt a hand land on his shoulder and grip him hard. Sterling winced and instinctively let go of the neural interface to pull the hand away. He saw that Razor was peering into his eyes, imploringly.

"Wait, I'm okay..." Razor said, struggling to force the words out through her clenched teeth. "It's... fighting me..." she continued.

The engineer pressed her eyes shut as sweat began to bead on her lustrous skin. Razor continued to fight the creature and Sterling could see that the alien's resistance was beginning to fade. The portable console that his engineer had been working on then chimed an alert. Sterling checked it and saw that the first of five firewalls she'd set up to protect herself and the others from the corrupting effect of Colicos' experimental device had already failed.

"You have five minutes, Lieutenant, then I'm pulling the plug. Literally," Sterling called out. He couldn't be sure that Razor had heard him, but whether she had or not no longer mattered. They had to get off the cruiser before the Sa'Nerran reinforcements arrived.

A low rumble through the deck plating caused Sterling to look toward the viewscreen. The Invictus' combat shuttle had just maneuvered past the windows of the alien bridge. Sterling switched back to the remote piloting interface on his computer and commanded the vessel to latch onto one of the porthole windows and begin cutting through. However, the bridge of the Sa'Nerran cruiser was thick and heavily armored. The process would take time – time they were rapidly running short of. He heard the combat shuttle thump against the porthole and its cutting beams activated. The countdown had begun, but he knew they weren't going to escape without a fight.

"We need to hold off the reinforcement for as long as we can," he called over to Lieutenant Shade. "It'll be down to you and me."

His weapons officer nodded and moved over to the door, holding one of the powerful Homewrecker heavy plasma rifles in her hands. Unlike his freakishly-strong first officer, Lieutenant Shade had to use all her strength to wield the mighty weapon. Collecting one of the plasma hand-cannons from a dead commando, Sterling moved up beside Shade on the opposite side of the door. The sound of heavy boots was already filtering along the corridor, signaling that the first wave of warriors was close. Sterling glanced back to Razor, expecting to still see her frozen in pain and concentration, but instead the engineer was on her feet and appeared calm. He noticed that Banks had released her grip on the alien commander. Incredibly, the warrior walked over to one of the computer terminals, seemingly of its own free will, and began to operate it. The puppet master was now in control.

Sterling's computer chimed an alert and he saw that the second of five firewalls had failed. A plasma blast slammed into the wall inches from his head and he pulled back into cover, cursing himself for dropping his guard. Shade stepped out into the open and returned fire with the Homewrecker, doing more damage to the ship than she did to the advancing horde. She pulled back into cover and two alien warriors rushed out, charging toward Sterling armed only with semi-circular blades. Sterling stepped out and allowed them to advance. The hand-cannons had limited range, but in close quarters they were even more devastating than the heavy plasma rifles. The rasping hiss of the warriors grew to a roar then Sterling unleashed with the hand-cannon, blasting the first warrior back along the corridor as if it had been hit by a truck. The second continued its attack unfazed by the fate of its companion. Sterling gritted his teeth then fired again, blasting the head and upper torso of the alien into charred chunks of flesh and bone. The smell of burning alien meat assaulted him, as vile and as nauseating as ever.

Sterling's computer then chimed again and he knew that the third firewall had fallen. He was about to call out to Banks for an update before four more warriors rushed out. They were only partially decked out in armor and only two had plasma weapons. Sterling assumed they had just thawed out and had merely grabbed whatever weapons and armor came quickly to hand.

Lieutenant Shade opened fire, obliterating one of the warriors with her first volley, then a plasma blast struck her chest and she fell back. Sterling returned fire with the hand cannon, temporarily halting the aliens' advance then glanced down at Shade. Smoke was rising from her armor and she was clearly in pain, but his weapons officer fought through it and pushed herself up. Sterling continued to fire, but the aliens were too far away from the hand-cannon to be fully effective. He felt a thump to his side followed by a burning sensation of pain. Returning into cover, he saw that his armor had soaked up the bulk of the energy. He'd been lucky – but fortune favored the brave, he told himself. Shade then fired again, killing the second of the two-armed aliens before her strength failed and she was forced to release her hold on the heavy weapon. Sterling's computer chimed again and he cursed. The fourth firewall was down. It was do or die time, Sterling told himself, but there wasn't a chance in hell he was the one doing the dying.

Stepping out to meet the two advancing warriors, Sterling fired at the closest and blasted the alien's leg off at the hip. A flash of plasma raced past his face, temporarily blinding him, but he pressed on and squeezed the trigger again. This time the weapon jammed. Cursing, he had just enough time to raise the cannon to block a strike from the warrior's serrated blade. The clang and scrape of metal on metal felt like someone raking fingernails across a blackboard. Sterling was then kicked to the chest and sent down, but he rolled back and was on his feet before the alien could make a killing blow. Shade grabbed the warrior's ankle as it raced past, still in pursuit of Sterling, toppling the alien to the deck. Seizing his chance, Sterling hammered the butt of the plasma cannon down onto the back of the alien's head, striking the Sa'Nerran's weak spot with deadly precision.

"We're in!" Banks shouted over to Sterling. "The data is downloading now."

Sterling checked his computer. The final firewall was holding, but he knew it could fall at any moment. Then the thump of boots and the hiss of alien cries again filtered along the corridor from outside.

"Hold them off while I ready the shuttle," Sterling called back to his first officer. He then rushed over to the porthole window where the shuttle was still cutting through. The seal was holding, but it was as precarious as Razor's firewall.

Banks grabbed another plasma hand-cannon then ran over to Shade and helped her up. There were no concerned words. No asking, "are you okay?" Banks and Sterling both knew that Shade would fight on even if she was dying. Whether she was 'okay' or not was immaterial. Shade took the hand-cannon while Banks picked up the Homewrecker, carrying it with the same inhuman ease as she had done earlier. Both unloaded their weapons along the corridor, creating such a torrent of plasma fire that nothing living could possibly hope to advance through it.

The cutting laser then finished and the porthole fell onto the deck of the alien bridge with a resounding crash. Sterling ran over to Razor and grabbed her shoulder, turning her to face him. Her skin was soaked through with sweat and blood vessels bulged in her neck and around her temples. Sterling turned her head to inspect the engineer's own neural interface. The skin around it was red and inflamed, but it showed no evidence of the spidery corruption that the first-generation neural control weapons caused.

"Lieutenant, do we have the data?" Sterling asked, but Razor was on the verge of collapse and unable to answer. Releasing his hold on her, Sterling turned to the portable console his engineer had been working on. They had about seventy percent of the alien ship's database. Then he checked the computer on his wrist and saw that the final firewall was about to collapse. They were out of time.

"Get back to the shuttle, now!" Sterling called out, directing the order at Banks and Shade, who were still unleashing hell on the Sa'Nerran reinforcements.

Sterling then turned to face the alien commander. It was standing like a statue, its yellow eyes wide and unblinking. Blood was leaking out from the modified neural translation matrix that had attached itself to the alien's brain and Sterling could see corruption spreading like wildfire. Grabbing the alien behind the back of the neck, Sterling took hold of the neural interface and dug his fingers into the alien's flesh. Then with all his might he tore the device out of the warrior's head, like pulling giblets from the neck of a turkey. Blood gushed from the wound, coating Sterling's hands and face in the hot, crimson liquid. The alien hissed wildly, its cries horrific and haunting, like an evil spirit being exorcised. The alien then collapsed to the deck, dead. Razor collapsed moments later, but Sterling caught her and threw her arm over his shoulder. He glanced at the computer on his wrist. The final firewall had fallen, but he had no idea whether it had failed before or after he'd torn the device from alien's brain. Banks and Shade then rushed past, still firing through the door to hold off the alien warriors.

"Go!" Banks called before unloading another fierce volley from the Homewrecker, obliterating two more warriors in an eruption of blood and guts, like bursting balloons full of water.

Sterling grabbed Razor's portable console, threw it into the backpack then grabbed the bag with his free hand. Dragging the barely-conscious engineer onward, Sterling shoved her through the hatch and inside the combat shuttle before hauling himself inside after her. Banks and Shade followed and the hatch sealed. Leaving Razor on the deck of the shuttle, Sterling jumped into the pilot's seat and blasted away from the alien cruiser, tearing a hole in the bridge as he did so. Seconds later, the remaining alien reinforcements were blown into space through the rupture. Incredibly, the dying warriors still tried to fire at the shuttle as it departed, despite their bodies swelling and asphyxiation setting in. Sterling almost admired their tenacity, but at the same time he enjoyed watching them suffer. The alien race had shown humanity no mercy and they would get none from him.

The Shuttle then cleared the cruiser and Sterling thumped the console and cried out, overcome by the euphoria of their victory and narrow escape. Banks whooped and cursed the alien warriors that had been condemned to a painful death in space. She then grabbed Shade and pulled her into an embrace, though the weapons officer's response was as austere as always. However, their elation was short-lived. The shuttle's scanners chimed an alert and Sterling saw that the three Sa'Nerran Destroyers were almost on top of them. Against all odds, they'd won the first round, but the fight was not over yet.

STERLING STEERED the combat shuttle toward the Invictus and increased power to the engines. He'd hoped to make it inside the protective cocoon of his ship before the alien vessels arrived, but it soon became clear that wasn't going to happen. An alarm rang out and Sterling threw the shuttle hard to port, narrowly avoiding a stream of plasma blasts that flashed past the cockpit then vanished into space.

"We've got Wasps..." Sterling called out, activating the shuttle's combat mode. "The destroyers must have launched them in advance."

"How many?" asked Commander Banks, sliding into the second seat of the shuttle. She was holding the backpack full of equipment that Razor had used to download data from the Sa'Nerran cruiser.

"I have six on my scanner," Sterling replied, pulling in behind one of the Sa'Nerran fighters and opening fire. The small attack craft exploded, showering the combat shuttle with fiery debris. "Make that five," Sterling corrected, though without any hint of boastfulness. "With these things buzzing around, there's no way I can dock with the Invictus before the destroyers arrive."

Banks pulled the portable computer console out of Razor's backpack and slotted it into the shuttle's systems. "I'm uploading the data from the alien cruiser to the Invictus now," said Banks, tapping out a short sequence of commands into the computer. "I'll run an analysis and try to extrapolate anything that looks like navigational scan data."

Sterling nodded then glanced over his shoulder. His chief engineer was now strapped into a seat in the rear of the shuttle. She was still unconscious, but was being attended to by Lieutenant Shade. However, at Sterling's instruction, Shade kept a pistol close by. He had no way to know whether the firewall had failed before or after he'd torn the neural translation matrix from the head of the Sa'Nerran commander. If there had been a moment when the two interfaces were connected without a protective barrier between them, he had no idea what effect that might have on Razor's brain. However, he wasn't taking any chances. If Razor showed any sign that she was about to turn then she'd have to be put down. It was that simple.

Sterling focused back on the controls and the Invictus soared into view ahead of the combat shuttle, plasma blasts flashing into space from its turrets. A Wasp was hit and exploded, burning a fiery trail through space to Sterling's right, like a comet. He adjusted course to stay close to the Marauder, in the hope that its more accurate and powerful guns would make short work of the Wasps. Slotting in behind the Invictus, Sterling then tapped his neural interface and reached out to Commander Graves.

"Commander, we have the data and are running an analysis now," Sterling called out to the temporary commander of his ship. "But until we have a new course, we'll have to stand and fight. Can you handle those destroyers?"

The Invictus initiated a full-power turn, putting itself between the combat shuttle and two of the attacking Wasps. Blasts from the Sa'Nerran fighters thumped into the Invictus' regenerative armor, but it was as ineffective as firing BB-gun pellets at a rhinoceros. Focused fire from the Marauder's turrets then obliterated one of the fighters, while the other narrowly evaded being hit. The alien combat ship panicked and turned away from the Invictus, allowing Sterling to pick it off with ease.

"We can handle the destroyers, Captain," Graves replied. His tone was so level that the medical officer sounded almost bored. "I would recommend you dock before they are in weapons range, however."

Sterling was about to answer when the shuttle took a hit and was buffeted like a dodgem car at a fairground. He glanced at the damage control console and saw that their armor had absorbed the bulk of the energy. The weapons systems of the older-generation Wasps lacked the punch of their modern equivalents and the damage was minor. Even so, Sterling knew they couldn't last long, especially with three destroyers closing fast. Sterling then glanced at the scanners and saw that the alien warships were already within weapons range. However, Sa'Nerran Destroyers hadn't yet opened fire. Sterling guessed that their alien commanders thought they were being smart by waiting until they were within optimal weapons range. However, they were unwittingly playing into Sterling's hands. When it came to close-quarters fighting, the Invictus was devastating, combining the grace of a ballerina with the punch of a heavyweight boxer.

"Finish off these Wasps then prepare for an emergency landing in the docking garage," Sterling replied to Commander Graves while also firing at, and missing, one of the nimble alien fighters.

"Understood, Captain," Graves replied. "We'll be waiting."

Sterling was about to close the link then he remembered about Lieutenant Razor and her possible neural injuries.

"And Commander Graves, as soon as I'm back on the bridge, I need you in the medical bay. Lieutenant Razor is injured."

"I will alert my medical team, Captain," Graves replied.

Another volley of plasma shot out from the Invictus, clipping the wing of one of the Wasps. The fighter spiraled out of control then collided with the Marauder, bouncing off the dorsal armor like a bug hitting a windshield.

"One last thing, Commander Graves," Sterling continued, as the burning remains of the Wasp sped above them. "Keep Lieutenant Razor restrained and watch for any signs that she is turning. If that happens, you know what to do."

"I understand, sir," Commander Graves replied, with barely a breath of pause before his answer. Perhaps more than anyone else on the ship, Graves had the least trouble with taking life. Considering that he was the officer responsible for keeping the crew alive, Sterling had always found this perversely amusing. Though mostly he found it disturbing. It was another reason why the stone-cold doctor creeped him out.

"I think I've found the raw data from the cruiser's navigational archives," said Commander Banks, momentarily distracting Sterling from watching his ship make mincemeat of the remaining Wasps. "Fortunately, it looks like nothing has come this way for a long time, so it's a good chance this is Colicos' shuttle."

"Send the data to Ensign Keller and get him to plot a course," said Sterling, pulling out of the shadow of the Invictus, ready to initiate the docking maneuver.

"Aye, Captain," replied Banks, returning to work.

Only a single Wasp now remained and the diminutive ship was running scared. However, Sterling was not about to allow the infuriating combat craft to escape. Like a fly continually buzzing around his head, he was determined to squash it. Increasing power to the engines, Sterling pulled in behind the Wasp and locked on. Beyond the engine glow of the fighter, now within visible range, were the three Sa'Nerran Destroyers. The safe and perhaps even smart thing to do would be to let the Wasp escape and return to the Invictus. However, that wasn't Sterling's style. Fleet had spent too much time trying to be smart and playing it safe, and look where it had got them. This was a war and as far as Sterling was concerned there was now only one rule of engagement. It was the same rule that had allowed the Sa'Nerran Empire to turn the tide of the war. The rule was simple; kill the enemy, any way you can.

Plasma blasts flashed out ahead of the combat shuttle and the Wasp exploded. Sterling turned hard and rammed all available power into the engines. Alerts rang out and plasma blasts from the destroyers flashed past their windows. However, Sterling was unafraid. All the alien destroyers were doing was depleting their own energy reserves. The more power they wasted shooting at the shuttle the less they had to take on the Invictus.

"Stand by, Invictus, we're coming in hot," warned Sterling over an open comm channel to the ship.

The shuttle bay had already opened and the Invictus had slowed to allow the combat craft to approach. Even so, their relative velocity was dangerously high, but it was the only way to get the shuttle back on board, without making the Invictus a sitting duck.

"Hold on, Lieutenant," Sterling called back to his weapons officer. Shade then planted herself in the seat opposite Razor and grabbed onto a combat harness. She had a pistol on hand, resting it across her lap, ready to use it should the engineer's neural interface show signs of corruption.

Sterling glanced at Banks, but there was no need for them to exchange words, verbally or through their minds. Both had experienced emergency combat landings before. Both hated them.

The shuttle hammered into the landing bay of the

Invictus and began to carve through the metal decking toward the end wall. A magnetic net caught the craft, arresting their forward momentum as suddenly as a pigeon flying into a window. The harness bit down tightly across Sterling's chest and he felt the breath being literally squeezed from his lungs. Forcing another breath into his bruised chest, Sterling popped the emergency escape hatch and unbuckled his harness. He could already see a medical team approaching, carrying a grav-stretcher for Lieutenant Razor.

"Stay with her, and keep her under guard until we're sure she's clean," Sterling said to Shade, as he stumbled toward the hatch. "Commander Banks will handle the weapons control station until you return."

"Aye, Captain," Shade replied, briskly.

Ordinarily, he would expect that an order denying Shade the opportunity to kill the enemy would generate a measure of discontent. However, it was clear that Shade considered their unconscious engineer to be a potentially greater threat at that moment in time. As usual, her judgement was sound. The Invictus could handle three old destroyers, but if their chief engineer was turned and retained her knowledge and access of the ship's systems, one rogue operative reaching the engineering level could wreak far more havoc than three aging alien warships.

Sterling jumped out onto the deck of the docking section and raced toward the main elevator, with Banks hot on his heels. He could feel the inertial negation systems working on overdrive to counteract the effect of the Marauder's high-energy maneuvers, and he could feel from the rattle through the deck plating and thrum of the engines that the ship was being pushed hard. A tremor ran through the deck as the elevator doors opened and Sterling ran inside. He recognized it at once as the result of their forward plasma railguns firing a full spread. A series of thumps then pounded the Invictus' hull. However, Sterling knew that these weren't the result of incoming fire, but from incoming debris.

"Graves has already got one," said Banks. She could feel the ship just as keenly as Sterling could. "Hopefully, he'll leave some for us."

Sterling loved how Banks could sometimes steal the thoughts from his mind, even when they weren't connected through a neural link.

The elevator doors swung open onto deck one and Sterling raced outside. "I take it you remember how to fire our plasma guns?" he said, smiling back at his first officer.

"Just watch me," replied Banks, picking up the pace and catching up with her captain.

The door to the bridge swished open and Sterling's ears were assaulted by the sound of consoles bleeping, weapons firing and plasma blasts thudding into their regenerative armor.

"Captain on the bridge," Commander Graves called out, immediately giving way to Sterling.

"Razor is en route to the med bay," Sterling said, jumping onto the command platform. "Lieutenant Shade has her under guard."

"Understood, Captain, I shall prepare my butcher's

knives," Graves replied, immediately setting off toward the exit.

Sterling almost called out to the doctor to reinforce the notion that he wanted Razor kept alive, but a blast from one of the two remaining destroyers focused his attention on more pressing matters.

"Time to impress me once again, Ensign Keller," Sterling called out to his helmsman, while Banks relieved the crewmember at the weapons control station.

"Aye, Captain," Keller replied, briskly. "Good to have you back, sir."

A wide grin appeared on Banks' face and she glanced at Sterling, eyebrow raised. However, despite her bravado and tough-talking, Sterling knew that his first officer found their helmsman to be endearing too.

Keller drove the Invictus in pursuit of one of the alien destroyers, embarrassing the Sa'Nerran vessel with the Marauder's superior agility and speed. Banks waited until the glow of the destroyer's engines almost filled the viewscreen, then unleashed a full spread from the forward plasma rail guns. The blasts tore through the older alien warship like a tank shell smashing through an old garden shed. A series of hard thuds rocked the deck and Sterling saw that their aft armor had taken a pounding. The remaining Sa'Nerran destroyer was directly on their tail. Unlike the Wasp, which had chosen to flee, this warship was not about to turn and run. Sterling respected its choice to stand and fight. Perhaps the alien commander believed it had a chance, Sterling wondered. Or perhaps it was too prideful or stubborn to back down. The outcome would be the same, either way.

"Ensign, hold your course and initiate a full-power y-axis turn," Sterling called out to the pilot. "Let's end this the old-fashioned way. A duel, face-to-face."

"Aye, sir," Keller replied. Sterling could sense the excitement in his voice. The young officer was learning to control his anxieties and live in the moment. Sterling glanced across to Banks, and saw she was ready. The fire was back in her eyes.

Sterling grabbed the side of the captain's console then felt the kick of the ship's thrusters. The starfield outside the viewscreen became a blur and moments later they were staring down the throat of the Sa'Nerran Destroyer.

"Fire," ordered Sterling, gripping the sides of his console more tightly.

The flash of plasma lit up the viewscreen as both vessels attacked. Sterling felt the impacts of the blasts land on the Invictus, but their regenerative armor soaked up the energy. The destroyer, however, was reduced to a burning cloud of wreckage.

Sterling glanced down at the scanner readout and saw that no other Sa'Nerran ships were in range. They'd found a back door into the alien's territory and with the Sa'Nerran armada engaged in Fleet space, there was barely anyone home.

"Do you have our next waypoint, Ensign Keller?" Sterling asked, glancing up at his helmsman.

"Aye, sir," Keller replied. "Long-range scanners have

detected an aperture. Based on the data retrieved from the Sa'Nerran cruiser, that's where Colicos went."

"Then set a course, Ensign, and take us there at maximum acceleration," Sterling replied.

The helmsman acknowledged the order as Sterling pushed himself away from his console and drew in a long, calming breath. His heart was still pounding in his chest from the adrenalin and excitement, but for now, at least, they were in the clear.

"We have a few hours until we reach the aperture," said Banks, who had moved back over to her own console beside Sterling's. "Repairs are under way, but we're still in good shape."

Sterling nodded, then glanced to the rear of the bridge, where Lieutenant Razor would normally be.

"Let's check on our patient," he said, meeting Banks' eyes. "The last thing we need right now is to surge deeper into enemy space without a chief engineer."

STERLING AND BANKS walked into the medical bay to see Lieutenant Shade standing guard over the Invictus' chief engineer. Razor lay unconscious in one of the surgical beds. Shade's pistol was holstered, but her hand remained on the grip. Commander Graves, as usual, appeared less concerned, and was across the other side of the room, peering down into the eyepiece of a microscope.

"What's the prognosis, Commander?" asked Sterling. He nodded to Shade, who took two steps back to make room for himself and Commander Banks. However, the weapons officer still did not remove her hand from the grip of her pistol.

"Lieutenant Razor has not yet turned," Commander Graves replied, without looking up from the instrument. "That is all I can tell you at this moment."

"Not yet suggests that she still might," Sterling replied, wary that his medical officer's response might come with a caveat.

Graves picked up a medical implement that Sterling had never seen before and removed a computer chip about the size of a matchstick from the tray beneath the microscope. He finally looked up and met Sterling's eyes.

"The truth, Captain, is that I do not know what will happen to her," Graves admitted, moving over to the side of the bed where Razor was lying. "Currently, Lieutenant Razor is stable and her brain shows no evidence of alteration. However, a detailed analysis of her neural interface suggests that there is some low-level corruption."

Sterling cursed under his breath. Graves was being cagey about the seriousness of his engineer's situation, but it still wasn't the news he was hoping for. Commander Graves then held up the medical device that he'd picked up from the tray of the microscope.

"The corruption is currently restricted to a small section of the neural device, but my analysis shows that it is spreading slowly," Graves continued. He turned the engineer's head to the side and delicately placed the device in his hand across Razor's neural implant. "This chip will disable the Lieutenant's implant. It may be dangerous for others to link to it at this stage." The matchstick-sized chip then appeared to melt into Razor's implant, like butter melting into hot toast. "It will also alert us, via the ship's computer, if the corruption reaches the point at which it begins to affect her brain. A paralyzing shock will then temporarily incapacitate the Lieutenant, but only for a couple of minutes at most." Graves placed the medical tool in a tray next to the bed, then gave Sterling a look that he'd seen dozens of times before. It was the look of a doctor who was about to give a terminal diagnosis. "At that point, Captain, there is only one course of action that we can take."

"I understand, Commander," Sterling replied, moving beside Razor and peering down at the softly iridescent skin on her face. "Do you know how long we've got?"

Commander Graves initially looked relucent to make a prediction. In many respects, Sterling realized it was no different to giving a life expectancy prediction for another kind of terminal illness. There was always uncertainty. However, the ship's medical doctor eventually gave an answer.

"Based on my studies of the brains of people that were turned by the generation-one neural control weapons, it may take several months for the corruption to Lieutenant Razor's interface to reach the same level." The doctor paused, and Sterling waited for him to deliver the inevitable stipulation to his estimate. "However, the rate of decay may accelerate as the corruption takes hold." The doctor shrugged. "In truth, Captain, this is as much a technological issue as a medical one. The person on this ship who is best equipped to 'treat' Lieutenant Razor's condition is Lieutenant Razor herself." Then the doctor raised his eyebrows, seeming to come up with another suggestion on the spot. "The only other who could help is, of course, the inventor of the device, James Colicos."

Sterling tapped his finger on the side of the bed's railings. Until they found James Colicos, Lieutenant Razor was her own best hope, which meant potentially allowing his chief engineer to resume her post. However, that was akin to allowing a walking bomb to roam the ship freely, without ever knowing when or where it might go off.

"This failsafe that you just inserted into Razor's interface, is it foolproof?" Sterling asked. Commander Graves looked like he was gearing up for another noncommittal answer, so Sterling quickly headed him off. "I know this is all uncharted territory, Commander, so just keep it simple. Yes or no."

"No," the medical officer replied, starkly.

Sterling turned to his weapon's officer. "I need you to rig a special kind of security monitor, Lieutenant," Sterling said, noting that Shade still hadn't taken her hand off the grip of her pistol. "Except this isn't just for monitoring and control. I need the option to initiate a lethal shock on command, to neutralize Lieutenant Razor should the need arise."

"Aye, Captain, I have something that will work," Shade replied. "They employ similar devices on high-security prisoners at Grimaldi, in case of riots."

Sterling had forgotten that his weapon's officer had once been an inmate of the military prison, and so would know this information first-hand. He was reminded of how little he still knew about her. However, Opal Shade had proven herself time and time again. He trusted the weapons officer to get the job done.

Sterling then turned to Commander Banks. "Authority to activate the charge should pass down the chain of command, should I be killed or incapacitated," he added. "That means if I can't do it, the duty falls to you."

"Understood, sir," Commander Banks replied, though

Sterling could sense that she had reservations about the order. However, his first officer knew better than to question them openly in front of the other members of the crew.

"Keep Razor sedated for now, until the modified security monitor has been installed," Sterling continued, now addressing Commander Graves. "Alert me once she's awake. I will explain the situation to her personally."

"As you wish, Captain," Commander Graves replied with his usual lack of bedside manner.

Sterling then turned to Shade. "Assign a commando to guard the medical bay until the device has been implanted, then have Commander Graves treat your injuries."

"I request that I return to my post immediately," Shade was quick to add before Sterling could turn for the door. "We're in enemy territory and could be attacked at a moment's notice."

"The fact we're in enemy territory is precisely why I need you fighting fit, Lieutenant," Sterling hit back. His weapons officer's request had not surprised him, but the last thing he needed was Shade collapsing at her post. "Get yourself fixed up then report to the bridge, that's an order."

"Aye, sir," Shade replied, though her disappointment at the order was clear.

Sterling left the medical bay, closely pursued by Commander Banks. He could tell she wanted to speak her mind about the decision to let Razor loose on the ship, but she remained silent. There were still other members of the crew flitting around the narrow corridors who might overhear them.

"We still have a few hours until we reach the aperture," Sterling said, choosing to be the one who broke the silence. "How about we grab a coffee? Then I'm going to try to get a couple of hours sleep."

"You know me, Captain, I'm never one to turn down a visit to the wardroom," Banks replied, smiling.

Suddenly, Jinx the beagle hound came bounding down the corridor, yapping vociferously. The dog stopped in front of Commander Banks and whined at her. Banks smiled as she picked the dog up.

"How the hell did you get out again?" said Banks, rubbing the dog's ears.

"That thing is some kind of Houdini," replied Sterling, scowling at the hound as they walked.

"It is a she, and she's very clever," Banks replied. "Aren't you Jinx?" she added, petting the dog more boisterously, while talking in the twee tone of voice that people reserve exclusively for pets and babies.

Sterling rolled his eyes. "We're supposed to be the most hard-ass crew in the Fleet, Mercedes," he said, still scowling at the dog, who was looking at him dotingly. "You're ruining our image."

Banks frowned then gestured to the empty corridor around them. "Who's here to see?" she hit back. "Besides, I'm training Jinx to pick up the scent of the enemy. She could come in useful."

Sterling laughed, though he wasn't entirely sure if Banks was being serious or not. "I wouldn't let that thing anywhere near the enemy," he replied. "They'll probably consider it a tasty snack."

"She, not it..." Banks corrected him again as they approached the door to the wardroom. "And if any Sa'Nerran bastard so much as looks at Jinx in a way I don't like, I'll personally reduce their homeworld to ash from orbit."

"That's the spirit, Commander," said Sterling, stepping inside the wardroom first.

Sterling had stood the ship down from battle stations, though they remained on high alert. Even so, the compact wardroom was quiet, save a handful of off-duty personnel, who all acknowledged the captain and first officer as they entered. Sterling grabbed a couple of mugs and set a pot underneath the processor. Meanwhile, Banks occupied herself with the more important task of finding herself something to eat. Taking the freshly-filled pot out of the processor, Sterling sat down at his usual table and waited for Banks to saunter over with her foil-wrapped tray. Jinx trotted along beside her then sat down underneath her chair.

"So, I guess you think we should just airlock Razor now?" Sterling said, as Banks tore the foil wrapper off her tray. His first officer laughed, which was not the response Sterling had expected.

"I think it's risky to let her loose, but we're behind enemy lines and we need everyone we can get," Banks replied, picking up a piece of meat and tossing it to Jinx. "The safer option is to airlock her, but when have we ever played it safe?" Sterling shrugged then poured the coffee. Banks had a point. "Besides, I know you'll take her out if it comes to that," she continued, in between mouthfuls of stew. "And, who knows, maybe this Colicos guy can help. He's supposed to be the genius."

Sterling added some creamer to his coffee and stirred it. "I hope he's worth it," he replied, grabbing a cookie off Banks' tray and dunking it into his coffee. Banks glowered at him as he did so. "If he can't help to fix this mess then I don't know what the hell we do next. In a straight-up fight against that Sa'Nerran armada, we could take the bastards down. But with each sector they take, more and more Fleet ships and crews get captured and turned against us."

Banks tossed another piece of meat to Jinx, who caught it skillfully before it hit the deck. "Maybe we should launch an invasion of our own?" she said, shrugging. "While the Sa'Nerra are pushing on Earth, maybe they've left their own world undefended, wherever the hell it is."

Sterling went to steal another cookie, but this time Banks was wise to his ploy and slapped his hand. The blow was meant playfully, but due to his first officer's strength, it smarted like a hornet sting.

"The Invictus is tough, but it's no planet killer, Mercedes," Sterling said, shaking his throbbing hand. "And unless Fleet drives the Sa'Nerran armada back into the Void, our ships are all trapped inside the inner colonies."

Banks considered this for a moment, while continuing to wolf down the contents of her meal tray. "We'll find a way," she eventually replied. She then grabbed a cookie from the meal tray and offered it to Sterling, smiling coyly as she did so. "We always do."

Sterling smiled and accepted the cookie, which he then proceeded to dunk into his coffee. Then he had a thought, though he knew immediately it was one that his first officer wouldn't like.

"Fletcher was pretty cagey about the number of ships he'd recruited to his cause," Sterling said, biting the end off the cookie and waiting for Banks' reaction.

"We're better off without that traitor's help," Banks hit back, tearing off a strip of jerky and holding it out for Jinx. The hound took the food politely in its jaws and began gnawing on it with relish.

"He still has all the mutineer ships," Sterling continued, still nibbling on the cookie while testing out his idea further. "And he hinted that there may be many more, recovered from the ruins of battles that took place over the last few decades." Sterling shrugged. "The fact the Sa'Nerra have left Middle Star alone suggests that the force Fletcher has amassed must be pretty powerful."

Banks shook her head then angrily tossed her fork down onto the empty meal tray. As usual, his first officer had polished off the contents in less time that it would take most people to finish the first course.

"If it comes down to needing that mutinous piece of trash on our side then we've already lost," Banks hit back. Her emotions were still running high and it hadn't taken much for her temper to fray. She appeared to recognize her slip and took a sip of coffee to calm her nerves.

"Let's hope it doesn't come to that," Sterling replied, relaxing his stance a little to help douse the flames that had sprung up in the belly of his first officer. "But something tells me that Christopher Fletcher's part in this war isn't over yet." Jinx then bayed and wagged her tail. "See, even that thing agrees with me," Sterling said, pointing to the hound.

"She..." Banks corrected again, rubbing the dog's ears. "And she agrees with you because you're the captain," she added, smiling. Then Banks' expressed turned suddenly more serious. "You should know that whether I agree with everything you do or not, I'll always have your back, Lucas," she said. The rapid change of tone took Sterling by surprise and he straightened up. "No matter what," Banks added, holding his eyes. Her stare was so intense, Sterling almost had to look away.

"I know, Mercedes," Sterling replied, with matching earnest. Then he finished his coffee, pushed his chair back and stood up. "Now, I'm going to try to grab a power-nap, before all hell breaks loose again," he said, rubbing the aching muscles at the back of his neck.

"Aye, Captain, let me know if you need a wake-up call," said Banks, while still stroking Jinx's ears.

"I doubt things will stay quiet long enough for me to need one," Sterling replied, pushing his seat back underneath the table. "But unless the ship suddenly catches fire, gets attacked by a giant space slug or is about to fall into a black hole, I'd appreciate it if I could be left undisturbed for the next couple of hours."

Banks nodded. "I'll see to it, Captain."

Sterling headed toward the exit then aimed a finger back toward Jinx as he went. "And if I step in that thing's crap on the way to my quarters, Acting Ensign Jinx will be going for a spacewalk..."

CHAPTER 23
PERMISSION TO SPEAK FREELY

STERLING WOKE with his heart pounding in his chest and his fists clenched so tightly that his nails bit into his skin. Cursing, he threw his legs over the side of the bed and forced his fists to unfurl, leaving his hands shaking.

"Damn it, get a grip..." Sterling growled, pressing his eyes shut and compelling his body to obey his commands, rather than the irrational impulses brought on by his subconscious mind. Quickly, his heart-rate relaxed and the tremors in his hands subsided. The vision of Mercedes Banks, dead at his feet by his own hands, then slipped deeper into the recesses of his waking mind. Soon, through a combination of controlled breathing and sheer force of will, the images sank away completely, like an old battleship lost at sea.

"Hello, Captain," said the computer, cheerfully. "Would you like me to conduct a brief session of psychoanalysis? Or perhaps we can meditate together. I hear that meditation can be effective in circumstances such as yours."

Sterling laughed and glanced up at the ceiling of his quarters, where he always imagined the omnipotent presence of the computer to be located.

"I'd like you to mind your own damn business and give me a ship's status report," he replied.

"As you wish, Captain," the computer said, breezily. "Perhaps later?"

"Perhaps not," Sterling answered, peevishly. He then dropped onto the deck and adopted the plank position, ready to execute his ritual set of push-ups while the computer intoned the status of the Invictus.

"Fleet Marauder Invictus is operating at eighty-one percent efficiency," the computer began. Sterling found the merry, balanced tone of the computer's voice to be helpful while performing his set. It was like a metronome ticking away in the background. "Regenerative armor is continuing to heal. The current projection is one hour, fourteen minutes from the point at which I finish this sentence until full regeneration is complete," the computer continued as Sterling rapidly reached the mid-way point of his set. "We are experiencing minor power fluctuations on decks three and four, sections seven through eleven. All other systems nominal. We remain on course for waypoint marker designation Sierra-Zero-Zero-Seven. Estimated time of arrival, twenty-three minutes, eighteen seconds from now."

Sterling completed his forty-eighth rep then remained in a plank position. "I don't suppose there's any news from the Fleet?" he asked, hopefully.

"Negative, Captain, we are far beyond the range of any aperture relays," the computer replied. "We are deeper inside Sa'Nerran space than any Fleet vessel has ever ventured before. It's quite exciting, don't you think?"

There was a sort of mystical dreaminess to the computer's voice as it said this. To Sterling, it sounded like the quirky AI had just announced something supernatural, as if they'd passed through the wardrobe into Narnia.

"I think I hate this part of space with a passion," Sterling replied, "but I'm happy you find it so fascinating," he added, sarcastically.

"Thank you, Captain, coming from you that means a lot," the gen-fourteen AI replied, apparently not getting the sarcasm.

Sterling huffed a laugh. "Was there anything else to report?" he added.

"Canine fecal matter was reported on deck two, section seventeen, but it has been dealt with," the computer intoned.

Sterling cursed the name of their adopted beagle hound under his breath, then cursed its owner for good measure. "Very well, computer, thank you," he replied. He then completed an additional ten push-ups, finding it easier than he'd expected. He missed the additional mass of Commander Banks on his back, forcing him to work harder. Springing back to his feet, he then felt a familiar link forming in his mind.

"I was just thinking of you," said Sterling before Banks had even spoken.

"Oh, really?" replied Banks. "Isn't there some Fleet regulation against that?"

Sterling shook his head. "I don't mean like that," he hit back, quickly changing his tank top and pulling on a fresh tunic. He threw his old one into the laundry processor then headed for the door. "I'm finding the press-ups too easy these days," Sterling went on, making a bee-line for the elevator to deck one. "I need the additional bulk of your solid frame to push me harder."

"Bulk?" Banks replied, clearly affronted by Sterling's choice of words.

"You know what I mean," Sterling replied, punching the button for deck one.

"And it's a good job too," Banks replied. "I've knocked teeth out for less than that..."

Sterling laughed then marched out of the elevator and onto the bridge. The short sleep had done him good, despite the rude awakening that was becoming a regular feature of his nighttime routine. Commander Banks was already at her post. She smiled as Sterling entered, the two of them exchanging the sort of knowing looks that suggested they were both in on a secret that no-one else knew. However, this exchange of glances went unnoticed by anyone else. Lieutenant Shade was curiously absent from her post and Ensign Keller's back was turned to Sterling as he entered.

"Lieutenant Shade is waiting in your ready room, with Lieutenant Razor," said Banks, answering Sterling's question before he'd had the chance to ask it.

Sterling nodded. "What's the status of the aperture?"

"The scanners are still clear, but we are picking up a mass near the threshold. It looks like it's the remains of a moored heavy cruiser, not unlike the one we encountered earlier. Except this one looks to have been pillaged for parts a long time ago. Whatever the reason, it's dead in space."

Sterling nodded. "Understood. Prepare to go to battle stations and surge as soon as we're in range," he replied, adjusting his route and heading for his compact ready room instead of his Captain's console. "I'll make this thing with Razor quick."

The door to Sterling's compact ready room swooshed open as he approached, revealing Lieutenant Razor in the chair opposite his desk. Shade was standing to the side of the door, ever vigilant. Sterling sucked in a deep lungful of the ship's recycled air then moved around to the desk, preparing to sit down and give Razor the bad news. However, his engineer surprised him by being the first to speak.

"Captain, I can save us both some time," Razor began. She sounded calm and appeared relaxed. "Commander Graves explained my condition. I accept that I may pose a risk to the ship and understand the conditions of my 'parole' as it were."

Sterling felt relieved that Razor had tackled the issue head on, and with such frankness. Then again, he expected nothing less from an Omega officer, and from the straight-talking Katreena Razor in particular.

"And you understand what I am required to do, should you begin to turn?" Sterling asked, since that was the one-part Razor hadn't been explicit about.

"Aye, Captain, I understand that you will activate the kill switch that Commander Graves installed while I was unconscious," Razor replied. The engineer glanced back at Lieutenant Shade. "Or the Lieutenant here will blow my head off. One or the other."

Sterling's eyebrows raised up a little at this last statement, though Shade's expression remained as still as a painting.

"Naturally, I'd rather not have that happen, Captain," Razor then continued, meeting her captain's eyes again. "But it is what it is." The engineer shrugged. "I guess all those commendations were for nothing, after all."

"They were always for nothing, Lieutenant," Sterling replied, flatly. "Commendations, medals, promotions and even your release from the service... all of it is meaningless if we lose this war. What you did was help us to get one step closer to victory. That's what matters."

Razor appeared to consider this for a moment then straightened her back. "Permission to speak freely, Captain?" she asked.

Sterling glanced up at Lieutenant Shade. "You can resume your post, Lieutenant," he said. Shade's already stiff posture stiffened further. "It's okay, Lieutenant, you no longer need to stand guard. We have an understanding."

Shade nodded. "Aye, Captain," she replied then promptly, albeit reticently, exited the ready room.

"Permission granted," Sterling then said to his engineer.

"This war already forced me to give almost everything to the Fleet, Captain," Razor began, sounding more relaxed now that the overbearing presence of the ship's weapons officer had gone. "I hated the Fleet for what it forced me to do. Losing my brother was hard enough, but then Fleet rewarded me for that act with this promotion and this post. The only reason I didn't tell Admiral Griffin where to stick her offer was the prospect of mustering out once this assignment was complete." Razor sighed and shook her head. "But now I know that there is no escape for me. No future. I don't like it, Captain, but I accept it."

Sterling listened, never taking his eyes off his engineer as she spoke. He had known that the young engineer wanted out of Fleet, because of what it had cost her. He hadn't considered that she resented her Omega Taskforce posting because of it. Maybe that was down to his own lack of empathy, Sterling realized, or perhaps he was just too cold-hearted to care. Either way, it changed nothing.

"Very well, Lieutenant, resume your station," Sterling said, standing to signify that their meeting was over.

"Aye, Captain," Razor replied. The engineer stood to attention, spun on her heels and marched toward the door.

"Lieutenant Razor," Sterling called out, causing his engineer to stop and glance back over her shoulder.

"I know I'm not the most personable commanding officer in the fleet," Sterling began, causing Razor to raise one of her white eyebrows a touch. "And I know this job is hard, thankless and cruel. It asks everything and gives nothing. But we're not here for commendations, Lieutenant. We're here to ensure that humanity survives, by whatever means necessary. If the cost is our lives, or the lives of the ones we care about or respect, then that is a cost we have to bear."

"I understand that better than most, Captain," Razor replied.

Sterling knew he was pushing her and as a result Razor's bitterness had become impossible to contain. However, he had to know that his engineer could still be trusted.

"But you should understand something too, sir," Razor added, unexpectedly. "This ship and this fight are now all I have left. You want to know if you can still trust me, and I get that. All I can tell you is that I'm all in." Sterling studied his engineer for a moment and for the first time since she'd joined his crew, he felt like he knew her. "Will that be all, sir?" she continued, looking eager to leave.

Sterling straightened his back and pressed his hands behind his back. "No, Lieutenant, not quite," he said, suddenly feeling anger swelling in his veins and causing a pit to form in his stomach. However, it wasn't anger directed at his engineer, but at the bind her situation had placed him under. "This ship and this crew are my responsibility," Sterling continued. "You should be under no illusion that I will sacrifice any one of you should the mission require it. But *only* if the mission requires it. Until that time comes, I will fight for you till my dying breath, and I expect you to do the same. This isn't over for you yet, Lieutenant Razor. I order you to fight this thing until we find a way to cut this cancer from your body. Is that clear?"

Razor turned and straightened to attention. "Yes, Captain, perfectly clear."

"You are dismissed, Lieutenant," Sterling said.

Razor turned and exited the ready room, leaving

Sterling alone with a fire in his belly that he had no way to quash. Only the heat of combat could give him the satisfaction he craved. A neural link then formed in his mind and the voice of Commander Banks entered his thoughts.

"We're approaching the aperture now, Captain," Banks said.

Sterling clenched his fists, realizing that in a few moments he was likely to get the tonic his soul required.

"Battle stations," Sterling replied.

STERLING STEPPED out onto the bridge and was bathed in the low-level red lighting that signified the ship was at battle stations. Ahead of them through the viewscreen were the remains of a timeworn Sa'Nerran Heavy Cruiser. Once it had been a gatekeeper, perhaps, Sterling thought as he studied the carcass of the once mighty vessel. Now it was a fossil in space, merely providing evidence of what had at one time been a Sa'Nerran fortification.

"The cocky bastards," said Banks, leaning forward on her console. "It looks like that old cruiser was carved up for parts pretty recently," she added, glancing across to Sterling. "They obviously think their space is no longer in danger."

Sterling stepped up to his console and slid his hands into the familiar grooves on the sides. "Why cannibalize an old cruiser like that, though?" he asked, tapping his finger on the console. "Could they really be that short of resources?"

Banks shrugged. "Building a war armada is expensive, especially when it includes a ten-kilometer-long monster like the Titan," she suggested. "And prior to the neural control weapon, when we had the upper hand, Fleet was destroying Sa'Nerran ships at a ratio of two or three to one. That had to have hurt them."

Sterling considered this while observing the remains of the cruiser. It was a tantalizing proposition. Perhaps the Sa'Nerra had been much closer to defeat than Fleet had realized. The neural control weapon may have saved their leathery skins literally in the nick of time, causing Fleet to hesitate and falter. Had they pressed the attack over a year ago and invaded Sa'Nerran space, perhaps the war would have already been won.

"It's all academic now," Sterling replied to Banks. "We missed our shot to finish them off and now they have us by the throat, unless we can do something about it."

"I have a data feed from the relay probe we sent through the aperture, Captain," said Lieutenant Razor.

The ship's engineer was at her post at the rear of the bridge, as if nothing had happened. Lieutenant Shade cast her watchful eyes in the direction of Razor, then returned to her work. However, it was clear to Sterling that his weapons officer was still wary of their engineer. In truth, he would have it no other way.

"There is another gatekeeper cruiser guarding the other side of the aperture, but it has also been stripped," Razor went on, undeterred by Shade's suspicious glances. "From the limited scans the probe made before it automatically shut down, it appears to be a six-planet system. The third and fourth planets are inside the goldilocks zone for Sa'Nerran life. There are signs of a settlement on the third planet, but the fourth appears uninhabited. However, there is a large space station in orbit around the planet."

Sterling scanned the readings as Razor detailed the findings in brief. "What about Colicos' shuttle? Can we say with certainty where it went?" he asked.

"It's impossible to be certain based on the data we have, Captain," Razor replied.

"Then give me your best guess, Lieutenant," Sterling replied, turning back to the viewscreen. "We'll just have to hope luck is on our side."

Razor turned back to her array of computers; fingers flashing across the consoles. A short while later she turned to face the command deck. "Head for the space station around the fourth planet, Captain," Razor said, announcing her findings. "It's our best shot."

Sterling was silent for a moment while considering his options. Simply passing through the aperture and emerging directly on the other side would allow them to make a more detailed scan and fix their destination with accuracy. However, any ships in the system would detect the surge and have ample time to intercept. Vectoring their surge so as to arrive as close to their target as possible would give them the element of surprise, but it also carried considerably more risk. However, risk was part of the game and they'd come too far to play it safe now.

"Ensign Keller, plot a surge vector that takes us as close to the orbital platform around the fourth planet as you can get us," Sterling said. He then pushed away from the console and pressed his hands behind his back.

"Exactly how close do you want me to get, sir?" Keller replied, peering over his shoulder at his captain.

"So long as you don't crash into it, Ensign, I don't care if we stop an inch away from its hull," Sterling replied, dryly. "Just get us close."

"Aye, Captain," Keller replied, setting to work.

A deathly calm then fell over the bridge, punctuated only by the soft bleeps and chirps of the different stations. Sterling glanced across to Shade and saw that she was poised over her console, like a tiger lying prone in the long grasses ready to pounce. To his left, Banks was focused ahead, arms folded across her chest. The definition of the muscles in her arms and shoulders showing through her tunic told Sterling she was also coiled and ready. To the rear, Lieutenant Razor appeared as calm as the space outside their viewscreen. She met Sterling's eyes briefly, then looked ahead. Sterling wondered how he would respond in her shoes, with a ticking time-bomb in her head. Would he have been so philosophical and accepting of his fate as Razor had been of hers?

Everyone dies, Sterling reminded himself, turning back to the viewscreen. *It's only a matter of when and how.* To Sterling, it was only the how that he really cared about.

"Ready to surge, Captain," announced Ensign Keller.

"Then take us in, Ensign," Sterling replied, without hesitation.

Keller acknowledged the order then eased the ship toward the threshold of the aperture. Sterling felt the pulse of the ship's engines and reactor build, along with the thrum of the surge field generator. Long surges were always risky and unpredictable, but the Invictus had made an art of bending probability to its will.

Seconds later the Invictus fell through the aperture in spacetime, temporarily removing Sterling from the confines of his own body and placing him into a thought-based limbo. Images of Ariel Gunn and Mercedes Banks invaded his mind, one rushing in front of another like the pictures of a flipbook. *Not now, not now!* Sterling told himself, fighting against the dark thoughts that plagued him like a dormant virus that couldn't be fully eradicated. Then the ship punctured the rift between dimensions and burst back into normal space. Alarms rang out, jolting Sterling into action more severely than the panicked awakenings from his nightmares. The Sa'Nerran orbital platform was dead ahead and danger was close.

"Reverse engines full!" Sterling called out as the nose of the Invictus raced toward the station.

"They've seen us," Shade called out, though that particular nugget of information was one Sterling could have guessed for himself. "They're launching Wasps. Weapons systems on the platform are charging and locking on."

"Turrets to automatic," Sterling replied. "Let them handle the Wasps while we focus on the station's weapons platforms." He then watched as the Sa'Nerran fighter craft shot out from the space station like darts.

Ensign Keller's quick reactions had pulled them clear of the station, affording Sterling his first good look at it.

He'd seen and attacked dozens of Sa'Nerran outposts in the Void before, but this installation looked somehow even more alien.

"Evasive maneuvers, Ensign," Sterling said as the ship was thudded by blasts from the encircling Wasps. "Pilot's discretion."

"Aye, sir," Keller called out, though he was already operating at a frenzied pace, pushing the nimble Marauder to its limits.

Sterling could feel forces tugging on his body as the inertial negation system struggled to keep pace with the talented helmsman. The Invictus' plasma rail guns then flashed and explosions rippled out across the station. Moments later they were hit and more alerts rang out.

"Minor hull breach, deck four," Banks called out. "Re-routing power to regenerative armor."

"Give us everything you can, Lieutenant," Sterling called back to his engineer, though like Ensign Keller, Razor was already flat out.

Two Wasps were caught by blasts from their plasma turrets and collided with the Sa'Nerran station. A second volley from the main rail guns then destroyed more of the installation's static gun emplacements. However, Sterling could see that the station's remaining weapons were again ready to fire.

"Keep the Invictus on the side of the station with the fewest guns, Ensign," Sterling ordered, adjusting the readout on his own console to a tactical view of the installation. One half of the station had only a couple of guns remaining, while the other side still packed enough firepower to obliterate them.

"Lieutenant Shade, launch torpedoes at these co-ordinates," Banks called out, adding to the cacophony of noise on the bridge. "We need to take out their hangar bays so they can't launch any more fighters."

Shade acknowledged the order then Sterling saw two torpedoes snake out from the rear launchers of the Invictus. Moments later they were hit by another blast of plasma from the station and Sterling was thrown hard to deck. Consoles blew out on the bridge and more alarms sounded.

"Report!" Sterling called out, pulling himself back to his station.

"Moderate damage, midships to port," Banks reported. "Armor depleted. Evacuation of sections ten through twelve on decks three and four underway."

The torpedoes that Shade launched then slammed into the station, sealing the hangar bays and also causing the installation's power levels to fluctuate wildly. Shade continued to fire, using every weapons system the Marauder-class ship had in its arsenal, while Keller tried desperately to keep them from being hit again.

"All the weapons platforms in this section of the station are disabled, Captain," Shade called out. "And the four remaining Wasps are running in the direction of the third planet."

Sterling checked his console then saw why the fighters had chosen that particular course. A squadron of six light cruisers had set out from the planet and were heading in their direction.

"Hull breaches secured, Captain," Lieutenant Razor called out. "I'll need to launch repair drones to patch up the damaged armor plating."

"How long until those cruisers get here?" Sterling asked, turning to Commander Banks.

"Three hours, maybe less," his first officer replied. "They're burning hard. Scanners show another three more warships launching from a station around the third planet, but they're only Skirmishers, and they're all phase ones."

"Phase one? Even the cruisers?" queried Sterling, frowning down at his own console to confirm the readings. "Those are decades old."

"It's like you said, Captain," replied Banks. "Maybe they've committed their newer ships to the invasion. All that's left out here are relics."

"That number of phase ones can still take us down," Sterling said, while scanning the orbital platform ahead of them. Their attacks had crippled its offensive capabilities and left twenty percent of the station damaged. Like the ships that were on their way to intercept them, the station was old and vulnerable. "We need to get onto the station, find Colicos, and get out again before those ships get within range." Sterling turned to Ensign Keller. "Latch onto the station at these co-ordinates," he began, sending the location to Keller's console from his own station. "Then scan for apertures, including any that might be unstable and hidden. We're may not have a choice over how we get out of here or where we end up."

Keller responded briskly then turned back to his

console and set to work. Commander Banks arrived at Sterling's side, muscles taut and eyes shining with purpose.

"Lieutenant Shade, assemble your commando team," Sterling said to his weapons officer. Shade was already staring back at him, her eyes betraying the same single-mindedness that he'd already observed in Banks. If he'd looked in a mirror at that moment, he'd have seen it in himself too. They were ready. "We assault the station at once."

ENSIGN KELLER SWOOPED the Invictus down toward the space station, like a kestrel diving at its prey. There was a thud through the deck plating as the ship set down then latched on with the ventral umbilical at the co-ordinates Sterling had specified.

"Cutting through now, Captain," Shade called out. "Sixty seconds." Shade and her commandoes were already geared up for the assault. As with the attack on the Sa'Nerran cruiser, the soldiers were equipped with Homewrecker heavy plasma rifles and plasma hand cannons. This time, Sterling had also assigned grenades. In general, blowing holes in starships and space stations you have boarded is never a good idea, but this time he needed every available weapon and option at his disposal.

"Once we've breached, make your way through the outer sections towards this central area," Sterling called out, highlighting the location on his wrist computer. "Scans of the station have shown it to have a honeycomb-like structure around the circumference, surrounding a larger, more open space in the center," Sterling continued, as his computer updated the images to match what he was saying. "Based on what we've seen on Sa'Nerran outposts in the Void, this should be a command center."

Sterling lowered his wrist and drew his plasma pistol. A Sa'Nerran half-moon blade was also attached to his armor. He'd could have a used a Fleet-issue close-quarters weapon, but he preferred the alien blade. It was brutally-effective and brutality was exactly what was required of him.

"We have no idea where Colicos is or even if he's still here," Banks added, dialing the power setting of her Homewrecker to maximum, "and we have less than two hours to get in, locate him and get out again before Sa'Nerran reinforcements arrive. I know it sounds impossible, but the impossible is our specialty."

There was a hiss of air as the pressure between the ship's docking section and the station equalized.

"We're through, Captain," Shade announced as the sound of the boarding tunnel extending into the alien station whirred through the cabin. The indicator then turned green and the hatch opened. "Go, move out!" Shade called, slapping the lead commando on the back. "Move, move, move!"

Shade and her squad had barely reached the inner corridors of the station before plasma fire erupted through the opening. Sterling and Banks followed, rushing through the boarding tunnel, weapons raised. A single commando then dropped down behind them and set up a gun emplacement to guard their entry point. Unlike the assault on the Sa'Nerran cruiser, there was only one way in and out of the station. They had to secure their route back to the ship or they'd be trapped inside.

"This doesn't look like any Sa'Nerran station I've seen before," Sterling commented, moving up behind the advancing squad. "These outer sections are more densely packed than normal. The Sa'Nerra prefer open spaces."

To either side of the corridor were doors, spaced only a few meters apart. As he advanced further into the station, Sterling saw that the same arrangement continued along intersecting corridors and appeared to run around the entire circumference of the station.

"Maybe they're storage areas?" Banks suggested, creeping forward, holding the powerful Homewrecker in one hand and a pistol in the other.

"I don't know what the hell they are, and I'm not sure I want to find out," Sterling replied.

The commando squad had advanced with ruthless efficiency and was approaching the open area in the center of the station. Stepping over the charred remains of Sa'Nerran warriors, Sterling got his first clear look at the central area. Unlike the boxy, honeycomb layout of the outer sections, the central area was a like a giant mesh scaffold, except built on the inside rather than the exterior of the structure. There was a long, sweeping staircase, spiraling down to the lower levels, plummeting hundreds of meters into the belly of the station.

"It could take days to search this place," said Sterling, coming to terms with the scale of their task for the first time. Despite his bravado about the Omega Taskforce specializing in the impossible, he wasn't foolish enough to believe that there was some supernatural hand guiding their journey. Perhaps naively, he had hoped that they would break into the station and find James Colicos merrily working at a console right where they'd entered. However, that hadn't happened and now he was faced with an entire space station and no idea where to look first. He didn't even know if the scientist was on the station at all.

Sterling felt a neural link from Lieutenant Shade form in his mind. He opened it to allow the rest of the assault squad to monitor.

"We're at the central area, Captain," Shade began, as more plasma blasts filtered down the corridor close to his position. "Emergency bulkheads have sealed off the decks below level three. We can't get lower, at least not from here."

"Any sign of Colicos?" Sterling asked, remaining hopeful.

"Negative," Shade replied, crushing Sterling's hopes with a single word. "There's extensive damage to this central section. We're meeting moderate resistance, but these warriors look tired and old. Their weapons and armor are outdated and are no match for ours."

"Understood, Lieutenant, secure your position and wait for instructions," Sterling replied. A link then formed from Commander Graves on the Invictus and Sterling opened it, allowing Banks to monitor.

"Captain, I have some new information from Lieutenant Razor," Graves began. Sterling was about to ask why his engineer hadn't formed the link herself, before remembering that her neural abilities had been temporarily suppressed.

"Go head, Commander, but make it good. We're searching for a needle in a haystack down here," Sterling replied.

"Breaching the hull of the station has allowed us to conduct more detailed scans of the interior structure," Graves continued. "Lieutenant Razor believes that the honeycomb structures surrounding your current position contain life signs."

"Life signs?" repeated Sterling. "Sa'Nerran or human, or something else?" It was the 'something else' option that concerned him the most.

"There is no-way to distinguish with any accuracy Captain," Graves continued, "but, given the distant location of the facility, coupled with the fact it was armed, perhaps it is a prison installation of some kind?"

Banks raised an eyebrow at this suggestion. "If they brought Colicos here to continue his experiments, that might make sense," she said.

"Thank you, Commander, keep us updated," Sterling said, tapping his interface to close the link. He then glanced over to one of the many doors lining the corridor. "I think it's about time we found out what this honeycomb contains," he said.

"I can try to bypass the lock," said Banks, reaching for her computer.

"No time," Sterling replied. "Just bypass it the unsubtle way."

Banks smiled as she stepped in front of one of the

doors. Aiming the powerful Homewrecker rifle she unloaded a barrage of plasma blasts, smashing open a section of the door and the wall beside it. Sterling wafted the smell of burning electronics and molten metal from his face then advanced, pistol raised. Banks also moved up to the new opening. It was dark inside and Sterling couldn't see anything other than smoke.

"Can you make the gap wider?" Sterling asked, still aiming into the darkness.

Banks slung the rifle then gripped the sides of the door with her armored gloves. Gritting her teeth, she pulled back, wrenching the door away from its housing. Sterling flicked on the searchlight built into the shoulder section of his armor and stepped nearer, shining the beam inside. The light fell first onto a narrow cot bed, then as Sterling swept it across the room, it shone onto the face of a man, huddled in the corner. The prisoner was emaciated, dressed in dirty grey overalls, and looked terrified. Sterling met Banks' eyes, each as shocked and surprised to see a human in the cell as the other. Sterling dimmed the light then lowered his pistol.

"It's okay, we're with Fleet," Sterling said, extending his hand to the man.

"Fleet?" the prisoner answered, climbing gingerly to his feet. "Fleet was destroyed. Earth too."

Sterling shook his head. "Not yet. The war is still going on."

The man took a few tentative steps toward Sterling, his hand raised to shield his eyes from the harsh light in the corridor outside.

"You're a rescue party?" the prisoner said. The man's

frail body remained guarded and his timid voice was filled with doubt. However, Sterling could also see the flicker of hope in the man's eyes.

"We're looking for someone," Sterling replied, dodging the question. "James Colicos. Do you know him? Is he here?"

The prisoner recoiled at the mention of Colicos' name and retreated further into the darkness.

"You're with him?" the man asked, suddenly terrified once again.

"No, but we need his help. The Sa'Nerra have a new weapon, one that controls our minds. We need Colicos to stop it."

The prisoner shook his head violently and began to laugh, though to Sterling he looked on the verge of tears. It was an unexpected, freakish sound. The sound of madness, Sterling realized.

"He's the one who hurts us," the man said, returning to the dark corner of the cell and sliding down onto the filth-stained floor. "He experiments on us. Hundreds of us. I've seen what he does!" There was now bitterness in the man's voice. The bile that had been festering in the prisoner's gut for who knew how long was oozing to the surface. "He says they make him do it, but he enjoys it," the prisoner continued, spitting out the words. "He's evil. He won't help you. He only helps them."

Anger swelled inside Sterling's gut at the way the prisoner had been treated. Seeing the man broken and tortured only further fueled the rage and desire he had to destroy the Sa'Nerra. However, he was unable to offer the prisoner sympathy or salvation. He needed to find Colicos and this man was his best hope.

"I'll make Colicos help me," Sterling said, using the prisoner's obvious hatred of the scientist to his advantage. "Tell me where I can find him, and I'll make sure he suffers. I'll hurt him, like he hurt you."

The man's eyes suddenly widened and he scrambled closer, remaining on all fours. "You can do that?" he asked, suddenly becoming alive. "You'll make him pay?"

Sterling nodded. "Just tell me where he is."

This time the man smiled, revealing toothless, rotten gums. He nodded, the movements so ferocious that Sterling thought the man would send himself unconscious through dizziness.

"His lab is on level three," the man said, stabbing his finger toward the deck. "That's where they take us, the aliens who do his bidding." His face twisted into a tortuous mix of revulsion and grief. "So many screams. So many corrupted. So, so, many dead..." the man was becoming lost in his own grief and Sterling realized they were losing him. Then the prisoner switched on again, becoming suddenly alert and excited. "You'll make him suffer, right? Torture him? Make him pay!"

Sterling nodded again. "I'll make him pay, of that you have my word," he promised. He then looked to Banks and they both stepped away from the cell.

"You'll take us all with you, right?" the man said, as Sterling and Banks moved away. "Once you have him? You'll rescue us all?"

Sterling sucked in a lungful of the foul Sa'Nerran air,

which was laced with Sulphur and the stench of the prisoner, soaked in sweat, feces and urine. It only made him more determined to find the cause of the prisoner's suffering and to bring Colicos to justice. However, he also knew that he could not help the man. The Invictus was not a rescue ship and Sterling was not his savior. It was a hard truth of the sort that required the cold, heartless logic of an Omega Captain to accept. He considered lying to the man, but he would not add insult to injury. He deserved to know the truth. That was the least – and the most – Sterling could do.

"I'm not here to rescue you," Sterling said, making sure to hold the man's eyes and not release them. "I'm sorry."

The man tried to crawl toward Sterling, pleading for him to change his mind, but his frail body collapsed underneath him.

"But you must!" the prisoner cried out. "I've been here so long. So long and so alone."

"I'm sorry," Sterling replied. He meant it, but he knew the apology was meaningless. Nevertheless, it was all he could offer.

Sterling and Banks stepped away from the prison cell and headed back toward the rest of the squad. To their backs, the man continued to cry out to them, his words becoming slurred and tainted by grief. Then the prisoner's sobs were drowned out by the hiss of Sa'Nerran warriors and the fizz of plasma weapons. And then they were absent completely.

STERLING HURRIED down the steps to level three, the thud of his heavy boots causing the open grating of the metal staircase to clang and rattle. More warriors appeared on the upper levels, filtering out of the honeycomb-like outer layers of the station like worker bees.

"Take cover!" Sterling called out as plasma blasts began to rain down around them, causing sparks and molten metal to fall from the levels above.

Sterling returned fire with his pistol, striking a warrior in the chest. Normally, the Sa'Nerran armor would have saved the alien's life, but this time the metal buckled, along with the warrior's sternum. The alien tumbled from the upper level, clattering onto the metal deck below. Moments later the thunderous pulse of multiple Homewrecker heavy plasma rifles drowned out the sound of his pistol. Chunks of alien flesh rained down on them as the powerful weapons blew the warriors to pieces. However, the Sa'Nerra had also claimed a commando in the exchange.

Reaching the bottom of the stairwell, Shade's commandos charged onto level three and obliterated a group of defending warriors like they were carboard cutouts on a shooting range. Sterling entered the level with Banks at his side. It was clearly a laboratory space. Like Colicos' lab on Far Deep Nine, it was well equipped and at least ten times larger than the science lab on the Invictus.

Sterling moved up to one of the consoles as Shade and the commando squad secured a defensive perimeter. He could see that the machines were clearly alien in construction, but it was also apparent they had not been designed for the long, spidery digits of Sa'Nerran hands. Whoever had used the lab was a human. Sterling felt hope swelling inside him again. They may have just found their needle, he realized.

"Take a couple of commandoes and check the surrounding rooms," Sterling called out, directing the order to Banks. "That asshole is here somewhere and we're not leaving without him."

Banks acknowledged the order then detailed two commandoes and began going from room to room. Plasma blasts continued to fly as Shade and the remaining commandoes picked off the Sa'Nerra like they were fish in a barrel. Remaining vigilant and watchful, Sterling continued to explore. Then he spotted a door close to the stairwell. Unlike the automated doors he was used to, this one had a long, wide-bodied handle, designed for alien digits. Wrapping his left hand around the metal, Sterling tested the handle and it turned. Flinging open the door he thrust his pistol into the room. A hand caught his wrist and pulled him inside. Stunned by the surprise attack, Sterling was then struck hard to the chest. Staggering back, he saw a Sa'Nerran blade embedded into his armor. He felt no pain, but couldn't be certain whether adrenalin had numbed his senses or if the blade had miraculously fallen short of slicing his flesh. Sterling raised his weapon, aiming it at the alien that had attacked him, but the Sa'Nerran quickly slapped the weapon from his hand.

"Captain!" Sterling heard Lieutenant Shade call out from the lab outside.

His weapons officer's shouts were soon lost as the alien slammed the door shut, then broke off the handle. Its yellow eyes studied Sterling with an intelligence and an intensity that was strange and unsettling. The warrior's attire was also different. In fact, it wasn't wearing armor at all. In all of Sterling's extensive experience fighting the alien race, he'd never see a warrior wear anything other than their distinctive protective shells. However, Sterling didn't care how unusual this alien was – its fate would be the same as all the rest. Pulling the Sa'Nerran blade from his armor, he aimed it at the warrior and prepared to fight. A sliver of red coated the very edge of the blade. The alien had drawn first blood – he would draw it last.

"You're too late..."

The voice shook Sterling like an earthquake. It seemed to have come from the Sa'Nerran warrior, though the alien's thin, slug-like lips had not moved.

"Yes, I speak your words, human," the alien said, again speaking without moving its mouth.

Sterling saw that the warrior had a device implanted in

the side of its head. It was similar to a Fleet neural interface, but the technology and materials used looked alien in nature. Then Sterling realized that he was not hearing the alien's words spoken out loud. He was hearing them inside his mind.

"You're the warrior that took Colicos from Far Deep Nine?" Sterling asked, also replying in his mind. He could scarcely believe it. Hubbard, the old man from Thrace Colony, who claimed the alien had spoken, had been telling the truth.

"Not warrior. Scientist," the Sa'Nerran hit back. "Your human made me a prisoner. Now the human is mine."

"Not for long," Sterling replied, angling the blade toward the alien's throat. "I'm taking him back, then I'm blowing this place to hell."

This time the Sa'Nerran's lips did move as the creature hissed at Sterling. At the same time the words in his mind turned to an angry white noise.

"You are too late, human," the Sa'Nerran continued, as it and Sterling circled around each other. "The weapon is perfected." There was a thump against the door and muffled cries, but Sterling ignored them. He was focused only on the alien. "Your species will soon die."

Sterling adjusted his hold on the Sa'Nerran blade. The droplet of his own blood pooled on the lower edge then dripped and splattered onto the metal deck.

"If you think that shooting holes in little moons is enough scare us, you're even more stupid than you are ugly," Sterling said.

The warrior hissed at Sterling and a garbled laugh

filled his mind, like something out of a haunted house of horror.

"You are stupid, human! You do not understand!" the voice said in Sterling's mind. "You think that is our weapon?" The alien hissed again, and more twisted laughter filled Sterling's mind. "It is a shame you will not live to see what our weapon really is."

Sterling swung at the alien with the blade, but cut only air. The Sa'Nerran scientist dodged back as the blade flashed in front of it then hissed at Sterling again. He hadn't intended to hit the alien; only keep it on its toes. The opportunity to interrogate this unique being was too important to miss.

"Oh, I'll see it," Sterling replied. He was conscious of time, along with the danger of fighting a Sa'Nerran one-on-one, but he wanted to learn more about the Titan. "I'll see that ship burn in space when our fleets destroy it, along with the rest of your armada."

Garbled laughter filled Sterling's mind, making him feel sick to his stomach. The alien then tore a metal leg from a table to its rear and raised it.

"Your fleet will become our fleet," the warrior said in Sterling's mind. "You cannot stop us. It is already too late."

The alien swung at Sterling, but he dodged then raked the serrated blade down across the side of the creature's face. Hot blood splashed onto the alien's unique attire and its hisses grew frantic. Then came the realization that Sterling could feel the warrior's pain and anxiety through their link. He believed he had glimpsed the possibility of fear in the yellow eyes of the Sa'Nerran before, but Sterling had never known for certain that the alien species was susceptible to the most crippling of human emotions. Now there was no doubt. The Sa'Nerran he was fighting feared death. More than that, the alien feared *him*.

The Sa'Nerran scientist swung again with its improvised club, but Sterling deflected the attack with his armored forearm and slashed the blade across the alien's chest. Again the creature hissed and Sterling felt pain and terror grip it like a bear trap springing shut. The alien attacked again, but Sterling anticipated the swing and ducked inside, opening a gash in the scientist's neck. This time the creature fell to its knees. The bar dropped from its hand as its long leathery fingers clamped around its throat, desperately trying to stem the blood flowing from the wound. Sterling pulled his arm back, ready to deliver a killing blow, but he withheld the urge. This unique alien was more valuable alive than dead, he realized.

"If you're lucky, you might survive long enough to see me torch your homeworld," Sterling spat, muscles still primed and ready to strike. "Until then you're coming with me. We're going to slice you open to find out how that brain of yours works. It's time for you to become the experiment, you alien piece of trash."

The warrior peered into Sterling's eyes and for the first time he saw something other than a monster staring up at him. The Sa'Nerra had always had a mystique surrounding them. They were savage, impenetrable and terrifying. Not any longer. Now Sterling did not see a monster, but a pitiable creature, beaten and on its knees. He was more repulsed by the race than ever before and his desire to wipe them out only grew stronger.

"I will not be human experiment," the creature said, the neural link between it and Sterling growing weaker. "My work is done. Your species...will... die..."

Suddenly, the alien reached out and snatched the half-moon blade that Sterling still carried on his armor. Sterling adjusted his stance, preparing to defend against the alien's strike, but instead of attacking, the warrior plunged the blade into its own throat. There was a shrill waspish hiss and the words in Sterling's mind became garbled and incoherent. However, even though the words were lost, Sterling could still feel the Sa'Nerran through their unique link, and he could feel it dying.

"Damn you," Sterling spat, as the warrior's yellow, egg-shaped eyes became glassier and more distant.

Sterling concentrated on the link, trying to push through the fog and haze to reach the alien's mind one last time. Anything he could glean from it could still be useful, he realized. However, all he could feel was the alien's terror rising to a peak, like an orchestral crescendo. Then then link was suddenly severed and the alien fell to the deck, dead. Sterling cursed and stared down at the body as blood pooled around his boots. He was angry at himself for allowing the alien to take its own life, but also lifted by the certainty that the warrior race was fallible. They felt. They feared. And that meant they could be beaten.

THE DOOR WAS SUDDENLY SMASHED open, snapping Sterling's focus away from the dead Sa'Nerran and back into the moment. He spun around, blade in hand, ready to fight off another alien. However, instead of a warrior he was confronted by Lieutenant Shade. Blood coated the officer's face and armor from head to toe, as if someone had thrown a pot of red paint over her.

"Captain, are you okay?" his weapons officer asked, hurrying inside and sweeping the room with her rifle. The question contained no emotion – it was merely a request for information, delivered plainly and without sentiment.

"I'm fine, Lieutenant," Sterling replied, with matching coolness. He then hooked the bloodied blade onto his armor and recovered his pistol from the deck. "Have you found Colicos yet?"

"Yes, Captain, but there's a problem," Shade answered, aiming the barrel of her rifle at the Sa'Nerran and kicking its boots to make doubly sure it was dead.

Sterling peered over Shade's shoulder and saw that Commander Banks was not with her. If anyone would have been able to break down the door it was her. His first-officer's absence explained the delay in reaching him.

"Where's Commander Banks?" Sterling asked, as Shade moved back outside.

"Colicos has her, sir," Shade replied, hustling out of view. "I'll take you to them."

Sterling cursed as he hurried after his weapons officer, moving back into the central area of the station's third level. Shade's commandoes were covering the stairwells and upper levels, but two more of the Invictus' soldiers lay dead on the ground. However, the counter-assault by the Sa'Nerra appeared to have stopped. The sound of plasma blasts was absent, giving the station a suddenly more alien aura. Sterling was not used to being in enemy terrain without the accompanying soundtrack of weapons fire.

Lieutenant Shade stopped outside a room and waited for Sterling to catch up. Two commandoes were already inside, weapons raised, as if they were part of a firing squad. A knot tightened in his gut as he advanced closer and stepped through the door. Then he realized why Commander Banks had not come to his aid. She was being held hostage by James Colicos. However, instead of there being a gun pressed to her head there was a neural control weapon instead.

"Stop right there!" Colicos blurted out. The disgraced scientist's voice trembled, as did the man's eyes. Colicos moved further behind Commander Banks, using her as a shield. "Don't come any closer!"

Sterling cast his eyes over to his first officer, but she appeared frozen, as if her body were paralyzed. Despite this, Sterling could see in her eyes that she was still conscious and fully aware of everything that was going on around her.

"Make any sudden moves and your officer is dead," Colicos added, staring at Sterling with terrified eyes.

"You're making a big mistake, Doctor Colicos," Sterling said. Sterling had tried to contain his anger, but the implied threat was not lost on the genius.

"Don't try to intimidate me, Captain, I'm in control here, so do as I say!" Colicos yelled. "In five minutes, this lovely young lady's brain will be mush. So let's not dally, shall we?"

Sterling observed the scientist's trembling hands and twitchy, frantic movements. Colicos would have been well-spoken, had it not been for his flustered squawks. It was clear to Sterling that the scientist was so on edge that even the slightest push would send him over. Realizing something other than force was required, he waved for the commandoes to lower their weapons, then turned to Lieutenant Shade.

"How did this happen?" Sterling asked, keeping his voice as calm and as level as he was able to manage. "Banks could tear this guy in half."

Colicos had the build of a fashion model – lithe and tall. Despite being over sixty years old, the scientist looked even younger in person than he had done in the images Sterling had seen.

"He was playing possum, Captain," Shade replied,

glowering at Colicos as she answered the question. "He was on the floor, pretending to be injured. Commander Banks moved over to check on him then he slapped that thing on her before anyone knew what had happened."

Sterling nodded then turned back to Colicos, keeping the pistol in his hand held at his side.

"I'm afraid you've picked the wrong captain to play these sorts of games with, doctor," Sterling began, taking a respectful tone despite wanting to tear the scientist's head off. "You have no idea who you're dealing with."

"I know who you are, Captain," Colicos replied, insulted that Sterling would suggest possessing any knowledge that the scientist lacked. "I see the silver stripe. You're Griffin's little troupe, aren't you?" Then the scientist became visibly angry. "That witch even stole my ideas!" he bellowed. "The Omega Taskforce was my suggestion. You only exist because of me!"

"If you know who we are then you know that holding my officer hostage won't get you what you want," Sterling replied. "One way or another, you're coming with me, Doctor Colicos. The only difference is how much of you ends up on my ship, after my officers and I have finished with you."

Sterling then slowly raised the pistol, but instead of aiming it at the fraction of Colicos' head that he could see, he aimed it at Commander Banks instead. Sterling locked eyes with his first officer, and though she was paralyzed, he knew she understood that he was serious. Suddenly, images of Ariel Gunn flashed into his mind and Sterling felt sick. His aim wavered for a moment, but he bit down hard on the inside of his lip, drawing blood. Focusing on the pain, he pushed the image of Gunn deeper, feeling the queasiness in his belly ease further from his conscious thoughts as the memory slipped away.

"Don't try to threaten me," Colicos hit back. The scientist appeared not to have noticed Sterling's momentary lapse. "You came all this way to find me, which means you won't kill me now." He then snorted and harumphed like a restaurant critic who had just been served an overdone steak. "You can't outsmart me, Captain, so don't even try."

"You're right, I won't kill you," Sterling replied, still aiming his weapon at Banks. "But if you force me to kill my first officer, you'll discover first-hand just how cold and callous an Omega Captain can be." Sterling then nodded toward Lieutenant Shade, who had been silently glowering at the scientist the whole time he had been speaking. "To begin with, I'll have the Lieutenant here peel off your fingernails, one by one. Then we'll start on your toenails. Then your teeth."

Colicos laughed. "Yes, yes, I get the picture, my dear Captain," he replied, scornfully. Then his expression hardened like granite. "You're bluffing. And now you have only two minutes until she's dead."

Colicos' animated style of talking had caused part of his body to appear from behind the shield of Commander Banks. His left hand was now peeking out from behind his first officer's thigh. Sterling seized the opportunity, swiftly adjusted his aim and fired. The blast tore past Banks' leg, burning her flesh but also blasting Colicos' hand clean off.

The scientist screamed then staggered away from Banks, clutching his freshly mutilated limb to his body. Seeing an opportunity to subdue him further, Shade took a step toward Colicos, but Sterling held out his hand to stop her.

"That's five fewer fingernails to pull out, doc," Sterling said, as the scientist sobbed in agony. "I'll just break five whole toes off you instead. Then if you still aren't compliant, we'll start on your feet, then your legs below the knees." Sterling then approached Colicos and leant in closer, bringing his hate-filled eyes level with the scientist. "Understand this, Doctor," he spat. "I don't need you whole. I only need your mind. The rest of you is surplus meat."

"Alright, alright!" Colicos yelled, dropping to his knees. He reached his one remaining, trembling hand into the pocket of his overall and removed a control device. Moments later, the neural control weapon on Banks' head deactivated. Banks fell to one knee and wearily tore the device away from her head.

"There, it's done!" Colicos yelled, tears flowing down his face.

Sterling holstered his pistol then looked over to his first officer. He knew better than to rush to her aid and so did Shade. Banks' pride would not stand for it.

"Are you okay, Commander Banks?" Sterling asked, calmly and professionally. Inside, however, his blood was boiling. Colicos had forced him to come within seconds of shooting her.

"I will be soon," replied Banks, through gritted teeth.

The first officer of the Invictus then rose to her full

height and stormed over to Colicos, who cowered from her like a frightened mouse. Grabbing a clump of the scientist's overalls, she hauled him up then hammered the back of the man's head against the wall. The scientist fell like a butchered carcass, knocked out cold.

"Now, I'm better," Banks said. She then glanced down at the burned patch on her pants and sighed. "Apart from needing a change of clothes."

Ordinarily, Sterling would have found her darkly humorous response amusing. However, on this occasion the close call had left him numb. He was still too angry to laugh.

"Take him," Sterling said, directing the order to the two commands in the room.

A neural link formed in Sterling's mind and Commander Graves appeared in his thoughts.

"Captain, the Sa'Nerran Light Cruisers will be within weapons range of the station in ten minutes," Graves began with his usual, smooth delivery. "I would recommend returning to the ship as soon as possible."

"Understood, we're on our way back now," Sterling replied. Then Sterling had a thought. "How are you with prostheses, Commander Graves?"

"I have some direct experience, but I've always been curious to do more, Captain," Graves replied, showing more interest in the question than usual. "Is one of the crew in need of a replacement limb?"

Sterling glared at Colicos, who was now being strapped to a battlefield stretcher by the two commandoes.

"Not one of the crew," Sterling answered. "Let's just call him an unwanted but important guest."

"Very well, Captain, I will make preparations once you return," Graves said. "It will be function over form, however. Our medical facility lacks the equipment necessary to fabricate a visually appealing prosthetic."

"So long as this asshole can still use a computer console, I don't give a damn what it looks like," Sterling replied. He then tapped his neural interface to close the link.

"I hope he's worth it," said Commander Banks, stepping to Sterling's side.

Sterling sighed then watched the commandoes carry Colicos out. "So do I," he replied. "But, if he's not, I'll kill the bastard myself."

STERLING STEPPED onto the bridge of the Invictus, closely followed by Commander Banks and Lieutenant Shade. All three officers still wore their scarred and blood-stained combat armor. Adrenalin was surging through his body, dulling the aches and pains of combat. However, Sterling knew that his injuries would make themselves known soon, providing they survived long enough to escape from Sa'Nerran space.

"Captain on the bridge," Commander Graves announced. He acknowledged his captain and stepped down from the command platform.

"Your patient is under guard in the med bay," Sterling said, sliding his hands into their usual place on his console. "Don't worry about too much pain relief. I want the asshole to suffer."

"Understood, Captain," replied Commander Graves.

There was a twinkle in the medical officer's eyes that suggested the opportunity to inflict and witness pain appealed to him. Sterling momentarily wondered whether he should back down on his request. Then he remembered how Colicos had almost forced him to shoot Mercedes Banks and changed his mind. Instead, he just watched Graves exit the bridge in an unhurried, processional manner that was more akin to an undertaker than a Fleet officer or doctor.

Sterling turned back to his console to update himself on the status of the ship. His engineer, who was absent from the bridge, had done her usual excellent job of patching up the Invictus. However, they were still far from one hundred percent.

"Captain, I've located several apertures in the system," Ensign Keller said, appearing eager to report his findings. The helmsman had already detached the Invictus from the Sa'Nerran space station, ready for their return journey to Fleet space. "The stable apertures are all several hours away at maximum speed. However, with the head start the enemy cruisers have on us, we won't be able to outrun them before we surge."

"Understood, Ensign," Sterling replied. He noted that his ensign was unusually calm, which he hoped suggested that these distant apertures were not the only options Keller had uncovered. "What about disused apertures, like the unstable one we travelled through to reach Sa'Nerran space?" Sterling added.

"I've located three, sir," Keller replied, obligingly. The ensign's fingers flashed across his console and the data appeared on Sterling's screen. "One is close to this planet and from the readings I've gathered it's deep," Keller continued. "I believe I could vector a surge close to the Fleet side of the void, just beyond Thrace Colony. That would then mean only one hop back into calmer waters, sir."

"And I suppose such a long surge isn't without complications, Ensign?" Sterling asked.

Keller was about to answer when the door swooshed open and Lieutenant Razor entered the bridge. Her uniform was covered in dirt and dust and an assortment of tools were attached to her belt. She enabled her engineering stations at the rear of the bridge then stood tall, hands pressed to the small of her back.

"I think Lieutenant Razor is better placed to answer that, sir," Keller replied. It was an impressive way to dodge what was clearly an awkward question to answer.

Sterling turned to his engineer, who looked like she'd been exploring the crawlspaces in the ship again, then awaited her analysis.

"To put it bluntly, sir, a surge like this will kick our collective asses," Razor said, maintaining her stiff posture. "We learned a lot from the last surge, which means I can mitigate some of the effects. But there's a reason these apertures aren't used. It's like trying to round the horn in extreme conditions, sir."

"No-one has kicked our assess yet, Lieutenant. We can handle it," Sterling replied. "The bigger question is, can the Invictus?"

"This is the toughest little ship I've ever seen, sir," Razor replied. "It'll take more than a surge to put it down."

For someone who took obvious pride in her work, the

engineer was not one to wear her heart on her sleeve. However, Sterling was buoyed to hear that his engineer had the same faith in the Invictus that he did.

"Make the arrangements, Lieutenant," Sterling said. He then turned back to his helmsman. "Set a course for that aperture, Ensign, and prepare to surge."

Keller acknowledged the order and set to work. The bridge quickly became a hive of activity and Sterling observed his crew with satisfaction. His Omega officers had performed exceptionally, but there was still more to be done. Unfortunately, one of the tasks Sterling still had left to perform was amongst the darkest he'd ever embarked on. However, he also accepted that it was necessary.

"Lieutenant Shade, lock torpedoes onto the station's reactor core and prepare to fire," Sterling said, glancing across to his weapons officer.

"Aye, sir," Shade replied, with a funereal tone, like an ER doctor calling the time of death for a patient.

No-one on the bridge questioned the order or said a word. Sterling knew that at some level, each of his officers would feel the weight of what he was about to do. Each would feel the shame of it, whether they showed it or not. Yet each would also accept that Sterling's actions, though abhorrent, were necessary. If he couldn't rescue the prisoners on the Sa'Nerran science lab, he'd be damned if he'd allow the sadistic aliens to use them as lab rats.

"Torpedoes locked on, sir," Shade said.

Sterling stood tall and folded his arms behind his back, staring out at the station as it began to slip into the distance.

"The Omega Directive is in effect," Sterling

announced, calmly. He then turned to Lieutenant Shade. "Fire."

Lieutenant Shade executed the order and two torpedoes snaked out of the Invictus' aft launchers. With the station's defensive systems disabled, it was powerless to intercept the weapons. Moments later the torpedoes impacted on their target, causing a catastrophic reactor breach that consumed the station in a sunlike inferno. Sterling did not know how many human prisoners he'd just scarified. Thousands. Maybe even tens of thousands. Whatever the number, they could no longer be a part of the Sa'Nerra's mind-controlled army. Nor could they be used as test subjects for the aliens' depraved scientific experiments. Perhaps this made the act no less abhorrent, Sterling realized. Nevertheless, he could live with it.

"Approaching the aperture, Captain," said Ensign Keller. The burden of the act was already pressing down on the young officer's shoulders.

"Surge field recalibrated, Captain," Razor chimed in from the rear of the bridge. "I've shut down all non-essential systems and sections in order to give the armor as much power as possible. Even so, it's going to be a rough ride."

"Understood, Lieutenant," replied Sterling, resting forward on his console and sliding his fingers into the familiar grooves. He was about to give the order to surge, when his console began sounding a strident alert.

"Surge warning!" Lieutenant Razor called out; her voice suddenly frantic. "There's something coming through the aperture."

"Evasive maneuvers, Ensign!" Sterling called out. He then felt the kick of the thrusters push the Invictus away from the interstellar gateway.

"Ship emerging," Razor added. "It's going to be close!"

There was a flash of brilliant white light from the aperture, then collision alarms rang out across the bridge.

"One Sa'Nerran Heavy Destroyer has just entered the system," Commander Banks called out. "Registry, M4-U1." Banks slammed the palm of her hand down on her console and cursed. "Damn it, it's MAUL."

Sterling fixed the viewscreen onto the battle-scarred alien vessel. To his eyes, the warship looked even more disfigured than the last time he'd seen it, and no less hungry for battle.

"Target that ship, all weapons!" Sterling called out to Shade. He then turned to Keller. "Get us back on course to the aperture, Ensign, and do it fast."

The cries of, "Aye sir," were drowned out by the thump of weapons fire hammering into their hull. Every bone in Sterling's body rattled from the impacts, but incredibly the Invictus was still in one piece. He peered down at his console, studying their scans of MAUL and realized why.

"Surging through that aperture has damaged MAUL too," Sterling called out. "Keep us away from its main guns and focus on its engines. Hold it together, people, we can get through this!"

Flashes of plasma erupted from the Invictus' turrets and blasts of energy raked across the pockmarked back of the infamous warship. MAUL returned fire and again the bridge was rocked.

"Point defense cannons just went offline," Lieutenant Shade announced.

Sterling cursed. That left the Invictus vulnerable to conventional weapons.

"Armor failing," Banks then called out. "Multiple hull breaches detected. Emergency bulkheads are in place and holding," His first officer's fingers flashed across her console before she spun around to address Lieutenant Shade. "Focus your fire on this section," Banks said.

Sterling glanced at his console and noted the location that Banks had targeted. It was a secondary system and of limited importance. Sterling met his first officer's eyes, full of questions, as more thuds hammered their ship.

"Trust me, Lucas," Banks said, fixing his gaze.

Sterling's questions remained, but his doubt vanished like a starship surging through the Void.

"Do it," Sterling called out, turning to Shade.

Shade reacted instantly, unleashing their forward plasma rail cannons onto the Sa'Nerra's most lethal warship. The blasts of plasma slammed into the ship, hitting one of its most densely armored-sections. The mighty vessel initially seemed to shrug off the attack, but then its engines faltered and stuttered, kicking the ship off-course.

"It won't last long," Banks said, as Sterling watched MAUL spiral into the distance. "We need to surge, now."

"You heard the Commander, Ensign Keller," Sterling called out, gripping the sides of his console so tightly his fingers burned.

"Aye, Captain," Keller replied, turning the nimble

Marauder back toward the aperture and kicking their engines into gear.

Another alarm rang out from Sterling's console, but his weapons officer had clarified the cause before he'd had a chance to check it.

"Torpedo launch detected," Lieutenant Shade called out. "Six weapons online and tracking, launched from the pursuing cruisers."

"Pedal to the metal, Ensign..." Sterling added, trying to urge the helmsman and their beleaguered little ship on even harder.

"Surge field generator online and charged," Sterling heard his engineer call out from behind him. "Parameters set. We're ready."

Sterling's eyes were now locked ahead. The ping of the torpedoes drawing closer chimed out from his console, the interval between each note decreasing rapidly. With their point defenses offline, there was nothing he could do about them now. It was a race and one they had to win.

"Ten seconds to aperture perimeter!" Keller called out; his voice barely audible over the roar of their engines.

Sterling tapped his neural interface and reached out to the entire crew. "All hands, brace, brace, brace!" he announced.

Then the pings from the approaching torpedoes vanished, along with the space outside, the bridge, the ship, Sterling's own body, and his entire crew. They were rounding the horn and there was no turning back.

THE LONG SURGE through the unstable aperture felt like falling into an abyss with no end. It was a curious paradox that Sterling had slipped between dimensions and essentially no longer existed, yet remained fully cognizant of this fact. Usually, a surge was so quick that there wasn't time for a person's mind to contemplate its disembodied state. However, this surge was different. This was truly a step into the unknown.

Suddenly, there was a bright flash of light, but instead of finding himself on the bridge of the Invictus, Sterling was back on the alien space station. A plasma pistol was in his hand and he was aiming it at the head of Commander Mercedes Banks.

"Don't try to threaten me!" Colicos snarled.

Sterling frowned. He knew that he'd been here before and played out these events already, but for some reason he was compelled to repeat them. It was like he was being controlled.

Have I been turned? Sterling wondered, as Banks stared back at him, her body still paralyzed by the neural weapon Colicos had attached to her implant.

"You came all this way to find me, which means you won't kill me now," Colicos snorted, unaware that Sterling was trapped inside his own body – a silent observer of actions he'd already taken. "You can't outsmart me, Captain, so don't even try."

"You're right, I won't kill you," Sterling replied. The words came out of his mouth automatically and he was unable to prevent them. "But I will kill her."

No, that's not what I said! Sterling thought as his finger added pressure to the trigger. *I didn't shoot her, I shot you! I blasted your hand off!*

Sterling fought against himself, but he was a prisoner in his own mind, unable to intervene.

"Captain, don't shoot me!" Banks cried, as Sterling continued to squeeze the trigger. "Captain!" she yelled again, but then her cries were silenced by the fizz of the plasma pistol. Moments later, Banks' headless body slumped to the deck and the smell of her burning flesh flooded his nostrils.

"No!" Sterling yelled, still unable to compel his body to bend to his will.

"Captain!"

Sterling opened his eyes and found himself face down on the deck of the Invictus' bridge. The voice of Mercedes Banks was ringing in his ears.

"Lucas, are you okay?" said Commander Banks, helping to peel Sterling off the dimpled metal deck plates.

Sterling rocked back onto his knees then pressed his hands to his head, which seemed to be throbbing in synchronization with the pulse of the ship's reactor.

"What the hell just happened?" Sterling asked, meeting Banks' eyes. The memory of her headless body and the smell of her singed flesh was still raw in his mind, but he fought the sensations away. However, the sick feeling in his gut remained. "Did we complete the surge?"

Banks lifted Sterling to his feet and helped him back onto the command platform, which was several meters away. At some point, he must have been thrown clear of it, though he had no memory of that, or anything else beyond the point at which they'd surged.

"We made it through, but we're in rough shape," Banks said, operating Sterling's console and bringing up the damage control screen. "Weapons are down and a dozen or more power conduits blew out after we emerged, but Razor is in engineering trying to sort it out."

Sterling studied the data as best he could, considering that his mind was still cloudy and banging harder than a blacksmith's hammer. Their engines were online and he could see that they were on-course for an aperture that would lead them to Thrace Colony. He glanced over and saw that Ensign Keller was at his post. However, the young officer was clinging on to the console for dear life, as if it were driftwood that he was using to stay afloat in rough seas.

"How long till we reach the aperture?" Sterling asked.

"A couple of hours at our current speed," Banks replied. "Less if Razor can get the engines tuned up."

Sterling nodded and switched the data feed on his console to show a readout of the unstable aperture. There was currently no indication that the Sa'Nerran ships were following them through, but Sterling knew they would. He'd taken their most prized, secret asset and the enemy would want Colicos back. Either that, or they'd simply destroy the Invictus to prevent the scientist from being returned to Fleet custody.

"MAUL and the other ships would have got a good scan of our surge field," Sterling said, beginning to feel stronger and less queasy. "It will take them some time to re-calibrate their surge generators, but we should assume they'll come."

Banks nodded. "How long do you think we have?"

"Twenty, maybe thirty minutes," Sterling replied, though he was merely guessing. The Sa'Nerra had engineered the apertures and so knew how they operated, but surging through them would still require a modification to their systems. "We know that surging through the unstable aperture kicked MAUL's ass, so we can safely assume those older cruisers will take a beating too." Sterling continued, dabbing blood from a cut on the top of his head. "We just have to hope it slows them down enough for us to reach the aperture and surge back into the Fleet side of the Void."

Sterling's console chimed, but Lieutenant Shade was quick to provide the update.

"Partial weapons restored, Captain," said Shade. "The main rail guns are still offline."

Sterling turned toward his weapons officer, who was

the only person on the bridge who didn't look like they'd been dragged through a carwash backwards.

"What about torpedoes?" Sterling asked.

"I can arm them, but the guidance systems are fried, sir," Shade replied.

Sterling then had an idea. "Arm them and eject them in our wake, Lieutenant," Sterling said. "Maybe we'll get lucky and any ships that come after us will run into them like mines."

Shade acknowledged the command and soon after Sterling felt a dull thud through the deck as one of the torpedoes was expelled into space.

"Smart call," said Banks. "The sensors on those old phase ones aren't so sharp. It's possible they'll run into one or two of them on the way."

Sterling then had another idea, though he suspected his first officer would like it less. "I'm going to launch a beacon through the Thrace Colony aperture, calling for help," Sterling said, configuring the probe on his console.

"Who the hell would come to the aid of a Fleet warship in the Void?" said Banks. Then Sterling could practically hear the penny drop. Banks glowered at him and thrust her hands onto her hips. "Fletcher? You really think a mutineer will risk his neck for us?"

Sterling shrugged. "He was Fleet once. And I think he still has something to prove, to himself more than to anyone else."

Banks sighed and shrugged. "I can't believe I'm saying this, but I hope you're right," she admitted.

The probe raced out ahead and quickly vanished into

the darkness. Sterling tracked the signal on his console. It was strong and clear.

"I think it's time we spoke to our guest," Sterling said, returning his attention to his first officer. "I want to make sure that asshole is worthy of all this trouble."

"And if he's not?" Banks asked, raising a curious eyebrow.

"Then we shove him in an escape pod and jettison him," Sterling replied, flatly. "Maybe that will be enough to stop the Sa'Nerra coming after us."

"And if he is worth it and we need to keep him?" Banks wondered.

Sterling huffed a laugh. "Then we'd better pray to whatever god or gods exist out here in alien space that we can outrun MAUL and those cruisers."

This didn't appear to be the answer Banks was hoping for, but it was the only one Sterling could give. He was used to being on the back foot, outnumbered and outgunned, but this time the odds weighed heavily against them.

Sterling glanced back to Lieutenant Shade. "You have the bridge, Lieutenant," he said, stepping down from the command platform. "If anything comes through that aperture, let me know at once."

"Aye, Captain," replied Shade, hustling over to the Captain's console as Sterling and Banks departed.

Neither of them spoke as the two Omega officers hurried along the short corridor outside the bridge and into the waiting elevator. The sudden absence of other thoughts caused Sterling's mind to wander back to his nightmare before Banks had roused him on the bridge. More than anything, these episodes were starting to piss him off.

"Thanks for not shooting me, by the way," Banks said, as the elevator descended.

"What?" Sterling replied, jerking back from Banks. He knew she wasn't in his thoughts at that moment, though she certainly seemed to be reading his mind.

Banks frowned. "Apologies, Captain. Just a bit of dark humor," she replied. Sterling's snappy response appeared to have confused her.

"No, don't apologize, Mercedes," Sterling said. He was used to Banks' dark and often ill-timed quips. However, he wasn't used to reacting in a knee-jerk fashion, as he had just done, and felt embarrassed because of it.

"Are you okay, Lucas?" Banks asked. "Maybe we should have Graves take a look at your head. You fell pretty hard."

"Later," Sterling replied, quick to dismiss the idea.

The elevator stopped and the doors slid open. Banks stepped out first then froze, as if she'd seen a ghost.

"Shit!" Banks cursed, darting off ahead into the corridor.

Sterling followed, though he was less sure-footed than his first officer was, and found Banks a few meters ahead. She was crouched down and Sterling could see that her body was shaking.

"What it is?" said Sterling, moving alongside Banks.

Then he saw the reason for his first officer's cry. Jinx the Beagle hound was lying on her side panting heavily. Sterling could see a trail of blood smeared along the deck, ending underneath the animal's patchwork coat. The dog's front-left leg appeared to be badly broken and the cause of its blood loss.

Banks picked up the injured hound and turned to Sterling. He was about to tell her to leave the animal where it was and explain that they had more important considerations than tending to a wounded pet. However, the expression on his first officer's face completely disarmed him. It wasn't a mawkish look, nor did Banks look to be on the verge of tears. Tears were not Mercedes Banks style. He doubted that Omega officers even had tear ducts. However, what was clear was that this particular Omega officer did not want the dog to die. He could see it in her eyes; if she could have given her own body and lifeblood to save the animal, she would have done so right there and then.

"Bring her with us," Sterling said, resuming his journey toward the med lab. "We'll see what Graves can do."

Banks carried Jinx along the corridor and, dripping a trail of blood in her wake, followed Sterling into the med bay. Six of the beds were occupied by injured members of the Invictus' crew, who were being attended to by the ship's medics. Sterling saw Commander Graves inside the compact surgical bay. He pushed through the door to find James Colicos on the operating table. Graves was working on the scientist's injured hand – the one Sterling had blasted off back on the space station. Resting on a tray beside the table was a bionic prosthetic. It was still in a raw format, lacking any artificial flesh or skin covering.

"Is he conscious?" Sterling asked, pointing to Colicos

on the table. He couldn't see the scientist clearly owing to a curtain shielding his face.

"Yes, I'm conscious," Colicos snapped back, before Graves could reply. "I just don't like seeing blood, that's all. I wanted him to put me under, but he said he didn't have a spare bed for me to recover in." The scientist's hostility and complaining was doing nothing to endear the man to Sterling.

"Is he secured?' Sterling directed the question at Graves.

"Yes, he's strapped me down like a lunatic, if that's what you mean," Colicos again interrupted. "It's degrading, I..."

"Shut your traitorous mouth!" Sterling barked, causing the scientist to stop mid-sentence and fall silent. "I don't want to hear another damn word from you until I ask you a question."

Sterling could not see the scientist's reaction, but Colicos remained silent.

"Commander Graves, give me a moment with the prisoner," Sterling said to his medical officer. The doctor turned to leave, then saw the injured beagle that Commander Banks was holding in her hands. "See if you can fix the dog while you're waiting," Sterling added. Then he again noticed the prosthetic hand on the tray next to the operating table. "Maybe you should test out your skill with prosthetics before you attach that asshole's hand. If he can't operate a computer console, we may as well airlock him now."

"Of course, Captain," said Graves, appearing oddly

amused by the order to attend to the dog before his human patient. Sterling nodded to Banks and she and Commander Graves left the surgical bay.

Sterling waited for them to close the door then stepped closer to Colicos. He could see the man's feet flinch with each thud of his bootsteps. He tore the curtain away and peered down at the scientist's startled and petrified face. Colicos looked away, too fearful to meet Sterling's eyes, but only succeeded in seeing the stump where his left hand would have been. Yelping like a dog who'd had its tail trodden on, Colicos twisted his head to the opposite side and pressed his eyes shut.

"Here's the deal, doc," Sterling began, grabbing Colicos by the jaw and turning his head to face him. The scientist forced his eyes open and reluctantly met Sterling's gaze. "The neural weapon that you so kindly developed for the enemy is causing us to lose the war," Sterling continued, still gripping Colicos' chin. "Since the weapon first appeared, the Sa'Nerra have captured almost a hundred Fleet ships and turned them against us. Colonies in the Void have been made to produce munitions and resources for the enemy, the people then taken and forced into labor. Now the Sa'Nerra are pushing toward earth with a super-weapon the purpose of which we have no idea." Sterling paused and drew his head closer to the scientist. The sweat from his brow dripped into Colicos' eyes, forcing him to blink away the hot, salty liquid. "You're going to tell me everything you know," Sterling went on, his words dripping as heavily as his sweat, "and you're going to find a way to reverse this neural weapon."

He drew back and released Colicos' jaw, then continued, "Or I'm going to have Graves perform some little experiments of his own on your body."

"You think I wanted this?!" Colicos screeched, struggling in vain against the restraints that held him to the surgical table. "What choice did I have? Griffin threw me to the wolves. She cast me out into the Void, and for what?!" The scientist was suddenly raging, though beneath the anger there was still a suffocating blanket of terror. "I was working for Fleet, helping the war effort. If you're looking for someone to blame, Captain, blame your precious Admiral!"

Sterling sighed and shook his head. He had wondered what the character of this supposed genius would be like. He'd hoped that the Sa'Nerra had perhaps coerced him and broken him down over weeks or months. Perhaps they'd even turned him using his own weapon. However, it seemed that Colicos was just as spineless and weak as he had imagined him to be.

"You had a choice, Doctor Colicos," Sterling said, toying with the prosthetic hand that Graves had prepared. "You could have fought the Sa'Nerra who took you. Perhaps tried to escape. Maybe even taken your own life." Sterling dropped the hand back into the tray. It landed with a loud clang, making Colicos jump, as far as his restraints would permit. "But instead, you helped our enemy develop a weapon that is already responsible for the loss of hundreds of thousands of lives. Human lives."

"That blood is on Griffin's hands, not mine!" Colicos hit back, clearly incensed by the accusation of cowardice.

"Why should I take my own life? Why should I care about a people that abandoned me, like an unwanted pet!"

Sterling's attention was caught by a tray of surgical instruments to the side of the operating table. It was typical of Graves to favor the tools of a bygone surgical era, when practitioners sliced into flesh using sharpened steel, instead of lasers. It also fit Sterling's own notion of his medical officer as a "Jack the Ripper" style persona. Sterling pulled the tray closer and removed an old-fashioned metal scalpel.

"Wait, what are you doing with that?" Colicos said, urgently, pulling his head as far away from the scalpel as possible. "Help!" the man yelled. "Someone, help me!"

Sterling brought the tip of the scalpel toward Colicos, twisting it in his fingers and admiring the way the spotless metal reflected the light.

"No-one on this ship will come to your aid, doc," Sterling said. "The only reason you're here is so you can undo the damage you've done."

"It's impossible," Colicos answered. "I've already tried to reverse the effects of the neural control device. I worked in secret, at night when the Sa'Nerra weren't watching. But it cannot be done!"

Sterling was already tired of the man's excuses and protestations of innocence. Leaning in closer, he laid the flat of the scalpel blade on top of Colicos' Adam's apple. The scientist froze as if Sterling had just placed a scorpion on his neck.

"I'm telling you the truth!" Colicos pleaded. "In nearly sixty per cent of cases, my subjects died instantly. More than thirty percent who survived were driven mad. The rest were like empty shells, as if I'd sucked the souls from their minds!"

Sterling lifted the blade off the scientist's neck. For the first time since they'd been talking, Colicos had actually revealed something of worth.

"You said that reversing the effects was impossible," Sterling said, still toying with the scalpel. "What you've just described sounds like your process had potential."

"Yes, yes, I misspoke!" blurted Colicos, apparently seeing an opportunity for a reprieve. "It is possible. Just challenging. And agonizing. It is a painful process, and one that so far no-one has recovered from."

Sterling lifted the tip of the scalpel blade so that Colicos could see it. The scientist's eyes grew almost as wide as the Sa'Nerra's egg-shaped orbs.

"Believe me, the suffering of your patients is nothing compared to what will happen to you if you fail, or refuse to help," Sterling said.

A neural link formed in Sterling's mind. He allowed it through and connected to Lieutenant Shade.

"Captain, MAUL has just surged into the system along with six phase-one Sa'Nerran Light Cruisers," Shade announced, calmly. "Two of the cruisers were torn apart on arrival from the surge stresses, and the four that made it through took heavy damage. Even so, they will intercept us before we reach the aperture to Thrace Colony."

"Understood, Lieutenant, I'm on my way," Sterling replied. He then tapped his interface to close the link.

"Saved by the bell, doc," Sterling said, dropping the

scalpel back into the tray by the side of the operating table. "We'll talk again soon."

Sterling then turned to leave, but Colicos' indignant screeching followed him.

"You can't just leave me here like this!" the scientist protested. "Where is the surgeon!"

Sterling peered through the glass and saw that Commander Graves was operating on Jinx the beagle hound. Banks was standing to Graves' side, watching the medical-doctor-turned-veterinary-surgeon like a hawk.

"My medical officer has a more important patient to attend to," Sterling said, as the door slid open. "He'll be with you when he's free."

Sterling stepped outside and waited for the door to slide shut behind him, cutting off the panicked squawks of Dr. James Colicos as it did so.

STERLING STRODE onto the bridge with Commander Banks close behind and jumped onto the command platform. The viewscreen was already focused on the squadron of Sa'Nerran vessels that were in pursuit.

"Report, Lieutenant," said Sterling, aiming the statement at his weapons officer. Then he noticed that Lieutenant Razor was also back on the bridge, in her usual place beside the aft consoles.

"We're receiving a hail from MAUL, Captain," said Shade, her voice containing the subtlest hint of intrigue.

"Well, you'd better put it on the viewscreen then," replied Sterling, also intrigued to hear what the commander of Sa'Nerra's most decorated warship had to say. Sterling glanced across to Banks, who appeared just as curious to learn the reason for the communication request as he was. Moments later, the image of the approaching Sa'Nerran warships faded and was replaced by Emissary Clinton Crow, dressed in Sa'Nerran armor.

"Captain Sterling, what a surprise to find you out here," said Crow, sounding not in the slightest bit surprised. "I would have expected you to be with the rest of your Fleet, attempting to stave off our invasion armada."

Sterling smiled. "Oh, we're just out here running some shakedown tests, you know? We have a few upgrades and I wanted to try them out."

Crow's eyes narrowed. "Let's not play games, Captain," he said, suddenly taking a more menacing tone. "I know why you're here and I know what you've done."

"Then you also know that no matter what you say or demand, my answer will be the same," Sterling replied, calmly.

"And what answer is that, Captain?" Crow spat.

"That you can kiss my ass, Emissary Crow," replied Sterling, with relish.

Sterling ended the transmission and turned to Shade. "What's the condition of the Sa'Nerran squadron, Lieutenant?"

"MAUL has fallen to the rear of the formation, Captain," Shade replied. "It's in bad shape, but our scanners detect its weapons are still online."

"What about the cruisers?" Sterling added, updating his Captain's console with the latest scan data.

"They all took heavy damage during the surge," Shade replied. "I'm reading multiple hull breaches and power fluctuations. They might fly themselves apart before they even reach us."

Sterling huffed a laugh. "I think we've used up our

quota of luck for this mission, Lieutenant," he replied. "What about the torps we jettisoned as mines?"

Shade worked her console then the viewscreen updated to show the location of the torpedoes and the course of the Sa'Nerran squadron. "They're heading straight for them, sir," she announced. Sterling detected a modicum of satisfaction in his weapons officer's voice. Killing Sa'Nerra was about the only thing that brought Shade close to appearing happy.

"At their current speed the enemy squadron will be within optimal firing range in five minutes," Banks then chimed in. "But it will take twice that length of time for us to reach the aperture and surge. Even then, there's nothing to stop the cruisers following us through."

Sterling turned to his chief engineer. "This is the part where you explain your genius plan to boost our engine power, Lieutenant."

Sterling's statement had been worded a tad facetiously, but he was deadly serious. The engineer was equally as deadpan in her reply.

"I can give you more power, sir, but it's the dirtiest hack job I've ever done in my life," Razor replied. "I can't promise how long the boost will hold, but I can promise you that it will be a close-run thing."

"Do it, Lieutenant," Sterling replied. "Give Keller everything you've got."

Sterling turned to his helmsman. "I'm afraid that's not the only miracle I need performing today," he said, meeting the ensign's curious eyes. "I need you to vector a surge deep into the Thrace Colony system. We need to emerge so far away from that squadron of alien killers that they have no choice but to give up the chase."

Keller twisted back toward his station and moments later a number of surge projections were displayed on the viewscreen.

"I took the liberty of running some calculations already, Captain," Keller said. The ensign's head was turned away from the command console, but if the young officer had been looking, he'd have seen his captain swell with pride. "I can get us close to the aperture to Middle Star. Close enough that they'd never reach us before we surged."

Sterling slapped his hand on his console in triumph. If they could reach Middle Star then Christopher Fletcher's fleet would deter the Sa'Nerra from continuing their pursuit. "Good work, Ensign. Enter the program and stand-by to surge."

"Aye, Captain," Keller replied, continuing to tap away at his helm controls. "There might not be much of us left once we emerge."

"I don't care if we have to get out and push the Invictus through that aperture to Middle Star, Ensign," Sterling hit back. "Just get us there."

Lieutenant Shade's console then chimed an update.

"Captain, the lead cruiser is approaching the minefield," the weapons officer announced.

"Put it on the viewscreen," Sterling said, sliding his hands into their familiar grooves on the sides of his console. "Let's see if lady luck is still with us."

A magnified image of the lead Sa'Nerran Light Cruiser appeared on the screen. Its three companions were clearly visible to its rear, though MAUL was trailing far behind. Sterling updated his scans of the alien's top gun and saw that it was faltering badly. Two surges through an unstable aperture were too much even for the Sa'Nerra's mightiest warrior, it seemed.

"Twenty seconds to impact," Shade called out.

Sterling held his breath and waited. If he could disrupt the alien's pursuit even for a moment, it might be enough, in tandem with the engine boost, to pull the Invictus clear of danger.

Several flashes lit up the viewscreen. Banks shook her fist and cried out, but Sterling's head hung low. He knew that the flashes were not caused by torpedo explosions, but by Sa'Nerran plasma weapons.

"The lead cruiser has targeted and destroyed the torpedo, Captain," Shade said, confirming Sterling's suspicions. More flashes popped off in the darkness. "They're targeting the other torpedoes too. It didn't work."

This time Banks slammed her hand down on her console. Despite the fact Razor had reinforced the stem, on account of the first officer's frequent, super-human outbursts, the metal still groaned like an old shipwreck.

"How the hell did they see them?" Banks said, throwing her arms out wide.

"They didn't," Sterling said, realizing what had happened. "But MAUL did."

Banks cursed then squeezed her hands into fists. "Damn it, one day soon that ship is going down," she said, seething with anger. "Even if I have to tear it into scrap with my own hands."

The Invictus was then rocked hard as if they'd collided with an invisible object directly ahead. Sterling was thrown over the top of his console and landed heavily on his back. Strident alarm tones pierced the air and Sterling was peppered with debris from exploding consoles and power relays.

"Engine one has overloaded, Captain," Razor called out, raising her voice to a yell to be heard over the commotion on the bridge. "I have to shut it down or it'll blow, taking half the ship with it!"

"Do it, Lieutenant!' Sterling called back, dragging himself to his feet. "What's the status of engine two?"

"It's stable, for now," Razor replied, rushing from console to console to perform the necessary actions. "But the momentum we're carrying, plus the thrust from the remaining engine won't be enough."

Sterling cursed as he clawed himself back around the front of his console. Banks was at her station, sporting several additional cuts and bruises, while Shade was also dragging herself back to her feet.

"Get down there and do whatever you can, Lieutenant," Sterling called over to his engineer. "If we can't reach the aperture before they're in weapons range, there'll be nothing left of us to surge."

Razor acknowledged the order and staggered off the bridge as Sterling turned his attention to the damage report. Despite the violent reaction to the engine overload, the additional damage to the ship hadn't been severe.

"Sir, the lead cruiser is preparing to fire," Shade called

out. There was an urgency in her voice that was rarely heard from his weapons officer.

"How? It should still be out of range," said Banks.

"They've pushed their engines beyond their limits to reach us, sir," Ensign Keller called out. He too looked shaken and was sporting a fresh cut to the side of his face. "Their engines are burning out. They sacrificed their ability to return to Sa'Nerran space in order to catch us."

"Strengthen the aft regenerative armor," Sterling called over to Shade. "Take power from anything but engines."

Shade acknowledged, then the ship was pounded by an initial volley of weapons fire from the lead Sa'Nerran Light Cruiser.

"Armor holding, but we can't take many more hits like that," Banks said.

"How long until we can surge, Ensign?" Sterling said. He could feel through the deck plating that the Invictus was tiring. It had already run a marathon and was now being asked to run a sprint. If it were any other ship, Sterling knew that it would have already faltered. However, the Invictus was no ordinary ship and she had no ordinary crew.

"Two minutes, Captain," Keller replied. Sterling could hear the despair in his helmsman's voice. Despite his inexperience, Keller had seen enough action to know that they wouldn't last another sixty seconds, never mind twice that.

"Get creative with your evasive maneuvers, Ensign," Sterling replied, maintaining the confidence in his voice. Keller and the rest of the crew had to believe there was still a chance, even if logic dictated otherwise. "We can make it. Just stay the course."

"Aye, Captain," Keller replied, immediately throwing the Invictus into a series of chaotic moves using their RCS thrusters.

Another blast rocked the ship, but Sterling could feel that it was only a glancing blow. Another slice of luck, though he knew that whatever good fortune had kept them alive this far was dwindling rapidly. He wracked his brain for another idea – anything that could buy them an extra sixty seconds – but he came up blank.

"Surge detected!" Banks called out.

"From where?" replied Sterling, suddenly feeling his heart thump harder in his chest.

"Thirteen ships, directly ahead. They're coming from Thrace," cried Banks. "And we're right in their lane."

"Hold your course, Ensign," Sterling ordered, aiming a finger at his helmsman before Keller could even contemplate steering them wide. They needed to carry all the forward speed they had.

Multiple flashes popped off ahead of them and thirteen new ships entered the system. Alarms wailed as the Invictus found itself on a collision course with one of them. However, unlike the battered Marauder, the new arrivals were fresh and agile, and their weapons were already armed. Plasma turrets flashed and mass cannons erupted sending a storm-front of death toward the Sa'Nerran Light Cruiser. The enemy vessel was obliterated in an instant.

"They're Fleet ships," said Banks, continuing her scan. "The lead vessel is a generation one destroyer." The

Invictus' first officer laughed and turned to him. "Well, I'll be damned..." she said, shaking her head. "It's the Bismarck."

The comm system chimed and Sterling immediately put the caller through. Like Banks, he already knew who it was.

"Need any assistance, Captain Sterling?" asked Christopher Fletcher, with a wry smile.

"You certainly know how to make an entrance," Sterling replied, suddenly feeling the muscles in his body go limp. "Thank you for responding to my distress call."

Fletcher nodded. "Any chance to take down a few more Sa'Nerra, Captain," the former Fleet officer replied. "The aperture is clear, so go ahead and surge to Thrace. We'll take care of this lot then meet you on the other side."

"Understood, Captain Fletcher," Sterling replied. "Be careful of the heavy destroyer to the rear of the group. It's wounded, but still dangerous."

"I'd love a chance to take down MAUL," Fletcher replied, "but it's already seen the writing on the wall and bugged out."

Sterling glanced down at his console and saw that Fletcher was correct. The alien's most decorated warship would live to fight another day.

"And it's just Fletcher, Captain Sterling," the commander of the Bismarck then added. "I gave up my chance to become a captain long ago."

"Maybe it's not too late," Sterling replied, standing tall. "I'll see you at Thrace Colony."

Fletcher nodded, then the comm channel closed and

the viewscreen switched to a display of the thirteen former Fleet warships. Each one of them had first seen action before Sterling was even born, but all of them were still going strong, as were their commanders.

"Ensign Keller, take us to Thrace Colony," Sterling said, meeting his helmsman's eyes. "Just a regular surge will do, Ensign. Nice and steady."

"Aye, Captain," Keller replied, smartly.

"It seems that luck is still with us, after all," said Banks, stepping beside Sterling and leaning on his console. For once, she looked as weary as he felt.

"That wasn't luck, Mercedes," replied Sterling, peering out at the warships on the viewscreen. "That was providence."

"Well, whatever it was, I'll take it," replied Banks.

Sterling's console then chimed and he saw that a message had been received. It was text only and transmitted from MAUL. Sterling opened the file and read it on his console.

"You can't run forever, Captain", the message began. "Whether out in the Void or inside Fleet space, I will find you, and I will personally put you down. Fleet is finished. Earth is finished. You are finished." Sterling shook his head as Crow signed off the message with the man's usual pomposity, employing his full title as "Emissary to the Sa'Nerra." However, it was the final two words that pissed off Sterling the most. Two simple words that highlighted the depth of Crow's betrayal. The message ended, "For Sa'Nerra."

STERLING PRESSED his back against the wall of the Invictus' narrow corridors to allow a maintenance crew to move past. It had been six hours since they'd landed at Bastion, after limping through Thrace Colony and surging to Middle Star. Chris Fletcher's squadron of veteran former Fleet warships had made mincemeat of the Sa'Nerran Light Cruisers, but Fletcher had been unable to catch MAUL. The Heavy Destroyer carrying Emissary Clinton Crow had escaped back into Sa'Nerran space using the safe, regular aperture routes. Sterling should have been disappointed and frustrated by Crow's narrow escape, but the truth was he was glad. Crow and MAUL were his. It was personal between them and if anyone was to take them down – Fleet or otherwise – it was going to be Captain Lucas Sterling.

The maintenance crew was followed by a team of engineers from Bastion, loaned by kind permission of Fletcher himself. Then Sterling was finally able to continue on toward the medical bay. The door slid open and Sterling stepped inside to see Lieutenant Razor in one of the bays. Commander Graves and Commander Banks were standing by one side of the bed. However, it wasn't the ship's medical officer that was tending to Razor, but none other than James Colicos. The scientist's robotic hand had finally been attached, but Graves had been unable to add any cosmetic enhancements with the time and resources the skilled surgeon had available. As such, the hand remained almost skeletal in appearance, with bare gunmetal-colored panels and visible mechanical joints. Nevertheless, the appendage appeared to function perfectly, responding as intuitively and naturally as a real hand.

"Nice work, Commander Graves," said Sterling, as he approached the medical bay. "Not that this asshole deserves it," he added, glaring at Colicos.

"Nice work?" Colicos replied, as indignant as ever. The scientist raised the hand and flexed all the joints, revealing the intricate inner workings of the device. "This is an abomination!" he screeched. "Once we are back in Fleet space, I demand a proper replacement."

Sterling took a step closer to Colicos, causing the man to recoil and knock into a cabinet to the side of Razor's bed.

"I'm sorry, I didn't quite catch that," Sterling said, raising a finger to his ear, as if he'd suddenly gone deaf. "But I was sure you just made a demand?"

Colicos quickly changed his tune. "Apologies, Captain Sterling, I did not mean to speak out of turn," the scientist hastily replied.

"I suggest you work on your manners, doc," said

Sterling, managing to keep a lid on his own resentment. "Because whether I take you back to Griffin, or cast you out of an airlock, depends entirely on how useful you are over the next couple of days." He gestured to Lieutenant Razor. "As a case in point, what have you been able to do for my chief engineer?"

With his organic hand, Colicos gestured to a medical scan of Razor's skull on the screen above her bed.

"Truthfully, it's actually remarkable that she's not already a gibbering wreck," the scientist began.

Colicos was smiling as if he expected the others to find his comment amusing. Sterling remained stony-faced, as did the others. The smile fell off Colicos' face and he coughed apologetically before adopting a more serious tone.

"The use of a firewall to prevent the Lieutenant's implant being infected by code from my neural translation matrix was actually quite inspired," Colicos continued. The switch to attempts at flattery in order to ingratiate himself was as obvious as it was unsubtle, Sterling thought. "Naturally, if I had devised the firewall it would not have failed, as this one did," Colicos added, seemingly unable to talk for ten seconds without making it about himself. "As it is, the level of corruption to Lieutenant Razor's implant is minimal, and, thanks to a rather clever technique I just developed, it is currently contained."

"Cut to the chase, doc, can you fix the damage or not?" Sterling cut in. He was already sick of hearing the man's self-aggrandizing, soft-spoken voice.

Colicos' puckered-up expression demonstrated his

obvious irritation at being interrupted. However, the genius scientist was smart enough to bite his tongue, rather than verbalize his grievances.

"In short, yes," Colicos said. "However, I will need access to a far more sophisticated medical facility than this quaint little ship offers."

Sterling felt like knocking the scientist out cold then and there, but managed to hold back. He could see that Banks' hands had already balled into fists and judged it best to end the conversation, before either of them murdered the man.

"I will need access to a facility on a command outpost at the very minimum," Colicos went on, unaware of just how close he was to being tossed through the bulkhead. "Though in order to do my best work, I will require a generation-three medical cruiser or access to the Fleet medical research facility on Earth," Colicos concluded.

"I'll see what I can do," said Sterling, speeding things along as best as he could. "Is there anything else you can do right now?"

Colicos peered around the Invictus' medical bay, his nose scrunched up as if he'd just caught the scent of fresh dog crap in the air.

"Not in here, no," Colicos replied, snootily.

Sterling gestured for the commando who was on guard to come over.

"Take our esteemed guest back to the brig," he said to the commando, whose name and face he did not recognize. Colicos opened his mouth and looked ready to protest before Sterling quickly added, "and if he causes any trouble, shoot him in the leg." This last part of the sentence caused the scientist to swiftly clamp his jaw shut again.

The commando acknowledged the order then roughly ushered James Colicos out of the medical bay.

"If I'm not needed here anymore, I'd like to continue repairs to the ship, Captain," Lieutenant Razor said, sliding her legs off the bed.

"Granted, Lieutenant," said Sterling. Colicos hadn't magically healed his engineer, as he secretly wished the scientist was capable of doing, but the fact Razor was no longer in immediate danger was reassuring.

Lieutenant Razor made her apologies to the room and departed. As the number of crew in the medical bay began to thin out, Sterling was suddenly aware that there was a patient missing.

"Where's the hound?" he asked, looking at Banks. He immediately felt a lump in his throat, worrying that the dog might have died on the operating table and he'd just put his foot in it.

"She's in the bar outside with Fletcher and his crew," said Banks. Sterling let out a silent breath of relief. "Fletcher asked to see you, once you were done in here."

Sterling nodded. "Let's not keep our mutinous savior waiting then," he said.

Sterling was about to head for the exit when he noticed that Commander Graves had already returned to his work. Sterling was not good at giving praise, especially where it concerned talking to his creepy chief medical officer. However, on this occasion, as on many others, he felt the effort was warranted, if not expressly required.

"Good work, Commander Graves," Sterling said, causing the dour-faced physician to look up from his console. "I'm going to need you to continue piecing us all back together with the same skill you've demonstrated over the last few days and weeks."

Commander Graves bowed his head graciously. "No thanks are necessary, Captain," the doctor said. "Though I appreciate the sentiment nonetheless."

The medical officer returned to his work and Sterling took his leave without another word. However, they'd only made it a few paces along the corridor outside before Banks highlighted his rare act of appreciation toward Graves.

"I think that's the first time I've seen you speak to Graves without looking worried he was about to suck out your brains with a straw," said Banks, smiling.

Sterling laughed and returned his first officer's smile. "He's earned it," he replied, honestly. "All the crew have. Graves, Keller, Razor, Shade. They've all proven they deserve to be on this ship."

"Aye, sir, that they have," Banks replied, her own voice and body language reflecting the same pride and admiration that Sterling had expressed.

Sterling was not surprised that Commander Banks hadn't highlighted his obvious glaring omission. He'd intentionally left out his first officer from the round of praise, simply to see whether vanity would compel her to fish for a compliment. However, as expected, Mercedes Banks did not fall into his trap. The respect and admiration that existed between the two of them did not need to be expressed. Yet, oddly, it was Sterling who found himself compelled to say more.

"And I'm glad you're with me, Mercedes," Sterling added. "I need you by my side, now more than ever."

He immediately regretted speaking the words, as it made him sound mawkish and sentimental. However, he had nearly been forced to kill his first officer on the alien prison station, an act that was suddenly playing on his mind. He half-expected Banks to react glibly and rib him for his sudden outpouring of emotion. However, his first officer was also unusually maudlin.

"Hey, you have me, Lucas," she replied, stopping and turning to face Sterling. "No matter what, remember?"

The two of them continued to look at each other, suddenly lost for words until another contingent of repair engineers bustled around the corner. This forced captain and first officer to separate and press their backs to opposite walls, like the parting of the waves. It was an unexpected, but timely interruption that cut through the awkwardness and allowed them to move on, as if nothing had happened.

"I feel it's my duty as first officer to highlight a concern, however," Banks then said as they as they entered the cargo hold.

Sterling stopped and scowled at his first officer, unsure of whether she was serious or being facetious. "And what's that?" he queried. He was curious, but also a little wary.

"This last mission has finally proved to me that your heart isn't pure ice after all," Banks said, her lips now curling ever so slightly up at the corners of her mouth.

Sterling snorted. "Nonsense," he hit back. "What makes you think that?"

Banks flashed her eyes at Sterling then continued on toward the lowered rear ramp.

"When I found Jinx injured in the corridor, you said, 'bring her with us', not 'bring it'," said Banks, her smile growing wide.

"I did not," Sterling hit back, wafting his hand at her. Then he stopped, genuinely unsure as to whether Banks was correct or not. "Or did I?"

"You did," replied Banks, smugly.

Sterling snorted again then stepped onto the ramp. He was suddenly hit by a blast of cool air from Bastion Colony, which made his entire body shiver. It was a late autumn evening in Bastion and the sudden drop in temperature took Sterling by surprise.

"It doesn't matter if I said, 'he', 'she', 'it' or any other pronoun," Sterling added, increasing his pace in the hope of escaping the conversation. "The fact remains that if I step in that hound's crap while I'm on the ship, it's still getting airlocked."

Sterling jumped down off the rear ramp and onto the landing pad at Bastion spaceport. However, while one boot made a satisfying thwacking sound on the asphalt surface the other was cushioned by something soft and malleable. Sterling cursed then peered down at his boot. Smeared across the sole was a smooth, dark-brown substance that he knew could only be one thing.

"That doesn't count," Banks said, breezing past Sterling a moment later. "It wasn't on the ship..."

AFTER A BRIEF DETOUR TO wipe the muck off his boot, Captain Sterling and Commander Banks arrived at the door of "Unsinkable Sam", the bar that Chris Fletcher and his twelve other former Fleet warships frequented.

"It looks like a chunk of this spaceport is devoted to Fletcher's ships and crew," said Sterling, peering up at the neon sign. In addition to the words, there was a picture of a black cat with a white chest sitting on a piece of debris floating in an ocean.

"I have to admit, I half-expected people with pitchforks chasing after us by now," said Banks, glancing around the exterior of the bar.

The bar was busy with numerous drinkers standing outside, chatting and smoking. No-one paid Sterling and Banks any attention, despite their Fleet uniforms and the modern Fleet warship on-stand a couple of hundred meters away. Suddenly, the distinctive howl of a beagle filtered out of the door, which was still open by a crack. Sterling saw

Banks' tense up and his first officer immediately pushed inside, presumably worried that Jinx was in trouble. Sterling cursed and followed her in, hoping that their first act on Bastion wasn't getting into a bar fight. However, it soon became apparent that there was no cause for concern. The dog's curious vocalizations were howls of happiness rather than distress. Jinx was merrily playing a game of "fetch" with Fletcher and several of the other patrons in the bar, all of whom wore similar outfits to that of the famous Fleet mutineer. The dog was clattering across the wooden floor of the bar in pursuit of an old tennis ball. The sound of her feet on the hard floor was accentuated by the fact that one of her legs was a metal, cybernetic replacement. However, the dog appeared entirely unconcerned by this fact and carried on as if nothing about her body had changed.

"See, everyone loves a ship's dog," said Banks, moving further inside and drawing up a stool at the bar.

"Not everyone," Sterling hit back, pulling up a stool beside his first officer.

"You're just the exception that proves the rule," said Banks, smiling.

Fletcher noticed that Sterling and Banks had entered and tossed the ball to another member of his crew, who continued the game.

"Captain, Commander, what can I get you?" Fletcher asked, leaning on the bar beside them. "It's on the house, considering I own the bar and all."

"Thank, you, Mister Fletcher," replied Sterling, but the old Fleet officer was quick to interject.

"Please, either Chris or preferably Fletch," the older man said. "No-one calls me Mister Fletcher except the rookies, and even then, I hate it."

"Okay, Fletch," Sterling said, feeling immediately more at ease. "We'll take whatever is good. Your choice."

Fletcher nodded then spoke to the barman, who placed three small wine glasses on the counter before moving off to fetch whatever the former officer had asked for. However, it was Fletcher's mention of "rookies" that had really piqued Sterling's interest, rather than the mystery drink he was about to be served. Fletcher had previously hinted that the forces under his command numbered more than just the thirteen mutineer ships. Yet he didn't want to immediately start off by grilling the man so soon after he'd warmly extended his hospitality toward them.

The barman returned and uncorked a bottle of port wine that looked at least as old as Fletcher's venerable warship.

"I haven't seen a bottle of port for a long time," said Sterling, accepting one of the glasses from Fletcher.

"I don't think I've seen one ever," remarked Banks, peering at the ruby red liquid.

"It's an old tradition from sea-faring nations of Earth's history," Fletcher said, finally picking up his own glass. "We had to invent, or at least repurpose, a few traditions of our own when we separated from UG and the Fleet." He raised his glass. "To a bloody war or a sickly season," he said, before drinking from the glass.

Sterling and Banks frowned at each other but followed Fletcher's lead and drank. The wine was sweet and – at least to Sterling's uncultured palette – had a powerful kick to it too. Fleet ships had been prohibited from serving liquor since the outbreak of the Sa'Nerran war.

"Thank you again for responding to my request for aid," Sterling said, setting the now half-empty glass down on the counter. "I honestly wasn't sure if you'd come."

Fletcher bowed his head then raised his glass again. "Well, you seem like a decent fellow," the older man replied. "Besides, I still have more of a beef with those alien bastards than I do with Fleet."

"Fleet could really do with someone like you right now," Sterling said, unable to stay off the subject of Fletcher's fighting force for long. "With the Sa'Nerran armada capturing G-sector, you command the only viable war fleet in the Void."

"I'll stop you right there, Captain," Fletcher said, raising the palm of his hand to Sterling. "I have no problem helping you out, but my responsibility is to Bastion and Middle Star. If I take my Fleet from this system, there's nothing to stop the Sa'Nerra rolling in and trying to finish the job they started back when I was a Lieutenant."

"If Fleet loses this war, the Void will fall next," Sterling countered.

"Then you'd better make sure you win it," Fletcher replied with a smile. He took another swig of port and topped up all the glasses. "I know what you're asking, Captain, and I understand why. But I can't help you without abandoning these people, and that's something I swore I'd never do, no matter what."

This time it was Sterling who bowed his head and

raised his glass. "I understand, Fletch," he said, earnestly, "and I'll see what I can do to help Bastion too. There must be the remnants of other Fleet outposts and hidden storage vaults on this planet and on Colony Two. I can give you the means to find and open them."

"That would be appreciated, Captain, thank you," Fletcher replied.

"Please, if I'm to call you Fletch then you can call me Lucas," Sterling said, starting to feel uncomfortable at the older man's formality. However, the veteran former officer just laughed and shook his head.

"A Lieutenant calling a Captain by his first name? Not a chance in hell!" Fletcher said, raising an eyebrow. "I may be a mutineer and a disgrace to the Fleet name, but old habits die hard."

Jinx then came trotting over and dropped the tennis ball at Banks' feet. The dog then sat down and peered up at her with its large, brown eyes. Fletcher laughed again and looked down at the cybernetically-enhanced hound.

"It looks like you have other duties to attend to, Commander," Fletcher said, nodding toward the dog.

Banks downed the rest of her port then yielded to Jinx's doe-eyed requests for attention. She picked up the ball and rolled it underneath the tables, sending Jinx scampering across the floor in pursuit.

"So, where to next, Captain?" Fletcher added, as Banks slid off her stool to continue the game with Jinx.

Sterling shrugged. "Back to Fleet space, if I can get there," he replied. "Unfortunately, there's an entire Sa'Nerran armada between us and F-sector."

"Any idea how you'll get past it?" Fletcher asked.

Just at that moment, Lieutenant Shade pushed in through the door. She scanned the room then met Sterling's eyes and approached, appearing ill-at-ease in the crowded and bustling surroundings of the bar.

"I'm hoping my officer just walked in with the answer," Sterling replied, acknowledging Shade's arrival.

"I'll leave you to it then, Captain Sterling," Fletcher said, sliding off his stool. He then refilled Sterling's glass and set off toward one of the tables occupied by his crew, bottle in hand.

"Mister Fletcher," Sterling called out after the older man. The mutineer commander stopped and raised an eyebrow. "Fletch, I mean," Sterling corrected himself. It still seemed wrong to refer to the man in such familiar terms. "I know you're not able to join the fight, but if you were to..."

"I'm not, Captain," Fletcher was quick to interject.

"I know, but indulge me," Sterling hit back. The older man shrugged and nodded to him to continue. "If you were, just how many ships are we talking about? Whether with rookie or experienced crews?"

Fletcher smiled and Sterling could tell that the man was itching to reveal his secret. He could see that Fletcher was rightfully proud of what he'd achieved at Middle Star. Few large colonies had survived inside the Void. To hold back the Sa'Nerra by training his own crews, using only wrecked ships salvaged from the war, was no mean feat. However, age and experience had clearly also taught the former Fleet officer how to keep a secret.

"Nice try, Captain," Fletcher replied as the tennis ball rolled past his feet, hotly pursued by Jinx. "But the only way you'll find that out is to attack Middle Star." The man smiled then continued toward his table before stopping and glancing back. "Though I wouldn't recommend it," Fletcher added.

Sterling conceded graciously then allowed the older man to retire to his new table. Shade then approached and stood to attention beside him.

"At ease, Lieutenant, this is a bar, not my ready room," said Sterling. Shade appeared confused by the order then adjusted her stiff posture by the slightest fraction. Sterling assumed this was what constituted "relaxed" for Opal Shade.

"Sir, I've been analyzing the data from Admiral Griffin, but I cannot see how I am the key to unlocking a route back into Fleet space," Shade announced. She sounded flustered and even a little embarrassed. Shade did not like to be defeated, whether in combat or any other challenge.

"What have you tried?" asked Sterling.

"Combinations of my name, date of birth, place of birth, parents, streets I used to live on, ships I've served on, commanding officers..."

Sterling held up a hand to stop Shade mid-flow. "I get the picture Lieutenant," he said. Whether his weapons officer had succeeded or not, Sterling need not question her thoroughness. "We're clearly missing something, so let's roll everything back to the most important question of all."

Shade's frown hardened. "What question is that, Captain?"

"Why did Griffin choose you, of course," replied Sterling.

However, Shade just shook her head. "I do not know, Captain."

Sterling then sighed and decided to attempt a new and potentially awkward approach with his guarded weapon's officer. He needed her to lower her shields.

"I'll level with you, Lieutenant," Sterling began. In addition to warming his insides, the port wine was also having the effect of lowering some of his own normally well-established emotional barriers. "Compared to the rest of my crew, I know very little about you," Sterling went on, deciding that if he required openness from Shade, he'd need to be more open himself. "I know that you came to the Invictus straight out of Grimaldi Military Prison." Shade's gaze immediately fell to the floor as Sterling said this. "And I know that Griffin personally vouched for you and got you out so that you could serve as my weapons officer." Shade had forced herself to meet her captain's eyes again, though it was clearly difficult for her to do so. "What I don't know, is why."

Shade was silent for a moment as she processed what Sterling had said. Then she straightened to attention again, suddenly appearing more comfortable and much more her usual, imperious self.

"Admiral Griffin is my aunt, Captain," Shade announced.

The Lieutenant was now speaking clearly and without awkwardness. She had clearly made a decision to reveal certain facts about herself and was speaking plainly, as if she'd been ordered to do so.

"Her younger brother was my father," Shade continued. "I never took his name and used my mother's instead. My father and I rarely saw eye-to-eye."

"Your father was William Griffin, Captain of the Warspite?" Sterling asked. The story of the Warspite's battle with the Sa'Nerra at Acadia Colony was one of the most famous war stories in the Fleet. He'd always assumed that it merely a coincidence that the ship's ensign had shared the same surname as her captain. Now he knew better.

"Aye, sir," replied Shade.

Sterling could see that some of Shade's barriers had already gone back up, but for now his weapons officer was still managing to be open with him.

"The Warspite took down four enemy warships single-handed and lived to tell the tale," Sterling said, thinking out loud. "Ramming the final destroyer after the Warspite's weapons had been destroyed was one of the gutsiest moves I've ever heard of." Then Sterling remembered the key detail about the engagement, which was more poignant now that he knew the identify of Opal Shade. "But Captain Griffin, your father, was killed during that attack?"

"Aye, sir, that's correct," Shade answered. "I was the ensign on duty at the time. The Captain and first officer were incapacitated, so I made the call."

Sterling could hardly believe it. "It was you that rammed that destroyer?"

"Yes, sir," Shade replied. "Then I left my father on the bridge to die."

Sterling knew the tale of the Warspite well enough to know that Shade's brutal summary of her actions wasn't the whole story.

"If I remember correctly, Lieutenant, you dragged three people off that bridge alive before the hull breach forced the emergency seals to fall," Sterling countered.

"It doesn't matter, sir," Shade replied. "The crew blamed me for the death of their captain."

It was all starting to make sense to Sterling now, including why Shade had ended up in Grimaldi. Over two hundred crew had perished when the Warspite rammed the enemy destroyer, including its captain. This was despite the fact the desperate act had saved the ship and won the battle. Emotions ran high in the aftermath of the incident, and plenty of blame was thrown around. Several fights had broken out at G-COP and one man had died. Sterling didn't know for sure, but he was guessing that Shade's incarceration was directly related to these events. However, he also knew the details of the court marshals that had followed, even if he hadn't paid attention to the names of those involved.

"The Fleet prosecuting authority found that your actions on the Warspite were warranted, and that you had no case to answer," Sterling said, speaking more sternly. Shade clearly blamed herself and was perhaps even punishing herself. However, from what Sterling knew of the facts, she had no reason to do so. "You would have been honored for your bravery, had what happened next not occurred."

"So you know about the fight?" Shade asked, clearly surprised that Sterling had brought it up.

"I didn't know it was you until just now, but yes," Sterling replied. "And if it's any consolation, I would probably have done the same in your boots." Sterling then slid off the stool and stood tall in front of his weapons officer. "I don't care about heroes or heroics, Lieutenant," Sterling went on. "I only care that when a decision has to be made, no matter how horrific the outcome, that an officer makes the hard call, not the easy call. You saved that ship. Your father was just another casualty of war. Screw anyone that thinks any different."

Shade nodded. "Aye, sir."

However, as fascinating as it was to hear Shade's story, it still got them no further forward in their quest to unravel Admiral Griffin's mystery message. Sterling swirled the stem of the wine glass on the counter, trying to think how any of this related to the encrypted file Griffin had sent them. However, he still drew a blank.

"I'm afraid I don't know how any of this helps, sir," Shade then said, sounding much more at ease. "I've already tried thinking of words or places associated with Admiral Griffin and myself, but nothing worked."

"Maybe we're over-thinking this," said Sterling. "There has to be something common between you and your aunt. Something special or unusual. Something that only you would know. Something you shared?"

Shade thought for a moment. "We share a rare genetic

condition, called adermatoglyphia," she added, almost as an afterthought.

"Is that serious?" said Sterling, recoiling from his weapons officer. "It sounds serious."

"It basically means I have no fingerprints, sir," Shade replied, holding out her hands, palms facing up and straightening her fingers. Sterling leant closer and inspected the tips of Shade's digits. They were completely smooth.

"Well, I'll be damned," said Sterling, rocking back on the stool. "That's going to make ID checks more challenging for you when you move up the ranks."

"I still don't see how it helps, though, Captain," said Shade, pulling her hands back to her sides.

Sterling continued to twirl the stem of his glass, peering at the ruby red liquid as if it were a crystal ball that could give him the answers he sought. Then the thick, crimson liquid gave him an idea.

"What if your DNA is the key?" said Sterling, holding up the glass and sloshing the liquid inside. "It would be just like Griffin to need you to bleed in order to get the answer."

Shade's pencil-line eyebrows raised up. "I suppose it is possible, sir," she said, sounding unconvinced. "With your permission, I'll see if Lieutenant Razor can use a sample of my blood for analysis."

"Very good, Lieutenant," said Sterling, raising his glass. "Keep me appraised."

"Aye, sir," Shade replied. She then stood to attention and spun on her heels before heading toward the door.

"And Lieutenant," Sterling called out, causing Shade to

stop and turn around. "For what it's worth, knowing what I know only makes me more certain that you belong on this ship," Sterling added.

"Thank you, Captain," said Shade.

Sterling could see that the weapons officer's shields had gone back up. However, there was enough of a flicker in her eyes to let Sterling know that his comment had hit home.

"You're dismissed, Lieutenant," Sterling said. He then slid back onto the bar stool, raised the wine glass to his lips and drained the contents in one.

THE INVICTUS SLOWED to a stop at the co-ordinates provided in the file Admiral Griffin had provided, prior to the Invictus departing F-COP for the Void. Sterling's hunch that the rare genetic defect that Griffin and Opal Shade shared was the key had been correct. As it turned out, Shade had not been required to let her blood in order for Lieutenant Razor to unlock Admiral Griffin's file. The cause of the condition was a mutation in the SMARCAD1 gene on Chromosome 4Q22. The passphrase had therefore turned out to be "SMARCAD14Q22". However, while Sterling's moment of insight had allowed his chief engineer to unlock the file and give them a location in the Void, it did not explain what to do once they arrived. As such, the Invictus was now in the middle of nowhere on the Fleet side of the Void, close to a Fleet colony that had been wiped out over thirty years earlier.

"Report, Lieutenant Razor," said Sterling, glancing to

his chief engineer at her station at the rear of the bridge. "Why the hell are we out here?"

As usual, Razor was flitting from console to console, running multiple scans and analyses at once.

"I'm running every standard scan I can think of, Captain," Razor replied, while continuing to work. "But so far, this just appears to be empty space."

Banks then turned around and rested back against her console, looking thoughtful.

"We're not looking for something standard," she said, trying to work through the conundrum. "Whatever the admiral sent us here to find must be out of the ordinary, and something that a standard scan won't pick up."

"Like what?" asked Sterling. He couldn't fault his first officer's logic, but he didn't see how it helped them.

Banks shrugged. "She suggested this would be a way back to Fleet space, so perhaps a wormhole?" she wondered. "Either that, or she hid a Fleet of warships somewhere in this system so we could surge back to G-sector and kick the Sa'Nerra off our lawn."

Sterling huffed a laugh, but then had a thought. "What if there is a wormhole out here, but it's not actually a wormhole, but another aperture?" Razor stopped working and started paying attention. "We know the Sa'Nerra established a number of long-range apertures, which they then abandoned for obvious reasons. What if Fleet was doing the same?"

From the thoughtful expression on Banks' face, his first officer appeared to be attracted to the idea. Razor, however, had already returned to her consoles. Several seconds later, Sterling's console chimed an update.

"You were right," said Razor, turning back to face her Captain. "There is an aperture at the co-ordinates Admiral Griffin supplied. The signature is similar to the unstable apertures we found in Sa'Nerran space. Not exactly alike, but close."

Sterling checked his console and saw that the location of the aperture was now showing on his scanner readout. He rested forward on the console, sliding his hands into the grooves on its side.

"The problem is we might ride this aperture and end up crippled again on the other side," Sterling said, tapping his finger on the side of the console. "Can we send a probe?"

"We're fresh out, I'm afraid," replied Banks. "This time we're going to have to ride it blind."

Sterling shook his head, though he'd already resigned himself to the fact that they really had no choice. It was either surge or remain in the Void.

"I can modify our surge field to compensate, but there's no question it will be a sporty ride, Captain," Razor added.

Sterling sighed and glanced at Banks, who also had a resigned look on her face.

"Okay, Lieutenant, make the modifications," Sterling replied. "But if we keep riding the rapids like this, we're going to have to get chairs fitted to the bridge," he added, tightening his grip on the console. Sterling then turned to Shade. "Take us to battle stations, Lieutenant, just to be on the safe side. Who knows where this thing will take us..."

The alert klaxons sounded and the bridge was bathed in red. It seemed to Sterling that they'd spent more time at battle stations than they had at any other condition.

"The new surge parameters are programmed in, Captain," said Razor, bracing herself against one of the consoles at the rear of the bridge.

"Very well, take us in, Ensign," said Sterling, nodding to his eager helmsman.

"Aye sir," replied Keller, smartly. "Approaching aperture threshold now. Ten seconds to surge."

Sterling cleared his head and tightened his grip further. He hoped that he wasn't about to experience a repeat of the disembodied hallucinations he was subjected to the last time they surged through an unstable aperture.

"Surging in three," Keller called out. "Two..."

However, there was no call of, "one", at least not that Sterling heard. The ship had already been consumed by the sub-dimension of space that facilitated aperture travel. Sterling again found himself conscious of his own lack of existence, and also swamped by images and memories of recent events. Scenes of battles they'd fought and alien warriors he'd slain were interspersed with more banal scenes with the crew. Then he found himself standing in front of Mercedes Banks, in the corridor outside the medical bay.

"I'm glad you're with me, Mercedes," Sterling said. He was again unable to stop himself speaking the words, as if he were an observer of his own past. "I need you by my side."

Mercedes Banks then moved closer and wrapped her arms around Sterling's neck.

This isn't what happened... Sterling thought, but then he was immediately unsure of himself. *Or was it?*

"You can have me, Lucas," replied Banks, pulling Sterling closer. "Whenever you want."

Did this happen? Sterling asked himself, as Banks' face drew so close that he could feel her breath on his skin.

Mercedes Banks then pulled Sterling's body against her own and kissed him passionately on the lips. Sterling was unable to resist, partly because of Banks' overpowering strength, but also because he didn't want to.

Suddenly the bridge exploded back into reality and Sterling found himself face down on his console. Alarms were sounding from multiple stations and the bridge lights were flickering chaotically.

"Captain?"

Sterling felt hands grip under his armpits and he was hauled upright. His head was thumping and his eyes were blurry.

"Captain, can you hear me?"

Sterling blinked his eyes and shook his head, despite the fact this made it throb even harder. Then his vision cleared and he saw Commander Banks standing in front of him. His cheeks flushed red, suddenly reminded of the vision he'd had during their recklessly-long surge.

"Are you okay, Lucas?" said Banks, lowering her voice.

Sterling took Banks' hands, which he realized were still holding him and gently pushed them away. "I'm fine,

Commander," he said, turning back to the viewscreen. "What's our status?"

Banks remained by Sterling's side for a moment, a questioning look on her face, but then moved back to her console.

"The reactor is offline, but emergency power cells are functioning," Banks said, working her station. "We're receiving reports of multiple minor hull breaches. The cargo bay has completely depressurized. Seventeen more wounded."

"There won't be anyone left on the ship at this rate," Sterling said, squeezing his eyes shut from the pain that was throbbing through his temples. "Do we know yet where the hell we are?"

"Star fixes and surge data suggest we're in F-sector, quadrant one," Banks replied.

"F-sector?" Sterling said, checking and confirming the readings on his own console. "That's one a hell of surge."

"Aye, sir," said Banks, echoing Sterling's sentiment. "It looks like we're close to Pandora, one of the evacuated outer colonies. That would put us about three standard surges from F-COP." Banks' console then chimed an alert and her brow furrowed. "There's a ship incoming," she said, working her console. The image of a Fleet Frigate appeared on the viewscreen. "It's the Corpus Christi, sir. A gen-two Patrol Frigate." Banks console then chimed another update. "It's hailing us."

"I suppose we should be glad they didn't just shoot us on sight," Sterling said. He then straightened up, drew in a deep breath and let it out slowly, ready to speak to the frigate's commander. Somehow, he had to explain how they'd just appeared seemingly out of nowhere. "Put them through, Commander."

The commander of the Corpus Christi appeared on the viewscreen. She appeared even more bemused than Sterling had expected her to look.

"This is Commander Rosa Dotson of the Fleet Frigate Corpus Christi," the commander began, still wearing a slightly pained expression. "Identify yourself and explain your purpose here. This is now a restricted area."

"I'm Captain Lucas Sterling of the Fleet Marauder Invictus, Commander," Sterling replied, managing to sound stronger than he felt. "However, how we ended up here is going to take a little more time to explain."

"I suggest you try to make it brief, Captain," Commander Dotson replied, skeptically.

Sterling's console chimed an update then he saw that the Corpus Christi had locked weapons onto them. If Commander Dotson had been standing in front of him at that moment, Sterling imagined she would have pulled a pistol and trained it on him with her finger on the trigger.

"I suggest you remove your weapons lock from my ship, Commander," Sterling replied, stressing Dotson's lower rank. "We're on the same side here."

Commander Dotson was not swayed. "Not until I've confirmed your identity and established exactly how you got here, Captain," the woman hit back. "Those are my orders. You and your crew could be turned for all I know."

Sterling appreciated the predicament that the commander was in. However, he also knew he could throw the same logic back at her.

"I could say the same for you and your crew, Commander Dotson," Sterling replied. "We could go around in circles all day trying to convince one another of who we are. At some point we're going to need to trust each other."

"Trust is in pretty short supply at the moment, Captain," Dotson answered. There was a fatalistic air to her statement that suggested the situation within the Fleet had worsened while Sterling had been away. "At least tell me how you got here. Give me something."

"My mission is classified, Commander," replied Sterling. He figured that if Griffin had been so secretive about the hidden apertures, she must have had her reasons. Sterling's console chimed, but he kept his eyes fixed on Commander Dotson.

"Light Cruisers Centaur and Champion just surged in, Captain," said Commander Banks. "They've set an intercept course and are charging weapons."

Sterling cursed under his breath. He realized he was in a bind with no way out. His only choices were to fight the Fleet ships then try to escape, or surrender and be escorted to F-COP like a captured enemy. However, one way or another he knew he'd have to answer for his actions by disobeying orders and heading into the Void.

"Commander, I request that you escort the Invictus to F-COP," said Sterling.

Dotson sighed. "I'm sorry, Captain, but I have my orders," the commander replied. "Any vessel that has potentially come into contact with the enemy or returned from enemy-controlled space must be seized and its crew quarantined under guard."

"That really isn't necessary, Commander," Sterling protested, but the officer held firm.

"I'm sorry, Captain, but these orders contain no ambiguity," Dotson cut in. "Now surrender your vessel and prepare to be boarded. Fail to comply and I will be forced to declare you and your crew aides to the emissaries and enemies of the United Governments."

Sterling glanced down at his console and saw that the two light cruisers were already in weapons range. Even a completely fresh Invictus operating at peak efficiency would struggle to take on two gen-three cruisers and a frigate. As it was, their reactor was still down, they had no engines or weapons and their atmosphere was slowly leaking into space.

"Very well, Commander Dotson, I surrender the Invictus to you," Sterling said, still managing to stand tall, despite the humiliating act. "I will make preparations to receive your crew."

"Thank you, Captain Sterling," replied Dotson. "And for what it's worth, I'm sorry."

"No apology necessary, Commander," replied Sterling. "You are only doing your duty."

Sterling was about to end the transmission when a question popped into his head. It wasn't especially important, but unless he asked it, he knew it would gnaw at him.

"One last thing, Commander Dotson," Sterling asked.

"Go ahead, Captain," Dotson replied, more than a little reticently.

"Who gave the order to capture any ships returning from enemy-controlled space?" Sterling asked.

"The orders were relayed by Admiral Wessel," Dotson replied.

Sterling laughed and shook his head. "Thank you, Commander," he replied. Dotson nodded respectfully then cut the transmission.

The viewscreen updated to show the Corpus Christi looming in space ahead of them, with the two cruisers slowly moving in behind it.

"Wessel..." said Commander Banks, spitting the word out like poison. "It would have to be him."

Sterling sighed and nodded. Wessel knew that there was only one Fleet ship out in the Void, so the order was specifically directed at them.

"Commander Banks, inform the crew to return to their quarters and cooperate with the boarding party," Sterling said, stepping down from the command platform. "And ensure that any data pertaining to how we got here is mysteriously 'corrupted' in the ship's logs."

"Aye, Captain," Banks said, setting to work.

"Then once you're done, meet me in the wardroom," Sterling added, heading for the exit. However, Banks appeared perplexed by the addendum to Sterling's last order.

"Why exactly am I meeting you in the wardroom, Captain?" she asked.

"For dinner, of course," Sterling said, continuing toward the exit. "After all, this might end up being our last meal."

LUCAS STERLING HAD NEVER CONSIDERED himself to be a proud man. He took pride in his work, the mission, his ship and his crew, but to him that wasn't the same thing. That was pride in duty and service, not himself. Even so, the act of having his ship seized and flown back to F-COP in disgrace while he sat alone in his quarters was difficult to swallow. He accepted it as a consequence of his actions, yet he regretted nothing. His actions were in support of the war and he had succeeded. They now had in their custody the one man who could potentially nullify the Sa'Nerra's key advantage. If the neural weapon could be rendered useless then the suspicion and fear that were running rampant inside Fleet command would end. They could throw their ships into a direct assault at the Sa'Nerran invasion armada and crush them, once and for all. Yet, as he waited outside the door to the room where his court martial hearing had been convened, he pondered whether he would be sitting out the rest of the war in Grimaldi.

Finally, the door opened and Sterling was invited in. However, rather than being confronted by the Judge Advocate General and a panel of other senior officers, he was met by Ernest Clairborne, the United Governments' Secretary of War.

"Come in, Captain Sterling," said Clairborne, ushering him inside. "You can remain standing. This won't take long."

Sterling moved inside and saw that Fleet Admiral Griffin was also in the room, along with Admiral Wessel and Admiral Rossi, the commander of the Third Fleet. The Judge Advocate General, however, was conspicuous by her absence.

"I'm confused, sir, I thought this was going to be a court martial hearing?" Sterling said, as Clairborne took a seat at the conference table. The admirals had all remained standing.

"Yes, well, certain matters have been brought to my attention that change things," Clairborne replied.

Clairborne shot a sideways glance at Fleet Admiral Griffin as he said this. Griffin, however, did not meet the Secretary of War's eyes and was instead focused on Sterling. The intensity of her stare was more unsettling than being brought before the secretary without knowing why.

"In light of this new information, you have no charges to answer, Captain," Clairborne went on. "In fact, we may end up pinning another damned medal on your chest," the politician added, with a gruff laugh.

"That's not necessary, sir," Sterling, replied. The last thing he wanted was another medal.

"There is a matter that remains unresolved, however," Clairborne added, becoming a touch sterner. "We have still not established how you found your way to F-sector when your last reported location was the Void."

Sterling shrugged. "As I detailed in my report, sir, I honestly don't know what happened," he lied. Sterling had already taken the decision to keep the knowledge of the unstable apertures a secret. "My chief engineer believes it could have been a wormhole, or perhaps a freak accident. We were badly damaged and our surge field generator was malfunctioning."

"I see," replied Clairborne. Though, even with a politician's tact for disguising their true feelings, it was clear to Sterling that Clairborne did not trust his answer. "In any case, we will continue to analyze your logs," the Secretary of War went on. "It is, however, a pity that so much of the data is corrupted."

Sterling shrugged again. "As I said, sir, we suffered heavy damage in the Void."

"Of course, of course," said Clairborne with the same forced politeness. "Anyway, I'll cut to the chase, Captain, to save us all time," Clairborne went on, becoming more upbeat. "By recovering James Colicos from the enemy, you have done Fleet and the United Governments a great service," the Secretary went on. However, despite the laudatory nature of the statement, Clairborne did not appear particularly enthused. "The damage, however, is already done. We may already be too late to do anything about the neural control weapon."

"Sir, if I may," Sterling cut in, but again Clairborne waved him off.

"I've read your report, Captain, and I understand your position," the Secretary interrupted. "You may be right, and we will utilize Colicos' talents in order to search for an 'antidote' to this neural disease." Sterling could tell there was a "but" coming, and Clairborne didn't disappoint. "But the fact remains the enemy is at our gates. Their armada, which now includes dozens of our own damned ships, outnumbers ours. And while our forces are superior in skill, the Sa'Nerran advantage remains."

"Sir, that is precisely why we need to counteract the neural control weapon," Sterling protested. He suspected that nothing he could say would change the outcome of the meeting, but he still wanted his voice to be heard. "If we can neutralize the emissaries and their aides, and prevent other ships and crew from being turned against us, the Sa'Nerran advantage crumbles."

Clairborne stood up, a sure-fire signal that the meeting – such as it was – was about to come to a close.

"Your opinion is noted, Captain Sterling," Clairborne said. The Secretary of War then slid a personal digital assistant across the table. "Here are you new orders, Captain."

Sterling frowned then glanced at Admiral Griffin, half-expecting her to interject. However, the Admiral remained silent, her eyes still fixed onto him. Sterling picked up the PDA and turned it on.

"I'm being posted to the Earth Defense Fleet?" Sterling said, scanning through the orders. His stomach knotted and he felt physically sick with anger. "But with a temporary attachment to the Special Investigations Branch?"

Sterling had not made any attempt to hide his clear displeasure at the orders and this had not gone unnoticed by Clairborne.

"That is correct, Captain Sterling," Clairborne replied. He had remained calm and personable, though it was also apparent his patience was wearing thin. "I believe your experience and knowledge would greatly benefit the SIB, especially as it seeks to uncover irregularities in the Fleet."

Sterling remained silent. He had a pretty good idea what "irregularities" Clairborne was referring to. And he couldn't deny that there was a certain cleverness to the act of assigning Sterling to the SIB. It would mean he would no longer be under the protection of Admiral Griffin. However, more importantly, it would mean that he was effectively tasked with uncovering his own covert operations. It would force him to give up the Omega Taskforce or lie to protect it. Then he noticed the names of the admirals present at the meeting. Griffin no longer held the rank of Fleet Admiral. Instead, Admiral Rossi now held the position. Sterling shook his head again. It hadn't been Sterling who had been court-martialed, but Griffin.

"You will report to me at oh nine hundred tomorrow, Captain Sterling," said Admiral Wessel, clearly enjoying himself immensely. "Bring your first officer too," he added in a smug, syrupy tone. "I want an opportunity to speak to you both to make sure you fully understand your new roles."

Sterling turned to Admiral Griffin, expecting – and hoping – that she would intervene. However, she merely remained silent.

"If there is no other business, then this meeting is over," said Clairborne, who then gathered up his personal effects and made a bee-line for the door.

Admiral Griffin and Admiral Rossi also left, but Sterling was still too stunned to move. It wasn't until Admiral Wessel was practically standing in front of him that he was able to gather his senses.

"It's time for you to fall in line, Captain," Admiral Wessel said, glowering at Sterling. "I know all about Griffin's little 'taskforce' and what you have been doing." He shot Sterling an oily smile. "It's ironic that as her favorite pet, you will be the one to bring Griffin down."

Sterling's mind was now as sharp as a scalpel. He knew what was happening and despite Griffin's silence during the meeting, his loyalties had not changed.

"I don't know what you're talking about, Admiral," Sterling said. He was outwardly calm, but inside he was still raging. "However, I'm very much looking forward to my new assignment," he added, sarcastically. "There are many irregularities in the Fleet. For example, I'm keen to explore how the offspring of senior Fleet officers appear to be promoted to positions of authority, without merit or due process."

Wessel's eyes narrowed, but he retained his oily smile. "You think you're so smart, don't you Captain?" he said, coming almost toe-to-toe with Sterling. "But you're mine now. And you will follow my orders to the letter, or you'll find yourself in a jail cell for the rest of your life."

Sterling smiled and held his ground. If the two men came any closer, they would have cracked heads.

"Will that be all, sir?" Sterling asked, politely.

"For now," Wessel spat back at him. Then he turned and headed toward the door. "Oh nine hundred tomorrow, Captain," Wessel called out as he went. "Do not be late."

Suddenly, Sterling found himself alone in the room. He had walked in expecting to be court martialed, but instead he'd suffered arguably a worse sentence. He'd had a bow tied around him and been presented as a gift to the most loathsome officer in the Fleet. Sterling flopped down into one of the meeting chairs, shaking his head. It had all happened so fast and he was still unable to process what it meant for the Invictus and his crew.

Then Sterling felt a neural link forming in his mind. He scowled and scanned the surface of the conference table, spotting a neural jammer. While scanners that were able to intercept and read neural communication were banned, neural jammers were permitted in rare circumstances. This was especially the case when members of the War Council were involved, as there had been during Sterling's meeting. However, Sterling could see that the jammer was still active, which meant that no-one should have been able reach out to him.

Tapping his neural interface to allow the connection he felt a presence fill his mind and knew immediately who it was.

"Sit tight, Captain," said Admiral Natasha Griffin. "Play along with Wessel and keep your nose clean. This isn't over."

The neural link then went dead, once again leaving Sterling utterly speechless. However, this time at least he knew he was not on his own.

STERLING LAY on his bed in his quarters, staring at the ceiling. The rest of the crew were on leave, pending yet another raft of repairs to the Invictus. Sterling was normally keen to speed up the work, so that he could get back into action. However, this time he hoped that the repairs would drag because as soon as they were done, he'd be heading away from the front line. His new commander, Admiral Wessel, would ensure that Sterling was kept under a tight leash and as far away from the action as possible. He'd hoped to hear more from Admiral Griffin, but as the new commander of the Third Fleet, she had already departed for E-COP.

Sterling closed his eyes and tried to clear his mind. Griffin's assurance that it was not over had given him some reason to hope that his mission and the Omega Taskforce would continue. However, at that moment, lying on his bed on his empty ship, he couldn't see how. With his mind quiet and his body still, Sterling suddenly heard a scratching sound. At first, he thought it was just a noise made by the repair crews filtering through the ship's structure. Then he realized it was emanating from somewhere inside his quarters. Sitting up, he tried to focus on the noise, but despite his keen hearing he couldn't quite place it.

"Computer, what is that damned noise?" Sterling said, aiming the question at the ceiling.

"There is a Beagle hound scratching at your door, Captain," the computer replied, cheerfully. "The animal's designation is Jinx. Shall I let her in?"

"No, you shall not," Sterling hit back. The noise then went away. Sterling waited for a few moments to make sure it didn't return then lay back down on his bed. "If that mutt craps outside my door, I'll devise a new meal tray based on Beagle stew," he muttered out loud.

"I do not believe there is enough organic material available in the Beagle hound to produce a sufficient run of new meal trays, Captain," the computer chipped in.

"I wasn't being serious, computer," Sterling said, closing his eyes. "And I also wasn't talking to you."

"Then who were you talking to, Captain?" the quirky AI asked.

"Myself. Or no-one. What the hell does it matter?" Sterling snapped. He was in a foul mood and since the computer was the only intelligence available to him, he decided to take out his frustrations on the AI.

"I have recently added some new counselling programs

to my repertoire, Captain," the computer continued, still in a cheerful tone. "Would you like me to begin an anger management session?"

Sterling laughed. "No, I would not," he replied. Then he frowned and opened his eyes. "Who the hell are you running these classes on, anyway?"

"Many members of the crew find my meditation and stress relaxation programs to be beneficial," the computer said. Sterling thought he could detect a hint of pride in the AI's voice, but then shrugged it off as his imagination.

"Like who?" said Sterling, growing more curious.

"I'm afraid that would violate my doctor patient confidentiality clause, Captain," the computer replied, this time sounding more subdued and suitably serious.

"You're not a damned, doctor, you're a collection of circuits," Sterling snapped.

Sterling was about to order the computer to reveal who it was running its courses on when the scratching sound started again. Cursing, Sterling got off the bed, muttering to himself then opened the door.

"Will you get lost?" Sterling snapped.

However, instead of seeing Jinx the Beagle hound, Sterling came face-to-face with Mercedes Banks.

"Is that an order, Captain?" Banks replied, folding her arms tightly across her chest. Jinx then trotted past and sat next to her boot.

"Sorry, Mercedes, I thought you were the damn dog," Sterling said, stepping back from the door and inviting her in. "It's been scratching at my door for last few minutes and driving me mad."

"She just wanted to say hello," Banks replied, stressing the word, "she". Sterling's first officer then moved inside and planted herself into his desk chair. Jinx trotted in after her and jumped up onto the bottom of Sterling's bed.

"Hey, what the hell do you think you're doing?" Sterling said to the dog. However, Jinx had already paced around in a circle and curled up on the covers.

"See, she likes you," Banks said, smiling at the hound. "Though I don't know why," she added, pointedly.

"How come you're still on the ship?" said Sterling, sitting back down on his bed. "I thought you'd be in the wardroom on the station, working your way through F-COP's supply of meal trays."

"I didn't like the company," replied Banks, spinning around in Sterling's chair. "Besides, I'm not really in the mood."

"It will all work out fine, Mercedes," said Sterling, choosing to be the optimist of the duo for a change.

"What makes you say that?" replied Banks, who was still spinning around in circles.

"Because the alternative is that I murder Wessel and his pissant son and end up on a penal colony for the rest of my life," said Sterling. Then he realized he was only half-joking.

"I'm wondering if that might be preferable to serving in his useless Earth Defense Fleet," said Banks, stopping herself spinning by planting her boots on Sterling's bed next to him. "They can't even defend against stray meteors, never mind a Sa'Nerran invasion force."

Sterling's computer console on his desk chimed an

alert. "Oh good, more orders," said Sterling, sarcastically. He turned the screen so that he could see it and switched on the terminal. There was a new message, transmitted on a secure, encrypted channel. Sterling glanced at Banks, who also appeared to recognize the unique frequency. It was the Omega Taskforce channel. It was Admiral Griffin.

"Grab the secure ID chip from my top drawer," said Sterling, pointing Mercedes in the right direction. His first officer swiftly obliged and Sterling slotted the chip into his console. He then placed his hand on the ID scanner and cleared his throat. "Unlock Omega Directive, authority Sterling Alpha One." The message unlocked and new data flooded onto Sterling's console.

"What is all this?" said Banks, frowning at the screen. "It looks like co-ordinates and surge-field configurations, but I don't recognize any of them."

Initially, Sterling was as confused as his first officer was. Then it dawned on him what Griffin had just sent them.

"These are the locations and surge-field configurations of other hidden apertures," Sterling said. Suddenly, he felt that things were starting to looking up. "Griffin has given us a route back out of Fleet space."

"But why?" Banks asked. "There's nothing else in the Void that's of use." She then reconsidered her statement. "Or is there?"

Sterling shrugged. "If there is, she's not said what, at least not in this message."

"Wait, there is more," said Banks, finding another file in the bundle of encrypted data. "It's just a plain message again, like the last one she sent us."

Sterling opened the file then read the contents out loud. "The Void Recon Unit has been disbanded but the Omega Taskforce remains. Do not let Colicos out of your sight. Standby for further instructions on this channel. The Omega Directive is in effect. Griffin."

Sterling let out a long breath as he rubbed the back of his neck. It was barely more information than Griffin had communicated to him after the meeting with Clairborne. If anything, it left him with more questions than answers.

"Can she even give us orders now that we're under Wessel's command?" wondered Banks, who was still frowning at the screen.

"It's not like all her previous orders were exactly above board, Mercedes," Sterling replied with a wry smile. "We've always operated outside the boundaries of the regular Fleet. I don't intend to stop now."

Banks nodded. "Fair point, though if she's no longer the Fleet Admiral, just how much can she get away with? How much can we?"

Sterling smiled. "I have no idea, but the way I see it, we have two choices. We take orders from Wessel and get used by him to take Griffin down. Or we carry on doing what we've always done."

"And what's that?" replied Banks.

"We do what's necessary," Sterling replied, suddenly growing in confidence. "We do whatever it takes to win the war, no matter the cost."

Banks nodded. "The Omega Directive is in effect."

"It always was, Mercedes," Sterling replied. "It never stopped being in effect."

Banks suddenly slapped her powerful thighs then sprang out of Sterling's desk chair. "Come on," she said, taking Sterling by the hand and hauling him up. Given his first officer's strength, there was no way to resist her.

"Where the hell are we going?" said Sterling.

"The wardroom, of course," Banks replied. She whistled to Jinx. The hound's ears pricked up and she jumped off the bed. "I've just got my appetite back."

Sterling laughed and followed Mercedes Banks out of the door. Jinx trotted along a few moments later, her robotic foot tapping on the metal deck plating in a brisk rhythm.

Sterling wasn't naïve enough to believe that recovering James Colicos was the end to their problems, but he had hoped it would have been the start of the solution. As it turned out, Fleet was already a long way down the road to defeat. If F-sector was to fall and the Third and Fourth Fleets took heavy losses, defeat was almost certain to follow.

In the war against the Sa'Nerra, there is only victory or death... Sterling reminded himself, as he walked side-by-side with his first officer. To continue his mission, Sterling would be required to not only exceed his orders, but disobey them completely. This troubled him almost more than some of the terrible acts he'd already conducted in the Void under the Omega Directive. However, he also knew that it was necessary. And above all else, Sterling would do anything necessary to win.

Orders didn't matter. Fleet didn't matter. The United Governments didn't matter. Only winning mattered. And he was going to win, whatever it took and whatever the cost.

The end (to be continued).

CONTINUE THE JOURNEY

Continue the journey with Omega Taskforce book four: Obsidian Fleet.

ABOUT THE AUTHOR

At school, I was asked to write down the jobs I wanted to do as a "grown up". Number one was astronaut and number two was a PC games journalist. I only managed to achieve one of those goals (I'll let you guess which), but these two very different career options still neatly sum up my lifelong interests in science, space, and the unknown.

School also steered me in the direction of a science-focused education over literature and writing, which influenced my decision to study physics at Manchester University. What this degree taught me is that I didn't like studying physics and instead enjoyed writing, which is why you're reading this book! The lesson? School can't tell you who you are.

When not writing, I enjoy spending time with my family, walking in the British countryside, and indulging in as much Sci-Fi as possible.

Subscribe to my newsletter:
http://subscribe.ogdenmedia.net

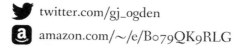

twitter.com/gj_ogden

amazon.com/~/e/B079QK9RLG

If you like Omega Taskforce then why not check out some of G J Ogden's other books? Click the series titles below to learn more about each of them.

Darkspace Renegade Series (6-books)

If you like your action fueled by power armor, big guns and the occasional sword, you'll love this fast-moving military sci-fi adventure.

Star Scavenger Series (5-book series)

Firefly blended with the mystery and adventure of Indiana Jones. Book 1 is 99c / 99p.

The Contingency War Series (4-book series)

A space-fleet, military sci-fi adventure with a unique twist that you won't see coming...

The Planetsider Trilogy (3-book series)

An edge-of-your-seat blend of military sci-fi action & classic apocalyptic fiction. Perfect for fans of Maze Runner and I am Legend.

Audiobook Series

Star Scavenger Series (29-hrs)

The Contingency War Series (24-hrs)

The Planetsider Trilogy (32-hrs)

Made in the USA
Monee, IL
20 March 2022

93254196R00197